Sweeter than Chocolate

AN IRRESISTIBLE
ROMANCE

LIZZIE SHANE

Hallmark
PUBLISHING

For all the romantic hopefuls.

Chapter One

HERE WAS NOTHING IN THE world so heavenly as the smell of fresh chocolate. Lucy Sweet had learned that at a very early age, standing at her great-grandmother's knee in the kitchen of her family's chocolate shop.

Burned chocolate, on the other hand? Not so great.

Which was why Lucy was currently hiding from the acrid, bitter scent—and the sneezing fit it had triggered—in the front area of How Sweet It Is. Her grandmother was training their new clerk, and Lucy was trying to stay out of their way, pretending to restock the display cases, while an ancient fan directed the charred chocolate fumes from the shop's kitchen toward the back alley. Away from the sensitive noses of any potential customers.

Lucy wasn't in the habit of burning chocolate. But then she wasn't normally as distracted as she was today, obsessing over the sign that had appeared this morning on the empty storefront across the street.

COMING SOON: LA VIE DOUCE. FRENCH DELICACIES.
La vie douce. The sweet life.

Her stomach had been in knots ever since she'd spotted it, and the burned chocolate wasn't the only casualty. She'd also ruined two batches of caramel before admitting to herself she was wasting her time... and ingredients.

Fortunately, her grandmother was too busy assisting their slow trickle of customers and training Georgie to notice the kitchen mishaps. She didn't want Nana Edda worrying. Lucy had taken over How Sweet It Is when her grandfather had passed. Keeping it running was her responsibility and no one else's. And she would figure out how to stay afloat— even if another sweet shop was opening right across the street.

Typically, when the shop was slow on a Friday afternoon, Lucy would retreat to the kitchen and take advantage of the quiet to whip up a batch of whichever sweet treat they were running low on, but she obviously couldn't be trusted in the kitchen today. So instead, she crouched behind one of the display cases, rearranging it for the fourth time and trying to pretend she wasn't quietly panicking, when the chimes over the etched-glass front door released a delicate cascade of sound, announcing a new customer.

Lucy looked automatically toward the entrance. Her best friend of twenty-five years struck a dramatic pose in the doorway, head thrown back, one arm in the air. At the sight, a smile broke through Lucy's La Vie Douce preoccupation. Lena could always be counted on to jolt Lucy out of her worry-spirals. She was a human tidal wave of energy, crashing through life and leaving chaos and laughter in her wake.

"It's official." Lena thrust her left arm forward, elbow locked, fingers down. "We're engaged!"

The diamond ring sparkled in the sunlight streaming through the shop windows as Tyler, Lena's boyfriend—no, fiancé, apparently—appeared in the doorway behind her. Tyler was tall and steady, as silent as Lena was talkative, and his lips quirked in an affectionate smile.

At the opposite end of the L-shaped counter, Nana Edda squealed with delight. "Lena!"

Her grandmother rushed around the counter toward Lucy's best friend, dragging the new clerk Georgie in her wake. Even the two teenage customers, who had been debating the merits of various cocoa bombs for the last five minutes, rushed to gather around the newly engaged couple, but for a single stunned moment, Lucy didn't move.

She crouched behind the display case, shock holding her in place as a single thought rang loud inside her mind.

She's leaving me behind.

She rallied quickly, shoving the thought away and kicking herself into motion, hurrying around the counter to join the knot of noisy congratulations and jewelry admiration.

Lena beamed, glowing with the attention. She looked so happy. Lucy couldn't imagine why she'd felt that little flicker of hesitation. It wasn't exactly a surprise. Lena had been hurtling toward this moment since the second she met Tyler nearly a year ago.

"I thought for sure he was going to do it on Valentine's Day," Lena gushed to her eager audience.

"Since that's the anniversary of the day we met. But he knew I was expecting that and that I would obsess about every little detail, worrying about what I was going to wear, and whether I had anything in my teeth, so he surprised me last night. There we were, in the kitchen eating takeout kung pao chicken, and suddenly he's down on one knee."

Lena shot her quiet fiancé a fond look, one that was returned with such affection that something twinged in Lucy's chest. Something that almost felt like envy. She pushed it away, reminding herself that no matter how thrilled she was for Lena and Tyler, she didn't have space in her life for romance right now.

Shoving aside her unexpectedly complicated feeling about the announcement, Lucy added an extra layer of cheer to her voice as she joined the chorus of well-wishes. "I'm so happy for you guys."

Lena's eyes locked on Lucy's, forgetting the rest of the crowd. "Oh, Lucy!"

Lucy's throat tightened at the joy in Lena's eyes. A year ago, Lena had been nursing a broken heart after her breakup with Awful Adam, and now she was radiant with love. It felt like a puzzle piece falling into place. So why was Lucy also fighting back the sensation that something was coming to an end?

Lena pulled her into a hug, squeezing tight, then stepped back to arm's length, her voice ringing with conviction as she declared, "It's all thanks to you."

"No, it isn't." Lucy's face flushed as she found herself the focus of everyone's gazes. Lena was a walking attention magnet, from her sunshine-yellow polka-dot dress to the hot pink daisy in her hair, but Lucy had always been happiest behind the scenes, tucked away in her kitchen in a chocolate-smudged apron.

She tried to step back, but Lena wasn't ready to let her escape the spotlight.

"Are you kidding?" Lena's grip tightened. "Of course it is! Tyler and I never would have met if it weren't for the Cupid chocolates. Your magic recipe led me to my true love. And I am *getting* my picture on that wall."

She thrust a freshly manicured finger toward the far wall, where a dozen framed photos were neatly arranged. The Cupid chocolate success stories.

Lena reached into the massive bag that was always hanging from her elbow. "I even came prepared." She pulled out a framed photo of her and Tyler beaming into the camera. "I'm not gonna lie, I had this baby framed months ago so I'd be ready as soon as it happened. Our very own happily-ever-after!" She made an exaggerated pleading face for Lucy. "Can we put it up now? I want to get a picture of the Wall of Love with us on it."

"The Wall of Love?" their new clerk Georgie asked, drawing Lena's attention.

"You don't know about the Wall?" She eyed Georgie's crisp red apron with the How Sweet It Is logo in white across the chest. "Don't tell me you've never heard of the Cupid chocolates?"

"It's her second day," Lucy explained, but Lena gasped as if she'd insulted St. Valentine himself.

"It should be the first thing you tell people! The Cupid chocolates are legendary." Lena marched over to the display case that held the Cupids, gazing at them with near religious fervor. "Every year on February fourteenth, anyone who eats a Cupid chocolate with an open heart is *guaranteed* to find their true love."

Lucy felt panic spike at Lena's words, especially when she saw the teenage customers exchange eager looks. "We don't actually guarantee—"

"That's how I met Tyler," Lena continued, oblivious to Lucy's liability concerns. "And how each of these couples met and fell in love."

She waved one artful hand, seamlessly transferring all three eager gazes—Georgie's and the two teen customers'—to the Wall of Love.

Lucy couldn't help but look, too. She was more than a little proud of that wall, even if she was nervous about claiming the Cupid chocolates guaranteed results. All of those couples had fallen in love after eating one of the Cupid chocolates on Valentine's Day. *Her* chocolates. Coincidence or not, it was pretty special to have had a hand in that many love stories.

Her kitten heels clicking on the hardwood, Lena led her disciples over to the Wall of Love—which was a short journey. The shop was only twelve feet across at its widest point. Glass display cases showcasing their wares lined the L-shaped counter, but the far wall was unobstructed—and filled with photos. Twelve in all. Soon to be thirteen.

Lucy let her gaze drift over the framed photos of couple after couple. Maybe she didn't need to worry about the shop across the street. Maybe the How Sweet It Is chocolate shop could survive a little competition.

"They really make absolutely anyone fall in love with you?" one of the teenagers asked.

"Oh, no, that isn't how the magic works," Lena exclaimed, her voice filling the shop—and Lucy tried not to cringe at the matter-of-fact, of-course-magic-is-real-and-we're-selling-it tone. She believed in the chocolates, mostly—almost completely—but she'd always been wary of promising things the shop couldn't deliver.

"The Cupid chocolates don't *make* anyone fall in love," Lena continued. "They guide whoever bites into them on Valentine's Day with an open heart toward true love, but it may not be with the person you expect. Tyler and I were both on dates with other people when we realized we were meant to be with one another."

"So they only work on Valentine's Day?" the teen asked, an edge of disappointment coloring her tone. V-day was still several weeks away.

Again, Lucy opened her mouth to confirm that was, indeed, the belief, but her grandmother got there first. "Well, the magic is certainly most *potent* on Valentine's Day, so be sure you come back then and bring your friends—"

"Nana..."

"I'll take two," the other teen ordered. Nana Edda quickly ushered the customers toward the main register.

Georgie went with them, and Tyler gave a sideways nod toward the Cupids. "I'll get us a couple to celebrate." He moved toward the others, leaving Lena alone with Lucy and the photos.

Lena held her picture up on the wall, trying out different spots, as Nana Edda waxed poetic about the family's secret chocolate recipe. Lucy held back the urge to intervene as her grandmother stretched the truth to the breaking point and beyond. Nana Edda had always liked a story. So much so that Lucy wasn't sure her grandmother even realized when she passed the threshold from truth into fiction. Lucy was the one who worried about the realities—such as the consequences for guaranteeing something they couldn't deliver. She was the one who flinched every time her grandmother promised untold flights of romance with every purchase.

"What if we moved your great-grandparents' picture?" Lena asked, pulling Lucy's attention away from the Cupid discussion at the registers. "Gave them a place of honor. Maybe at the top? We can put Tyler and me in their old spot and then we won't have to move the others around to make space for this one. What do you think?"

"That sounds good," Lucy agreed. "I trust your eye more than mine."

Lena was the one with artistic vision. Her family had run the flower shop down the street for nearly as long as Lucy's had run the chocolate shop, and Lena did all their arrangements.

"You're going to need a bigger wall after this year," Lena commented, moving the photos around. Then she pulled a hammer and nail out of her giant purse to hang Lucy's great-grandparents' photo at the top, reigning over all the happy couples. Never let it be said that Lena didn't come prepared to get what she wanted. She slanted a quick glance at Lucy. "And you'll need a special spot for your own photo."

Lucy groaned. "Don't start."

"I'm just saying that you have to try one this year!

You're the romantic enabler, making the dreams of all the people around you come true. Now it's your turn to grab a little of that magic for yourself."

"I'm fine just the way I am," she insisted. She had too much on her plate to be adding romance to the mix. Ever since she'd taken over running How Sweet It Is, they'd been hanging on by their financial fingernails. Now, with La Vie Douce about to open across the street, she couldn't afford to get distracted.

"This is not fine." Lena frowned. "All you do is work. And I love this shop, but all work and no play isn't *fine*." She took one last look at her handiwork, and then turned to focus the full force of her attention on Lucy. "And besides, don't you want to be more than fine? Don't you want to be incandescently, deliriously happy?"

"I'll leave that to you."

Lena made a face, clearly prepared to argue more, but Lucy's grandmother spoke before she could.

"Don't mind her." Nana Edda rounded the counter to join them. Lucy hadn't noticed the other customers leaving. Tyler was still quietly taking photos of the Cupids while Georgie studied them as if looking for traces of magic. "She's been grumpy all morning. Ever since they put up that sign across the street."

Lena's face twisted with sympathy. "I saw that."

Lucy met her grandmother's gaze. "I thought I'd done a good job of pretending not to notice." She'd been trying so hard not to let her worry spill over onto anyone else.

Nana Edda's eyebrows arched high over her glasses. "You burned two batches of caramel. And charred that dark chocolate to a crisp."

"Oh, honey, are you okay?" Lena asked and Lucy squirmed under Lena and Nana Edda's combined concern.

"It's fine. I'm sure it's fine."

Lena's face told her what she thought of fine, but this time, she didn't argue. As one, they looked out the front window and across the street.

How Sweet It Is was a cozy little shop with an old-fashioned feel. They'd upgraded the display cases and added a credit-card reader since the days when her great-grandparents had first opened the shop on Watson Corners' Main Street, but it still had an antique cash register that cheerfully binged every time they made change.

The kitchens were twice the size of the shop and gleaming with the results of the small-business loan Lucy had taken out to upgrade them when she took over the shop. The tiny little office in the back was lined with photos of her grandparents and great-grandparents, the history of the place surrounding her every time she sat down to do the books, a reminder of those who had come before.

And a reminder that if she didn't manage to pay off the last of that small-business loan, she might lose everything that they'd built.

Watson Corners had been a cute little town when her great-grandparents had emigrated from Belgium and settled there. But in recent decades, the nearby city had expanded, and a posh suburb had slowly surrounded Watson Corners. The charming downtown area had stayed intact, but subdivisions of gorgeous new homes and manicured lawns had sprung up where open fields used to be.

Big businesses had followed, as well as many not-so-big businesses that flocked to the upscale suburb to cater to its posh new residents.

Like the fancy French whatever moving in across the street.

The hardware store in that space had closed down last year, the older couple who ran it for decades retiring and moving to Arizona. The storefront had been vacant for so long that the other shops along Main Street had started a betting pool on what would finally move into the massive space. It was easily triple the size of How Sweet It Is, even if she included the kitchens and the apartment above.

When construction had started, the windows had stayed covered with brown paper so no one could see what was being done inside, and the betting pool had gone wild. Lucy herself had wagered it would be a microbrewery. Or a new restaurant—maybe some fancy Michelin-star place that would draw more people to the area.

She hadn't expected direct competition.

The swirly cursive of the "Coming Soon" sign had gone up this morning. And her stomach had instantly knotted.

"Maybe they're a bistro. Or a savory-only French bakery," Lena suggested with her usual degree of optimism. "Quiche and *croque monsieur* and baguettes and nothing else."

"They're *huge*," Lucy said, staring at the building. She'd been so eager for a new business to open, but now she was dreading February first, the opening date listed on the sign. "It could be a chocolate factory for all we know. A French Willy Wonka."

"Soups," Nana Edda declared. "It's all French onion soup and *pommes frites*, I bet."

"Even if they are a bistro, they'll have sweets, too," Lucy said, always the voice of logic. "Pastries and tarts and chocolate croissants. And if people are already eating over there, they're hardly going to walk across the street to get their dessert from us. People want one-stop-shopping, and all we are is chocolate."

"We have a loyal customer base," her grandmother insisted. "We're a Watson Corners institution."

And we're barely hanging on as it is.

Lucy kept that thought to herself, just like she'd hoarded all the financial worry over the last few years.

Her grandmother was magic with the customers, but Lucy was the one who had taken business classes at night so she could run the shop when her grandfather passed away. It was all on her now, from placing the supply orders to making the chocolates to keeping the books. She'd grown up in these kitchens, learning the recipes from her grandfather and great-grandmother. How Sweet It Is was home. And she would not be the one who let it fail.

"I should get back," Lena said. "But don't worry, okay? I know that's a big ask for you, but you've got this. Everyone loves How Sweet It Is."

"Thank you, Lena." She squeezed her friend's hands, feeling the unfamiliar presence of the ring. "And congratulations again! Today is all about you and Tyler."

"You bet it is." Lena beamed, linking her arm with her fiancé and sharing a look that made Lucy feel like she was standing outside on a snowy night, looking through a window at a warm, cozy fire.

Lucy waited until the bells above the door had rung over the exiting lovebirds before turning to her grandmother and arching her eyebrows. "Did I hear you tell those girls that the Cupid myth dates back through seven generations of Sweet women?" she drawled. "Don't you think you got a little carried away with the lore there?"

"What?" Nana Edda asked with artful innocence. "We don't know that the legend started with Gigi. Her ancestors probably meddled in love lives for centuries."

"But they wouldn't even have been Sweet women," Lucy argued.

"They wouldn't?" Georgie's gaze pinged eagerly between Lucy and her grandmother. The grad student had been hired to give Lucy's grandmother a break, but that had been before Lucy realized she was about to have competition directly across the street. Now she had yet another person on her payroll to worry about if the shop went under.

"Gigi married into the family," Nana Edda explained. "Just like me."

"And my great-grandparents changed their name to Sweet from Van Suyt when they emigrated to this country from Belgium. Which gives us, at most, four generations of Sweet women. If we include my mother, who also married into the family and has never made a chocolate in her life. Any more than that is just—"

"Adding a little flourish to the truth. It's harmless." Her grandmother dismissed her concerns with a wave of her hand. "People know I'm not serious. And they like the story."

"They *don't* know you're not serious. And if they realize we're lying about how many generations of Sweet women chocolatiers there have been, they might start wondering what else we're lying about."

"You mean the chocolates?" Nana Edda's chin tipped up in affront. "We aren't lying about the Cupid chocolates."

"You can't go around guaranteeing people that the Cupids will make them fall in love, Nana. We're going to get sued by someone when it doesn't work for them."

"I didn't guarantee. Who guaranteed?"

Lucy arched an eyebrow and her grandmother relented.

"Okay, yes, my language may have been a little on the guarantee-ish side of things, but no one is going to sue you over something your sweet little grandma said." She fluttered her lashes, somehow making herself look small and helpless.

Lucy snorted, incapable of keeping a straight face. "Just try to go easy on the promises, okay? And maybe stop telling everyone the recipe is seven generations old? The fact that it was Gigi's secret recipe is impressive enough."

"It is when you say it. You can call her your great-grandmother, and it sounds like an ancient family secret. When I say it was my mother-in-law's recipe, it has much less gravitas. Less sense of *history*."

A history that might not last much longer if Lucy couldn't keep things afloat.

She rubbed at her chest, worry pressing against her, tightening her lungs—and her grandmother caught the gesture.

"You should bite into one of those Cupid chocolates yourself. Fall in love. Let loose a little. You've gotten entirely too serious, Lucy Sweet."

Lucy met her grandmother's eyes, smiling helplessly at one of her favorite people on the planet. "I figure one of us ought to be."

"Nonsense." Nana Edda flapped a hand dismissively. "Seriousness is entirely overrated. Now *love*. Love is something the maker of the famous Cupid chocolates should fall into as soon as possible."

What was it about one engagement that made everyone start looking for romance everywhere? "I'm fine just the way I am. Thank you."

"I know, I know. Too busy for romance." Her grandmother eyed her shrewdly. "But I also know you aren't really worried about my harmless little exaggerations. You're worried about that French place across the street."

Lucy's gaze went back to the frost-edged front windows of How Sweet It Is and the street beyond.

"Why don't you do more to advertise the magic of the Cupids?" Georgie inquired. "I know someone who works for the local news station. I bet they'd love a story about magic Valentine's chocolates."

"Oh, that's a wonderful idea!" Nana Edda exclaimed. "The Cupids are always our biggest sellers this time of year. People may not cross the street for any old candy, but they'll come for love. Especially if we get the word out. I bet people would come from all around—"

Lucy held up both hands in stop signs. "No. No reporters." She needed to keep her grandmother and her true-love guarantees as far away from reporters and their recording devices as possible. A lawsuit for false advertising was the last thing they needed. "The legend can spread the same way it always has—by word of mouth from happy customers."

How Sweet It Is would survive the latest changes to Watson Corners. Just like it had for the last seventy years. Everything would be fine.

And if the current maker of the famous Cupid chocolates had never actually been in love...well. There would always be time for love later. Right now, she had a business to run.

Chapter Two

"*N*ORA WANTS TO SEE YOU."

Dean pulled out his earbuds and looked up as Alex Ramos, one half of *Alex and Anna in the Mornings,* breezed past his desk in the open bullpen area of Channel Five. "Now?" he asked.

"Is there any other time with Nora?" Alex knocked twice on the edge of Dean's desk as he continued toward his office, adding, "Nice work on that fake charity story. Really good stuff."

Dean didn't bother to temper the satisfied grin that spread across his face. There was no point in pretending to be modest when he knew he'd done a great job. "Thanks, man," Dean called to the retreating morning anchor, already locking his computer and standing to head toward Nora's office.

She must want to compliment him on the fake charity exposé. That story had been over a month in the making, and this morning, it had aired for the first time. He couldn't think of any other reason the executive producer would be calling him into her office.

Unless she wanted to give him a raise. Or maybe

a shot at the weekend anchor slot. Or even evening anchor. He grinned to himself as he took a shortcut across the set toward Nora's office. Why not dream big?

The set was dark now, since the morning broadcast was complete and the midday crew wouldn't go into hair and makeup for another hour. Still, there was that hum in the air. That barely contained energy. The newsroom was never completely silent. There was always something going on. Always the possibility of a story about to break, even though Channel Five was just a local affiliate. For the really big stuff, they threw to the national broadcast team. But people had been plucked out of the Channel Five lineup to go to the national team before. It could happen again. He just had to work his way up.

Dean liked the stories he covered for Channel Five. He'd built a good reputation for himself as the champion of the little guy. He was the reporter viewers could rely on to parse through all the local and state political mumbo jumbo and break it down into clear, comprehensible information that explained how it would affect everyday people in their area. And he was the one they could call when there was a local injustice that needed some light shone on it, such as the "charity" that had raised thousands promising to revitalize local parks and then siphoned that money into the personal bank accounts of the organization's directors.

It was the kind of story that could get national attention. Maybe it already had. Maybe that was why Nora wanted to talk to him. Excitement pushed his steps a little faster.

He may have been a little too preoccupied mentally rehearsing the conversation with Nora where she'd send him to New York to be the next Edward R. Murrow—so he was completely unprepared for what she told him when he tapped on her door and walked into her office.

"Magic chocolates?"

He couldn't have heard that right.

Dean Chase, Defender of the Little Guy, crack investigative reporter, stared at his executive producer and mentally calculated the odds that he was being pranked. Nora Nguyen wasn't usually a joker, but she couldn't be serious. Because honestly, magic chocolates?

But Nora didn't crack a smile. "Magic chocolates," she confirmed. "Apparently, there's a cute little chocolate shop up in Watson Corners where people fall madly in love if they eat a certain chocolate on Valentine's Day. One of the customers—recently engaged, apparently due to some chocolate noshing last Valentine's—posted about it on social media last night, and it's already gone viral."

Dean's fraud-and-corruption spidey senses shivered awake, and he nodded slowly, the assignment starting to make sense. "So you want me to do an exposé? The chocolate shop that's preying on the desire to find love and manipulating people with this magic nonsense?"

Nora was a petite woman, but her sigh filled the room. "No, Dean. It's a puff piece. A cute little human-interest story to run in the C block around Valentine's."

"But it's obviously a con."

"I don't care. Our viewers won't care, either. They're going to eat this up."

"Magic chocolates," Dean repeated, his skepticism clear.

Nora went on as if he hadn't spoken. "I need you to go up there, dig into the story, and get us a cute segment or two we can use in the lead up to Valentine's."

"You want me to do a Valentine's segment?"

He was the fraud and corruption guy. The one who protected the viewers from deceit. The one who was never taken in by the stories everyone else was so eager to believe. Like *magic chocolates*. Nora may say she was sending him there for a puff piece, but there were other reporters who did that stuff all the time. She wouldn't assign this one to Dean if she didn't want him to go for the jugular.

Unless...

He winced internally. "Is this a punishment?"

Nora steepled her hands, watching him. "It concerns me that you consider an assignment about love a punishment, but you could consider this a sort of penance, if you like."

Dean groaned, raking a hand through his hair. "I never meant to imply Anna's marriage was doomed to failure—and I never would have said it if I'd realized she was right behind me—but you have to admit that, statistically, most marriages do end in divorce."

Nora stabbed a finger in his direction. "And that right there is why you're doing this story. It'll be good for you. Go soak in some dewy romanticism."

He barely stopped himself from cringing. "There are three different resolutions coming up for a vote in the next state House sessions. You always say I'm the only reporter on your staff who can make dry legislation relatable and interesting to the average viewer."

"That is your superpower, and we love you for it," Nora said. "But I have faith in your ability to continue to make politics fascinating while also delivering a story that makes magic love chocolates relatable and interesting for our viewers. Multi-task."

"Yeah, but, magic chocolates." He shook his head. "Nora. It's ridiculous." And insulting to his intelligence.

"Valentine's stories are popular. I'm giving you a *gift*. Say, 'Thank you, Nora. You're the best boss ever, Nora. I can never thank you enough, Nora, but I will try by delivering a magic chocolates story that's so sweet you'll get cavities.'"

He opened his mouth and managed, "Thank you, Nora."

She grimaced. "Try for a little more sincerity next time. Now go. The sooner you get me that footage, the sooner you can get back to watching politicians bicker about funding."

He stood, taking his dismissal and moving toward the door, trying not to think about how much a story like this would undermine his credibility as the defender of the public.

"Oh, and Dean?" Nora called when he was in the doorway. "Good work on that charity story. Great stuff."

"Thanks," he grumbled, pretty sure he didn't sound any more sincere than he had a minute ago.

That was the kind of story he needed to be digging into. He'd worked hard to make himself the man the viewers could trust. He'd taken the low-man-on-the-totem-pole beat of recapping city council meetings and turned it into a segment people made sure to tune in for. He'd built a strong social media following because viewers knew he could be relied upon to cut through deception and get the real scoop. And in turn, they tipped him off about corruption, depending on him to get to the bottom of it.

He had a *reputation.* And he needed to protect that if he was going to have any kind of shot at making anchor or going national.

He liked the work he did. He liked being the good guy, digging into the stories no one else was paying attention to and protecting those less jaded than himself—which was, admittedly, most of the population. But he wanted more.

The only reason he hadn't gone straight to New York and tried to find a job there when he graduated six years ago had been his little sister. Their parents had never been what qualified as steady, and she'd still been in high school. He'd wanted to stay close to home to provide some stability for her. Be someone she could always rely on. The job at Channel Five had been perfect...at the time.

But she was in grad school now. Doing well. Established in her own life. She didn't need a protective older brother hovering over her anymore. And he'd still be just a phone call away. It was the perfect time to take the next step in his career, whether that was a local anchor position or as part of the national team.

And this new story wasn't going to help him do that.

"Dean." Anna Robinson, the other half of *Alex and*

Anna in the Mornings and the woman whose romantic future Dean had inadvertently maligned, strode toward Nora's office, her perfectly made-up lips pursed tight in barely suppressed irritation.

"Anna. Nice to see you," Dean replied, smiling an apology, as he had every time since that stupid moment when he'd shoved his foot into his mouth so hard he was still choking on the shoe leather. One of his coworkers had told him about Anna's engagement and he'd decided to run his mouth about divorce statistics and the likely demise of any new marriage—with his freshly engaged colleague standing a few feet behind him.

"Good work on that charity story," Anna said. Her dark brown eyes stayed as icily closed off as they had been since his little foot-in-mouth moment.

"Thank you. You guys were great this morning."

She nodded her thanks, but didn't slow down to chat, moving past him toward Nora's office.

Dean grimaced when she closed the door behind her, wishing again that he could take back the tactless moment and erase the flash of hurt he'd seen in her eyes that day—even if he hadn't technically said anything that wasn't a statistically proven truth. It wasn't his fault half of marriages ended in divorce or that there had been over seven-hundred-and-eighty thousand divorces in the US last year alone. Based on his own experience, he was surprised those numbers weren't even higher.

Love was a con. A collective delusion. And no one was better at exposing fraud than Dean Chase.

His thoughts circled back to the magic chocolate shop. All he had to do was find some way to satisfy

Nora's mandate for a puff piece while also doing a little investigating into this so-called love magic.

Dean smiled to himself as he moved back toward his desk. He just had to frame it the right way. Nora wouldn't want someone who was taking advantage of customers and their eagerness for love to go unchecked.

He'd go down. He'd dig into the story. And Dean would check them.

It was what he did.

And he'd ride that success all the way to New York.

Chapter Three

"**WE'RE OUT OF THE CUPIDS!**" Georgie burst into the kitchen, her panicked shout echoing off the stainless steel.

The spoon in Lucy's hands slipped from her fingers, clattering onto the counter.

Nana Edda had gone to meet a friend for coffee, which usually meant she'd be gone for at least an hour collecting all the latest gossip, but Georgie had seemed confident managing the shop on her own. She'd insisted she had it all under control, so Lucy had decided to take the opportunity to hide in the kitchens and make another attempt at the salted caramel cocoa bombs. She couldn't quite seem to perfect them. The flavor was good, and the cocoa-filled chocolate balls erupted into decadent hot chocolate when melted in hot milk just like they were supposed to, but there was something off about the texture, a grainy residue that didn't seem to dissolve no matter how hot she steamed the milk before pouring it over the bomb.

She was trying out a new mixture, adjusting the ratios of cocoa and caramel, but she hadn't even finished filling the shells to make the egg-shaped bomb, so she wasn't anywhere near the testing phase when Georgie flung herself into the kitchen as if she was being chased by an angry mob.

If the panic edging around Georgie's wide eyes was any indicator, the new recipe would have to wait. Her new clerk clearly wasn't ready to be left on her own out front.

"Don't worry," Lucy soothed Georgie, setting aside the half-filled cocoa bombs. "We'll just pull the description card and put something else in their place. We're always rotating through different flavors."

Georgie shook her head, eyes still wide. "People are requesting them. *Specifically.* They're asking when we'll have more. They're *waiting* for them."

"Okay." Lucy blinked. That was unusual, but still no cause for panic. "Well, that isn't going to work because the Cupids take hours and I won't have time to make them until we close tonight." She moved to the sink to scrub the clinging caramel from her fingertips. "But we can steer them toward other chocolates or take advance orders for tomorrow so they're guaranteed to get them in the morning."

Georgie's face scrunched with anxiety, and Lucy smiled with sympathy. She was probably only five or six years older than Georgie, but sometimes the grad student seemed incredibly young. Georgie stood twisting her hands, visibly daunted by the idea of telling a customer they couldn't have the exact chocolates they wanted exactly when they wanted them. Lucy's heart went out to the girl.

"Would you like me to tell them?" she offered.

Relief poured across Georgie's face. "Oh, would you?"

Lucy smiled, briskly drying her hands on the towel hanging from her crisp red How Sweet It Is apron. "Of course."

Smiling brightly for the customers, she swept through the swinging door into the shop—and stopped so quickly, Georgie bumped into her back.

She'd expected one or two people. Three, tops. Maybe including one particularly insistent customer who was giving Georgie pause.

She hadn't expected *this*.

The shop was *packed*.

Patrons were crammed into the cozy public area, elbow-to-elbow. A concern that they were verging on a fire code violation flickered through Lucy's thoughts—but she didn't have long to dwell on that because the restless customers had noticed her entrance.

The crowd had been mingling as best it could in the tight quarters, glancing at the sweets in the various displays, but the second they saw Lucy, a swell of sound hit her as they all rushed forward, speaking over one another.

"When will there be more?"

"Are you sure you don't have any more of the Cupids in a back room?"

"Can we get on a waiting list for them?"

"If we buy them now and save them until Valentine's Day, will that work the same as coming into the shop on Valentine's Day to get them? Or does the magic only work here?"

"Do they only work on Valentine's? Because your

clerk was saying the magic was stronger then, but can we get a small dose if we eat them now?"

"Why wait? I'm going to eat one every day until Valentine's, just to be sure!"

Lucy held up her hands, and thankfully, a hush fell over the crowd. All of them seemed to lean forward at once. She'd never had so many people hanging on her words, and it was a little daunting. The Cupid-seekers did tend to get a little excited the closer they got to Valentine's, but that was still three weeks away, and she'd never seen so many flood into the shop on a single day. What on earth was going on?

"We won't have any more Cupid chocolates until tomorrow," she announced, to a chorus of groans. "However, we *do* take advance orders—so you can reserve as many as you'd like to be picked up on the future date of your choice. We'll have them packaged and ready for you. Georgie will take advance orders at the far register, while I fill orders for our other delicious chocolates which you can take home today. And if you're looking for something with a similar flavor profile to the Cupids, may I recommend the raspberry creams?"

"But are they *magic*?" one girl, who couldn't be more than twelve, called out.

Lucy leaned toward the girl and grinned. "The magic is how delicious they are."

The girl smiled. Another voice called from the back of the crowd. "So you'll definitely have more of the Cupid chocolates tomorrow?"

"First thing in the morning," Lucy promised.

The woman at the front pointed to the nearest display case. "In that case, I'll take two of the cherry cordial chocolates now and see you tomorrow."

Lucy got busy filling the orders while Georgie filled out advance slips at the far end of the counter. Time seemed to pass in a blink, as it always did when there was a rush. Her hands moved smoothly with the practice of two decades helping in the shop, her smile ready and cheerful as she chatted with each customer while ringing them up. She'd always felt that the welcoming atmosphere at How Sweet It Is was nearly as important as the exquisite chocolate recipes her great-grandmother had passed down to her.

People came into How Sweet It Is to indulge, to celebrate, to cheer themselves up or reward themselves. Lucy always wanted her customers to leave smiling a little brighter than they had when they'd come in, even if they were taking their chocolates to go and hadn't had that first delicious hit of sweetness yet.

It was why she'd hired Georgie on the spot, even though her resume had been heavily stacked toward academia and she'd never held a retail job before. Her sunny smile had radiated the kind of warmth that Lucy wanted in her shop.

It was also part of why she'd encouraged the legend of the Cupids at first. She'd wanted How Sweet It Is to feel like the kind of place where magic was possible. Where true love could blossom at any moment. A place the stresses and realities of the real world couldn't quite touch, because in here, enchantment held sway.

But it was still a business, and as the legend of the Cupids had grown, so had her nerves about any potential liability.

After the bell had rung over the head of the last customer departing the shop—the twelve-year-old girl and her mom who had spent ages dithering between the caramel pralines and the mint-chip fudge before deciding to get both—Lucy leaned against the counter with a satisfied sigh. Georgie slumped against the opposite end of the display case, wide-eyed.

"Thank you," Georgie said with feeling. "At first, it was just one or two, but then there were so many of them and they all wanted the Cupids and we'd already run out. Everyone coming into the shop today has bought some."

Lucy frowned at the empty display area. "They usually don't go that fast except on Valentine's Day. I wonder why everyone seems to want the Cupids today."

As if in answer to the question, the front door burst open in a jangle of bells, and Nana Edda swept in, waving her cell phone over her head. "Darlings. We're *trending*."

Chapter Four

$\mathcal{I}$T TOOK TEN MINUTES AND a great deal of patience to find the Instagram post on Nana Edda's phone, since she'd accidentally deleted the link in her enthusiasm to rush back to the shop and show it to Lucy. When Lucy did finally clap eyes on it, her heart seemed to go up and down at the same time, as if it couldn't decide whether to be elated or terrified.

"Lena, what did you do?" she whispered, reading the first, ominous words.

How I Found the Love of My Life—And You Can, Too!

There were photos. Yes, the picture Lena had taken of the Wall of Love was prominently displayed, but there were others, too. The red awning out front. The Cupids themselves, including the tiny, laminated sign describing them. Lena had to have been planning this while she was in the shop the other day, snapping those pictures. Lucy'd had no idea she planned to go public with her engagement story.

Though, really, she should have known. Lena loved her love story. Loved telling people about it. Especially about the Cupids.

And it wasn't that going public about the Cupids was bad, necessarily. It was just risky in the way it exposed the shop, made it look like they were making promises—and Lucy had never been comfortable with risk. The only risky thing she'd ever done in her life was taking over Gigi's shop when she'd felt like she was too young and inexperienced to properly run it. She'd wanted it to stay open, to stay in the family, and neither her mother nor Nana Edda had ever been as involved with making the sweets as she was. They'd both enjoyed the social aspect of the front-of-house work, selling the chocolates and chatting up customers, but neither of them had cared nearly as much about carrying on the family chocolate-making legacy.

So Lucy had taken the one big leap of faith of her life—and had been braced to smack into the hard ground of reality ever since.

Was this going to be it? The thing that finally drove How Sweet It Is out of business? Were unhappy customers going to come out of the woodwork and complain that *they* hadn't gotten love as advertised?

"This is *awesome*," Georgie gushed, reading the post on her own phone while Lucy tried to absorb some of her enthusiasm by osmosis. "No wonder so many people wanted the Cupids!"

"You'll need to double your usual batch size," Nana Edda insisted, waving her phone. "Or even triple it. This isn't just Watson Corners. This is the *world*."

Lucy fought the urge to sink down to the floor and hug her knees. "How many likes is it up to?"

"Seventy-two *thousand*," Georgie said, beaming.

"Oh, wow."

She wanted to call her mother—not that her

mother had ever been a source of grounded, practical advice. Helen Sweet-Carter didn't believe in worrying about consequences. Definitely the "better to beg forgiveness than ask permission" type. She was always telling Lucy not to borrow trouble, which had only made Lucy want to plan more, organize more.

Her mother's advice would be terrible—undoubtedly something about enjoying the ride—but Lucy still wished she wasn't on a cruise ship halfway around the world with her new husband so Lucy could just hear the comforting sound of her voice.

The bell rang over the door as another customer hurried into the shop. "Is this the place with the magic chocolates?" the young woman asked eagerly. Lucy felt her stomach twist as Georgie and Nana Edda both nodded enthusiastically.

A distant droning started in her ears. She had to get out of here. She was going to have a panic attack in the middle of her own shop, and then the news of *that* would probably go viral, too.

"I have to..." She started toward the kitchen door, her breathing coming a little too quickly. "I need more..." Her grandmother looked at her questioningly, and she blurted out the first thing that popped into her head. "My secret ingredient. If I'm going to make triple batches, I'll run out. I'll just, um, I'll run out and grab some more. So I'm ready. To make the chocolates."

She was babbling. The wrinkle between her grandmother's brows showed Lucy exactly how strangely she was behaving, but she bolted through the kitchen door before she could start blathering again.

"This is good," she whispered to herself as she grabbed her purse off its hook on her way to the rear exit. "It's good exposure. Nothing is going to go wrong. It's just a few more customers."

She kept whispering reassurances to herself as she unlocked her little Ford Fiesta and slid behind the wheel. It wasn't until she was three blocks away that she realized she was still wearing her bright red apron, a chocolate-smudged hand towel tucked into her apron strings.

But everything was *fine*. It was just a little story. Things would settle down. She just had to keep things from getting any more out of control.

Chapter Five

WATSON CORNERS WAS AN ARTFULLY cultivated blend of old and new. Dean drove slowly down the absurdly charming Main Street, eyeing the gingerbread-trimmed gazebo holding down one corner of the square—which definitely appeared to be shaped like a triangle. A little creek wended through that square and across Main Street, visible more through the abundance of bridges than for the width of the waterway itself.

Mixed in with the original faded brick buildings were shiny new businesses designed to blend in with them, to preserve the character and feel of the town. No high-rises, no box stores. At least not in the Main Street area with its wide sidewalks and old-fashioned-looking wrought iron streetlights.

The whole thing was too cutesy to be believed. And How Sweet It Is fit right in, with its bright red awning dangling lace trim.

Dean was forced to park halfway down the block thanks to the cars overflowing the designated spaces for How Sweet It Is and spilling over into the alley beside the shop. A line snaked out the door and down the sidewalk, customers craning their necks to peer through the frosted windows.

Apparently, the taking-advantage-of-romantic-gullibility business was booming.

He left the camera gear in the back of his car for now, hoping to get the lay of the land—and maybe the inside scoop on these magic chocolates—before anyone knew he was press. He kept his ears open as he approached. One trio of twenty-somethings huddled in a knot, chatting so animatedly he was sure they were old friends until he got close enough to hear their words and realized they were strangers, sharing their stories of how they found out about the chocolates.

"One of my friends reposted that engagement story on Instagram, and as soon as I saw it, I *knew* this was just what I needed to get the guy in my building to finally notice me."

"I don't even have a crush. I'm just so ready for love to find me."

"Oh, I have a crush," the third one chimed in, "but I somehow doubt the chocolates are going to make Tom Holland fall madly in love with me. But a guy can dream. I mean, you never know."

The trio seemed so young, reminding him of his baby sister and stirring all his protective instincts. Someone needed to save them from themselves before they got their hearts trampled on.

Love was all well and good in the fairy tales, but no one ever talked about what happened after the happily-ever-after. Dean had gotten a front-row seat to the catastrophe that was his parents' marriage. Then he'd watched them both jump right back into what they called love, had heard all the promises that this time would be forever—only to witness two more divorces before he made it out of middle school. And his own romantic relationships hadn't exactly been straight shots to happily-ever-after.

So yes, maybe he was a little cynical about romance. But he had good reason to be. And to want to warn everyone waiting in that line not to trust their future happiness to a piece of chocolate.

There were dozens of industries sustained by the myth of True Love—flower shops and wedding venues and the entire made-up holiday of Valentine's Day—which was bad enough. But at least most of them were just capitalizing on pre-existing relationships. They weren't preying on the romantically desperate by promising to deliver love everlasting. What kind of predatory, profit-hungry chocolatier actually lured people in with the promise of love?

Chimes tinkled sweetly in the winter afternoon as the door opened and a swarm of customers emerged, making room for the twenty-something trio. Dean slipped in behind them. Immediately, the scent of rich, creamy chocolate surrounded him. The place smelled heavenly, but Dean kept his fraud-detection senses on high alert and blocked out the delicious scents.

It was a cute little place with a vaguely European feel. Wood floors, wood paneling, and tons of sweets on display, identified by tiny signs with elaborate cursive script. To the left of the entrance was an old-fashioned register. It was a massive brass fixture that took up an inefficient amount of counter space, but the customers seemed charmed by it. And by the sweet, round-faced grandmotherly type behind the counter.

Dean didn't let himself be charmed. The adorable elderly could be scammers, too. Crooks came in every demographic.

Display cases lined two of the walls, but he could only catch glimpses of the chocolates inside, his view blocked by the shifting crowd. Half of the people crammed into the shop seemed to be pushing toward the counter, while the other half angled toward the right-side wall crowded with photos of smiling couples.

"The Wall of Love!" the trio in front of him gushed in unison, pushing toward the photos.

"I'm going to be up there next year," one of them vowed, and Dean resisted the urge to roll his eyes.

Who would believe for a second that those were actual happy couples? "Grandma" had probably used the pictures that came in the frames.

He'd read the post that had sparked this frenzy before heading to Watson Corners. The brand-new bride-to-be had gushed about the legend of the "Cupid" chocolates, explaining how she'd finally gone to her friend's chocolate shop last Valentine's to change her luck in love. She'd bitten into the chocolate, and true love had followed. It was all very convenient, but hardly conclusive proof of anything magical.

The whole thing was undoubtedly a PR stunt, cooked up by the chocolate shop and the bride to drum up business for Valentine's. He hadn't missed the part where she wrote that she'd gone to her "friend's" chocolate shop. A quick search had shown that the bride-to-be also worked for a florist down the street. Any extra publicity, and the subsequent extra foot traffic in the area around Valentine's, could only help her as well.

He knew he was here for a sappy puff piece for Valentine's Day, but Nora had said he was supposed to dig into it. And he had a feeling if he even scratched the surface he was going to find a whole lot of smoke and mirrors.

The chimes over the door sounded again, and Dean glanced toward the new arrival as a petite brunette stepped into the shop. His gaze lingered as his instincts caught on something different about her, though it took his brain longer to deduce what it was that had caught his attention.

He found himself drifting closer as he studied her. Chestnut hair shifted around her shoulders, catching the light as she looked around the shop with wide, pale blue eyes. Her face had a sweetness to it, but what held his attention, he realized, was the fact that she looked just as alarmed by the crowd as he was. Her arms were full of shopping bags, and she stared at the crowd in open disbelief bordering on horror.

A kindred spirit in the trenches of romantic skepticism, perhaps? Or just an unsuspecting chocolate aficionado who'd had no idea what she was walking into.

The crowd shifted and Dean edged closer.

Another customer, visibly dejected, brushed past her, pausing to say, "Don't waste your time, honey. They're all out of the Cupids."

The woman's eyes widened, and she stammered, "Oh, I'm not..." But the chimes had already rung on the other woman's exit.

Dean was close enough now for his shoulder to brush his anti-romance soulmate's. "Can you believe this?"

Those wide blue eyes landed on him, still overwhelmed and slightly disturbed. "I'm sorry?"

"All these people are here because someone on social media told them a chocolate could make them fall in love," he explained. "It's such a scam. I mean, brilliant, as marketing schemes go. People will do anything if they think it will help them find the kind of love they see in movies. Look at all those dating websites. But a chocolate that makes people fall in love? I can't believe anyone is actually that gullible. And the people who came up with this? Mercenary. Taking advantage of all that foolish hope. Quite the con."

An expression he couldn't read moved across her face. "You think it's a con?" she asked, her tone neutral and curious.

"Absolutely. I'm pretty much a specialist when it comes to fraud."

She released a soft, breathless laugh, murmuring something so quietly that he nearly didn't hear it. It almost sounded like she'd said, "Perfect."

Her smile was wry. Taking that glimmer of dry humor as encouragement, Dean lowered his voice, leaning closer. "What do you think?" He tipped his head toward the wall of pictures. "Stock photos downloaded from some website? Or just the ones that came in the frames?"

Her eyebrows arched up and she asked lightly, "You think the photos are fake, too?"

"Of course. Don't you? If they put pictures of real

couples up there, the people in them could debunk the myth. They can't have that." He jerked his chin toward the faded vintage photo presiding over the others. "The old one's a nice touch. Who do you suppose they say that is?"

For a moment she seemed lost for words. Her mouth opened, and nothing came out, but then she shook her head, smiling slowly as she seemed to come to a decision. "Those are my great-grandparents."

The words were as sweet as spun sugar, and it took him a moment to process them. When he did, Dean laughed. "Right. Good one."

She met his eyes, her smile never faltering.

The first inkling that he may have just made a *major* tactical error whispered through Dean. "Wait. You aren't serious...?"

The sweet little grandma-type behind the counter chose that moment to call out, "Lucy! There you are!"

The woman—Lucy—answered the woman behind the counter. "Sorry it took so long, Nana. Parking was a nightmare."

Dean's stomach dropped. "You're..."

By now, her smile was almost aggressively blinding. "Lucy Sweet. Mercenary chocolatier. Nice to meet you."

Dean groaned internally. So much for stealth and catching them with their guard down.

He extended his hand. "Dean Chase. Channel Five News."

Chapter Six

*H*E WAS A REPORTER. BECAUSE *of course* he was a reporter.

The shop had been nearly empty when she'd escaped, but Lucy had returned to find How Sweet It Is even more overrun with customers than before. There was actually a line out the door. Her usual parking space was tucked behind the building, but the alleyway leading to the employee entrance was completely blocked by illegally parked cars, so she'd had to park down the street and hadn't even been able to get to the back door to sneak in quietly.

She'd taken off her apron before going into the market, so at least she was inconspicuous as she came in the front door.

Inconspicuous enough to unwittingly gain the confidence of the man at her side.

She was already feeling overwhelmed, as though Lena's post had strapped her to a runaway train and all she could do now was hold on tight as it barreled down the tracks. And then the dark-haired man with the perfect haircut and glinting dark eyes had started calling her a con artist.

The fact that he hadn't known who she was didn't make her feel any better.

TV reporter made sense, now that he'd said it. He had that highly polished, photogenic look of a nightly news anchor, and a confident, persuasive way of talking. Engaging. His smile was so addictive, it should come with a surgeon general's warning. She'd bet the viewers loved him.

But what was he doing here?

Please don't let him be doing a story on How Sweet It Is.

"So you're the woman with the magic touch," he murmured, his hand still closed warmly around hers.

"That's what they say," Lucy answered, reclaiming her hostage digits. She began to thread her way through the crowd toward the counter, and he fell into step beside her like he'd been invited.

"I hope you weren't insulted by what I said. I didn't realize you were the owner."

"Yeah, I figured that much out."

"But I really am impressed by what you've done here." His confident smile was back in place—it had barely slipped for a moment when he'd realized who she was.

"My scam?" she asked sweetly, ducking behind the counter and turning to face him when he would have followed. "Sorry, employees only."

He took a step back, hands held up in surrender, and she pushed through the door to the kitchen before he could flash another of those trust-me smiles.

Her grandmother was right on her heels.

"It's been a zoo ever since you left!" Nana Edda exclaimed, breathless with excitement. She held the door open an inch to keep an eye on the browsing crowd. "I can't take more than a moment. I've never seen it like this."

"Where's Georgie?" Lucy asked as she set down the shopping bags and fished out her apron.

"She had class, remember?"

"Right. Sorry. I should have hurried back."

"It's fine. I think most of them are here as much to talk to each other and gawk at the Wall as they are to get chocolates. It's all about the *experience*. And the crowds make us look so successful. We're in demand!" Her grandmother patted her silver curls. "I'll see you out there!"

Nana Edda swung back through the kitchen door and Lucy turned away from the counter where she'd set the shopping bags, pausing to slip her apron over her head and take a moment to ground herself.

She'd thought things through while she was shopping, processing the development of their newfound fame. It could be a good thing, she'd nearly convinced herself. She would still be able to protect the shop—probably.

And she wasn't going to panic just because a fraud-debunking specialist reporter had shown up on her doorstep.

But she couldn't stop thinking about Gigi's words.

Her great-grandmother had never sold the Cupids. She'd always believed the magic would turn on the family if they tried to profit from it.

Lucy had rationalized when she started selling the secret family-recipe chocolates that they weren't truly profiting from the legend if it was just word of mouth, if they weren't *promising* things. But now that they'd gone viral, had the magic turned to a curse? Was that why that reporter was here?

She should get back out front. Who knew what her grandmother was telling the customers?

Or the reporter.

Oh no.

The realization that she'd left her grandmother alone with a TV reporter hit and Lucy rushed back through the swinging door, panic hurrying her steps.

Thankfully, Nana Edda was occupied with a customer at the far end of the counter, and the reporter hadn't yet identified her as the source of over-the-top quotes that she was. Lucy took a deep, relieved breath. She just had to keep the two of them far apart until she could get him out of the shop.

Sadly, he hadn't given up and left.

He was lying in wait, as close as he could get to the employee area without crossing the invisible line she had drawn.

"I think we got off on the wrong foot," he said with a smile so smoothly charming that he probably instantly got his way eighty percent of the time he deployed it. Lucy was determined to be part of the twenty percent to resist.

"Do you?" she asked without an ounce of sarcasm. "I think we got off on a very truthful footing. You think my shop is a scam." She turned to the customer at the front of the line. "Can I help you?"

"Can I reserve two of the Cupids for Valentine's and also get one of those milk chocolate strawberry pralines for now?"

"Absolutely," Lucy replied with a sunny smile, as

the reporter sidled along the display cases to stay in her line of sight.

"I will admit I don't personally believe in magic or love at first sight," he admitted, "but I would love to do a story about the phenomenon of your shop."

"No, thanks. We're good." She crouched to place one of the strawberry-shaped filled chocolates into a tiny box. When she straightened, he was still there, and he kept pace alongside her as she moved back to fill out the advance order form.

She completed the order and turned to the next customer without sparing him a second glance, hoping he would take the hint and leave. But he just lingered at the edge of her vision as she helped one customer after the next, periodically interjecting new comments.

"I thought pralines had nuts," he said, evidently trying a different tack to slip past her defenses as she filled another order.

"These are Belgian pralines," Lucy explained as she carefully boxed the selections. "Chocolate shells with a soft filling. The French and American pralines both have nuts—and you can find them in the far case, between the fudge and the cocoa bombs."

She smiled brightly at her customer and rang him up, the reporter waiting semi-patiently until she had completed the transaction to interject again.

"And which kind are the Cupid chocolates?" he asked as soon as the customer had left with his purchase. "Belgian? Or is the magic American?"

Lucy sighed as she traded places with her grandmother at the cash register, moving down the display cases. She had to respect his persistence. "Mister..."

"Chase. Dean Chase. But please, call me Dean."

"Dean." She met his gaze, trying to impart all her conviction in hers. "You are wasting your time. You made it very clear what you think of my shop and me, and you are now the last person I would ever trust to do a story on us, if I even wanted to be on the news. Which I don't."

That should have been the end of it.

Something shifted in his eyes, and she almost thought she'd won, that he was going to take his questions and go home—but then a high, eager voice spoke from behind her.

"The *news*?" Her grandmother appeared at her side like she'd teleported. "Lucy! Of course we want How Sweet It is to be featured on the news."

The charm in Dean's smile ratcheted up to eleven, and Nana Edda went instantly gooey in the face of it as he extended his hand. "Dean Chase. And may I say, I am *delighted* to hear that."

Nana Edda fluttered. "Edda Sweet, Lucy's grandmother. Did you know How Sweet It Is has been family run for four generations? Be sure you put that in your story."

"There isn't going to be a story." Lucy shot her grandmother a quelling look.

"Of course there is." Nana Edda flapped a hand at her. "Don't be silly. We just love the local news." She turned to Lucy and stage-whispered, entirely too loudly, "And he's so *handsome*."

Lucy blushed, not meeting Dean's eyes, because yes, she had also noticed he was rather easy on the eyes, but of course he was. He was a television personality. That was practically in the job description.

"No, thank you," she said firmly, and looked around for another customer. The latest rush seemed to have passed, and they were in a very inconvenient lull. Lucy couldn't even pretend she was too busy to argue with him. The last trio of customers were taking selfies in front of the Wall of Love, already holding their purchases.

"The Cupid chocolates are her great-grandmother's secret recipe."

"Nana!" Lucy yelped. "We aren't giving an interview about the Cupids!"

"Well, *you* aren't, but I'm my own person, and I can talk to whomever I please."

"Perhaps I should go get my camera," Dean said.

"No TV cameras in the shop," Lucy insisted, giving her grandmother a stern look. "My name's the one on the lease, and I say no cameras."

"We can film out front," Nana Edda offered.

"Nana, can you please go to the office and get some more advance order forms?" Lucy asked. "We're running low."

"Of course," Nana Edda promised sweetly, heading toward the back, but not before making exaggerated *we'll talk later* gestures at the reporter.

"I saw that," Lucy warned, but her grandmother just smiled innocently.

"Saw what?"

She vanished through the swinging door, and Lucy turned her full attention to the reporter. "Please don't take advantage of my grandmother's eagerness to be on camera. I've already said no."

Chapter Seven

*D*EAN FROWNED, SWALLOWING THE FULL-COURT-PRESS persuasion he'd had locked and loaded in the face of her plea.

"I don't take advantage," he said, hearing an edge of unwelcome defensiveness in his own voice. "I'm the good guy."

"I'm sure that's what you tell yourself. But you're just going to have to go expose fraud somewhere else."

"If you have nothing to hide, what are you so afraid of?"

He knew it was the wrong thing to say as soon as the words left his mouth, but he couldn't unsay them.

She hadn't exactly been receptive before, but at that, the grumpy chocolatier's face closed off completely, lines tightening around her mouth as her eyes narrowed and she folded her arms tightly across her chest. "I think it's time for you to go."

The door to the kitchen swung open again, her grandmother appearing beside her. The older woman glanced anxiously between Dean and Lucy, picking up on the tension in the air. "Is everything okay?"

"Mr. Chase was just leaving," Lucy bit out, staring him down.

"Oh no!" Nana Edda exclaimed. "Well, I do hope you'll come back soon." She reached for a display of small cream-colored chocolate boxes with the How Sweet It Is logo stamped on the top in gold, and plucked one off the top, thrusting it at him. "Here. Just a little thank-you for coming by."

"*Nana.*"

"Thank you," Dean said, accepting the box before Lucy could snatch it back. He set his business card on the counter beside the antique cash register, sliding it toward her. "Just in case you change your mind."

The look of utter disbelief on Lucy's face spoke volumes about how likely she was to change her mind, but Dean didn't give her a chance to verbalize the when-pigs-fly odds. He knew when a strategic retreat was called for.

He took his chocolate box and slipped quickly out of the shop, back into the bracing cold of the late January wind that whipped along picturesque Main Street.

He wasn't giving up. Just regrouping.

Dean didn't give up easily. His tenacity was responsible for virtually all his success in life. But he'd royally screwed up in there.

He didn't usually run his mouth like that, especially not to someone he didn't know. It had to be her. There was just something about her that had brought out the worst in him, making him want to impress her by bragging about how he was the Fraud Exposer, like it made him some kind of superhero.

Or, if he was honest with himself, it was probably that place. The energy in it. All love and lies. That nonsense always set him off. It had gotten his hackles up, and he'd just wanted to take the place down a few pegs, poke a few holes in the shared delusion. Introduce some *rationality*.

Just like he had when he'd shoved his foot in his mouth with Anna. The second someone started talking true love, he couldn't keep his opinions to himself.

But it had been a boneheaded move. Nora would not be amused.

He could always get the story without Lucy Sweet. If he could get a few eager customers and the bride-to-be on the record, that would probably be enough for the kind of piece Nora wanted. The grandma would undoubtedly give him enough on-camera quotes to fill the segment all by herself. But Nora would ask why there was no footage inside the shop. She would ask if the grandma was the owner, and Dean had gotten the distinct impression she wasn't. And Nora would want to know how he could have botched the puffiest of puff pieces.

Back at his car, Dean settled in the driver's seat, starting the engine to warm the car up but not immediately putting it into gear. He sat studying the delicate gold-topped box in his hands. It looked like something from an exclusive, imported chocolatier. Featherlight, but when he shook it, he heard a soft rattle inside.

Maybe if he gave the chocolate to Nora as a peace offering, she wouldn't take his head off for screwing up the easiest assignment he'd ever had.

Or maybe this was an opportunity.

Maybe he could use Lucy Sweet's defensiveness, her refusal to do the story, as evidence that something fishy was going on to get Nora on board with the exposé plan.

That could work.

He felt a little flicker of something—almost like guilt—remembering Lucy's reaction when he called himself the good guy. *I'm sure that's what you tell yourself.*

He pushed away that whisper of *something* at the back of his mind. Of course it was what he told himself. Because it was true. He was the good guy. He was the defender of the defenseless. The gullible and the downtrodden.

He had a responsibility to them.

Now he just had to convince his boss.

Chapter Eight

"*No.*"

"Nora," Dean pleaded, "hear me out."

His boss rocked back in her chair, her head cocked and her black hair sliding to one side as she studied him. "I thought I was clear. I thought I requested an adorably sweet chocolate shop story."

"You did. You were." He paced restlessly in front of her desk. "But it's such a scam. Her name is Lucy Sweet. That's not even a real name! And you should have seen how she clammed up when she realized I was a reporter. They're obviously hiding something."

"They aren't even the ones claiming the chocolates do anything!"

"But they're profiting from it. And that bride who made the post? She's friends with the owner and runs a flower shop just down the street. All those people flocking to buy chocolates—you think they aren't placing some Valentine's flower orders, too? There's a story here, Nora. I can sense it."

"It's a piece about love! It's a warm, fuzzy hug of a story, and the viewers don't need you to rain all over it in an attempt to protect them from the possibility that love might exist."

He grimaced, spreading his hands. "I know you wanted me to learn my lesson about being bitter about the love stuff, but in my defense, I went in there with an open mind." Mostly. "I'm telling you, there's an angle here."

"Dean!" Nora raised her voice, then reined herself in, closing her eyes and taking a slow, deep breath. When she opened them again, she'd reclaimed her calm, and her expression was pitiless. "Close the door."

His heart instantly slammed against the inside of his ribcage. Nora only closed her office during confidential conversations.

Like when she was about to fire someone.

Dean moved slowly to her office door, replaying the last few minutes in his mind. Nora was fair. She wouldn't fire him just for disagreeing with her, would she?

Even if he'd done it over and over again and hadn't listened to her?

When the door clicked shut, she nodded to the chair he'd been circling opposite her desk. "Sit down."

"Look, Nora..." Dean began as he sank onto the edge of the chair, but she held up her hand to stop him.

"This story isn't a punishment, Dean. It was never a punishment or a lesson. It's an *opportunity*."

Dean frowned, shaking his head, trying to make sense of the words.

Nora steepled her fingers, meeting his gaze meaningfully. "Alex's wife just got a major research grant. It's a huge opportunity for her, but it means moving to New Mexico. Alex has already started sending his reel to local news stations down there, but he told us that whether he gets another anchor job or not, he's going with her. Apparently, they agreed it was time for her career to take priority." She met his eyes, spelling out the realization he'd already come to. "We're going to need a new morning anchor."

Suddenly his heart was pounding for a whole new reason. Morning anchor hadn't even been on his radar. Alex and Anna were wildly popular, and they were *young*. He'd known they wouldn't be retiring any time soon and that only a major gaffe could get either one of them off the air. But if Alex was moving...

Words clogged in his throat, but Nora wasn't done.

"The senior producers decided not to tell anyone yet because we didn't want you all circling around like sharks scenting blood in the water."

Dean found his voice. "Am I...?"

"You're in the running," Nora confirmed, and Dean struggled to keep his victory dance entirely internal, one of his hands closing automatically into a tiny fist pump of satisfaction. "The morning anchor position relies heavily on charm—and you have plenty of that. But you've seen how we stack the shows. The hard-hitting news pieces are for the evening broadcast. In the morning, we're trying to ease people into their day. There are cooking segments and feel-good pieces. And yes, the morning anchors read the important headlines, but it's not about exposing scandal over cornflakes. It's about being a resource in the community. A friend they turn on every morning. We do shorter cuts of the investigative pieces and get people back to the feel-good stuff faster."

Dean nodded along. He could do this. He could really make anchor without having to leave his sister behind.

"You're a great investigative journalist, Dean. And you're terrific at communicating with the audience, keeping things interesting and approachable, even when it comes to something as convoluted as some of our ballot measures. But you have to be able to do warm and fuzzy stuff, too, in order to be the morning anchor. The viewers want a feel-good morning show. Not someone to give them the hard truth about divorce statistics." Nora frowned. "And then there's Anna. Whoever we pick will have to have good on-air chemistry with our current co-host, who isn't your biggest fan right now."

Dean cringed, and Nora delivered her conclusion.

"Frankly, Dean, if you want a shot at the morning anchor desk, you need to lighten up your image—and convince Anna that you actually have a heart. Which means not raining all over the viewers' parade right before Valentine's Day when we all just want a cute story about love."

He closed his eyes briefly, groaning to himself. "I might have been a little overeager with the con artist angle."

"You might," Nora agreed.

"I can do warm and fuzzy," he assured her.

"Great. I look forward to seeing it."

"I'll go back tomorrow. Talk to the owner." Who would hopefully not throw him out on his face.

"Excellent plan," Nora confirmed, and Dean sensed his dismissal. He stood, moving toward the door. But as he opened it, Nora called out to him. "Dean?"

He turned, and she chucked the tiny How Sweet It Is chocolate box at him, forcing him to catch it before it could hit him in the face.

"Eat that. You need it more than I do. And no bothering Anna about this."

"She doesn't know Alex is leaving?"

"She knows. But she was part of the decision not to tell any of the candidates they were being considered. She doesn't want the parade of kiss-ups trying to get in her good graces any more than we do. So take my advice and just leave her alone. Let your wonderful piece about the virtues of love be your apology to her and leave it at that."

"Got it. Thanks, boss."

"And Dean?"

"Yeah?"

"Good luck. Something tells me you're going to need it."

"No luck required," he assured Nora, with every drop of confidence he possessed.

He would go back to How Sweet It Is tomorrow. He would make this work. He wanted that anchor job, and he wasn't going to let one little miscalculation today stop him from proving he could do this.

He took the shortcut through the studio on his way back to his desk. The six o'clock team was getting ready for their broadcast, the anchors reviewing last-minute changes with the producers.

Dean had always wanted to be that steady voice

on camera, reading the news, ever since his high school media class when he'd first sat down at an anchor desk—even if it was just broadcast on his high school's website. Anchors were always composed, always in control. They had the facts at their fingertips, and they made sense of the world.

His life hadn't always seemed to make sense, but sitting at that desk, he'd felt for the first time that he knew exactly who he was, and that he was exactly where he was supposed to be.

If he could do that every day...if he could be the person who woke up with the city, his voice making sense of a chaotic world for all the viewers tuning in...

When. It wouldn't be *if.* He would make it happen. He was too close to let this opportunity slip past him.

Provided he hadn't already spiked his chances.

Dean ducked out of the studio before the broadcast could begin, moving to his desk in the middle of the bullpen. When he was anchor, he'd have an office. He'd have journalists doing field pieces for him, rather than the other way around. He'd have finally made it.

Sitting on the edge of his desk, Dean eyed the chocolate box in his hand as if it was his blue-eyed adversary. All he had to do was find some way to get her to trust him.

Slipping his thumb under the seal, he popped open the box, peering at the solitary chocolate nestled inside.

It was square, with a swirling design gently imprinted on the top. He lifted it out of the box, and the scent of milk chocolate teased his nose.

Know thine enemy.

He popped the chocolate into his mouth. And groaned.

Creamy rich chocolate. Smooth vanilla cream filling. *Heaven.* The praline was silky, sweet heaven in a bite.

Dean closed his eyes as he savored the flavors melting together on his tongue, decadent and lingering.

No wonder people thought her chocolates were magic. The taste alone was almost enough to make him believe in the legend. If anything could make a person fall in love, it would be a chocolate like this one.

Bless sweet little Nana Edda. She'd given him the perfect excuse to come back. He had to find out what kind of chocolate she'd given him.

He'd wait until tomorrow, but Dean Chase was about to become Lucy Sweet's number-one customer. Right until he got his story.

Chapter Nine

ℒUCY SAT IN THE TINY office, cluttered with yellow-ing family photos, and stared at her computer screen with a creeping feeling of impending doom.

She should never have picked up Dean Chase's business card and shoved it in her pocket. She'd felt the shape of it against her leg for the rest of the day, a constant, nagging reminder. And she *definitely* shouldn't have searched online for the name on that crisp, white card as soon as How Sweet It Is closed and she was alone.

She loved this time of day, the perfect quiet of the shop at night, when there were no distractions and all she had to do was make a batch of whichever choco-lates they'd run out of during the day. She should be making Cupids right now. They had stacks of orders to fill. But instead, she was watching clip after clip online of Dean Chase exposing fraud with a grim de-termination.

He spoke into the camera with a steady confidence that made you want to trust him. Believe him. It would have been appealing—the dogged protector vibe, the subtle nobility of the champion for the little guy, his dark trust-me eyes—if he hadn't been targeting How Sweet It Is.

The man was good at his job. And now they were in his sights.

A loud buzzing rang through the kitchens, and Lucy jerked toward the sound. It was much too late for deliveries, and her first, panicked thought was that the reporter was back to do his exposé—which made so little sense that she firmly yanked herself out of her doom spiral and headed toward the rear door to the shop.

The buzzer was sounding rhythmically now, the person outside tapping a pattern into the button. Nana Edda had a key, and so few people dropped by the back door after hours that Lucy had a good idea who'd be on the other side even before she opened the door. Sure enough, she found Lena standing on the doorstep wearing a neon pink pencil skirt and a bright smile.

"Were you surprised?" Lena stepped inside as soon as Lucy opened the door, swanning into the kitchen and doing a little twirl. "Tyler told me I should tell you in advance about my plan so you could prepare extra chocolates just in case, but I wanted it to be a surprise. And I never imagined it would be as huge as it is! We passed half a million. *Half a million* people have liked my little post!" She spread her arms wide as if to scoop up all the accolades coming her way. "You can thank me any time you want."

Lucy groaned, slumping against an empty counter where she really should be preparing a batch of the Cupids. "Thank you? I don't know whether to hug you or wring your neck."

"What?" Lena blinked, confused. "Why would neck wringing even be a possibility? You had a line *out the door* today! I saw it every time our shop quieted down enough for me to pop my head out to look. Our receipts were *insane* today, and yours can't have been bad, not with those crowds."

Lucy grimaced. She had to admit the sales today had been on a level she'd never seen, even on Valentine's Day. Not during her entire tenure running the shop. She had dozens of preorders to log into the computer. Almost all of them were for Cupids on Valentine's, but there were a few others scattered in around the edges.

It had been a good day. An incredible day. And she knew Lena's story going viral had propelled those sales, but she still couldn't stop the anxiety crawling up the back of her throat.

"The receipts were fantastic, but I never wanted to go public about the Cupids."

Lena frowned, shaking her head in befuddlement. "If you don't want people to know about the legend, why do you have the Wall of Love?"

"It's not that I don't want people to know, I just..."

"Don't want to tell them?" Lena filled in when Lucy couldn't find the words.

Lucy flushed. She knew it didn't make sense, but selling the Cupids had always tangled her up inside. She'd had mixed feelings about it since day one. "Gigi always said the magic was fickle. That we shouldn't try to profit from it. I thought if we just sold them quietly..."

"Then the magic wouldn't realize what you were doing?" Lena asked, her voice thick with skepticism.

"I know it sounds crazy."

"Well, we are talking about magic chocolates. Which I fully believe in," Lena quickly assured her. "And which you have been quietly selling for years with no adverse effects. Even if the magic was sentient enough to be bothered that someone was trying to use it for financial gain, wouldn't it come after me because I'm the one who spilled the beans?"

"It's not logical," Lucy argued. "It's just..."

"Fear?"

The word seemed to land between them, taking root, and Lucy tried not to flinch away from the accuracy.

She was scared. She was always scared. Scared of losing the shop. Scared of failing her grandmother, failing her family legacy. Scared that the shop, the one place that had always represented security and stability in her life, was going to slip away.

Lena said, "I know things with your mom weren't always—"

"It isn't about that," Lucy insisted, though they both knew it was.

Lucy adored her mother. They were friends as well as mother and daughter. That was part of what had made today so stressful: the knowledge that her mother was out of the country and completely out of reach at a time when things suddenly felt so out of control.

She'd missed having her mother as a sounding board. Even if Helen Sweet-Carter was also a wild card: all instinct and reaction. She never thought ahead. She never *planned* ahead. Growing up with her, the ground had never felt completely steady beneath Lucy's feet. For as long as she could remember, she'd always been waiting for the next rug to be yanked out, always trying to predict where the next anvil was going to fall from. Lucy'd had to be the responsible one.

But How Sweet It Is had been her sanctuary.

She would come stay with her grandparents and Gigi, and they would talk about tradition, teaching her about ways of making chocolates that stretched back centuries, and making her feel grounded in a way nothing with her mother ever had.

Lucy ran a hand over the smooth, familiar surface of the countertop. She hadn't been ready to take over the shop when it had suddenly been her turn to carry that tradition into the future, but she wouldn't have had it any other way. She wanted this legacy to be in her hands.

She just hadn't expected it to be quite so hard to carry forward.

Until today. She'd been so worried about the publicity, but if business kept up like today, they'd be able to pay off the loan and easily weather any dip in sales when the French place across the street opened.

But how long would the story drive new customers to the store? Viral posts had a tendency to disappear from the public consciousness as quickly as they exploded onto it. Unless another scandal fueled them.

Her stomach clenched as she remembered the reporter and his determination.

"Why are you so worried?" Lena asked gently. "The legend holds up. Look at all your success stories." She waved a hand behind her to the darkened shop, in the vague direction of the Wall of Love.

"But what if someone starts digging, or the story starts spreading and it gets out of control? It can go from being a cute story with a few successes behind it to a fraudulent promise like *that*." She snapped her fingers.

Lena shook her head. "You aren't promising anyone anything that isn't true. People just want a chance at love."

Lucy couldn't share Lena's optimism. "A reporter came by today. Dean Chase from Channel Five."

Lena's face lit up. "The 'Five on Your Side' guy? He's sharp. A little cynical, but smart."

"Exactly. And he thinks we're con artists."

Lena cocked her head. "He said that?"

"He didn't know I was the owner when he said it, but yeah. He said the Wall of Love was probably all stock photos and that we were preying on romantic desperation."

"But it isn't, and you aren't," Lena argued. "A news story could be great. If you could convince Dean Chase that the chocolates are legit, people would *flock* to the store."

She wasn't wrong.

"It's just too risky," Lucy protested, reaching for the ingredients to start a batch of the Cupids. "If we promise people true love and they don't get it, we're the ones they'll be mad at. There's a fine line between a nice old family story and getting sued for false rep resentation."

"No one is going to sue you," Lena said, as if that much was obvious, settling in to watch her make the chocolates. "People don't sue the person who reads their tarot cards if they don't like the mysterious stranger they meet. And I have yet to hear of a single pregnant lady suing that eggplant parmesan place that promises anyone full-term will go into labor within twenty-four hours of eating there. People just want hope. They want something they can try when things feel like they're beyond our control. And that's what you give them. If it doesn't work out, at least they had the hope."

Lucy looked up from the chocolate she was heating and studied her best friend. Was she right? Was it just about hope?

"What does your grandmother think about the reporter?" Lena asked.

"At first, she was on your side," Lucy admitted. "All publicity is good publicity. I could barely stop her from inviting him to bring his camera in here. But after he left, I told her he'd called the Cupids a hoax, and she changed her tune."

Lucy could vividly recall the horror on her grandmother's face when she'd realized Dean Chase was a nonbeliever. Nana Edda had grumbled all afternoon that she couldn't believe she'd given that "lousy snake" one of her favorite chocolate creams.

"The fact that he thinks it's a hoax is what makes it even better," Lena insisted as Lucy's hands went through the familiar motions. "If you can convince him, you can convince anyone. *Everyone.*"

"But I don't want to convince everyone. More exposure means more people believing in the myth. It means more pressure to deliver true love. What if it doesn't happen this year?"

"Then you still have thirteen success stories hanging on your wall. And your customers still have hope. Don't you owe it to your community to give that hope to as many people as possible? Really, you should hold out for the national news."

Lucy groaned. "No, thank you. I just want to make chocolates and look after Nana Edda and not torpedo the family legacy."

The chocolate shop wasn't big business, its success or failure wasn't life or death, but it was hers. It was Gigi's and Nana Edda's. It was past, present, and future for her family. And she hadn't realized when she'd decided to take it over how heavy the responsibility of that tradition would be. If the shop failed, she wouldn't just be failing herself, she'd be failing her family, her heritage. Every decision seemed more important when looked at through that lens. Even the decision of whether or not to have a reporter do a story on the Valentine's legend.

"I know what's happening," Lena declared. "Fear of success."

Lucy rolled her eyes. "Look, Miss Psych 101, I don't have a fear of success. I just have the regular kind—a very healthy fear of very possible failure."

"Has it ever occurred to you that focusing so much on avoiding the things you're scared of means you never go after the things you want?"

Lucy narrowed her eyes at her best friend. "I have the things I want. I have the shop. I have my family. I have you."

"And love?"

"Not everyone needs romantic love to be happy. Don't judge me just because I haven't been brainwashed by the fairy-tale-princess-must-have-her-prince propaganda."

Lena's gaze was skeptical. "You say that, but you

see how happy the couples with the Cupids are. You saw how great your grandparents were together. How they helped one another, balanced each other. Look at your mother."

Her mother was a human tornado, but when she'd met her current husband—with the help of the Cupids—she did seem to have found the person who could bring out all her strengths while tempering all her wild winds.

But Lucy shook her head. "I'm not my mother."

"No, but that doesn't mean you have to do everything on your own. Wouldn't it be nice to have someone to rely on? To share the burdens, and the joys?"

It would be nice. She'd always wanted what her grandparents had. Two people who had hitched themselves together with love and were pulling together through all the highs and lows of life. But somehow, that had never felt entirely possible for her. It was part of why she'd never tried the Cupids on Valentine's. What if she did...and they didn't work?

Lucy looked down at the chocolates in her hands.

"Just don't let fear stop you," Lena encouraged, reading her mind. "From any of it."

"I won't," Lucy promised. Though she had no intention of eating a Cupid this year. Or calling that reporter to do a story on How Sweet It Is. Some things were just too risky. She smiled at Lena as she reached for a chocolate mold, changing the subject. "So tell me all about your wedding plans. I know you've already planned out ninety percent of it even though you've only been engaged forty-eight hours."

"You know me so well." Lena beamed and settled

in to tell her all about the centerpieces she was envisioning.

Chapter Ten

THIS MORNING, THERE WAS NO line out the door, but Dean could see a small crowd inside as he looked through the frosted-glass window of How Sweet It Is and reviewed his strategy.

He'd tried the flower shop down the street first, hoping to enlist the bride-to-be as an ally, but she'd seen him coming, and he hadn't gotten more than one sentence of his very persuasive speech out before she'd stopped him.

"You're going to have to get Lucy on board first," Lena had declared as she'd pointed him back toward How Sweet It Is. "If she gives me the green light, I'll tell you everything you want to know, but until then?" She made a zipping motion over her mouth and closed the door behind him.

And so here he was. Standing outside How Sweet It Is, regretting his attack of foot-in-mouth disease yesterday.

This wasn't make-or-break for the anchor position, he assured himself. There would be other factors. But it suddenly felt like his dream job, his entire future, hinged on convincing one very justifiably reluctant chocolatier to give him this story.

Luckily, he'd always liked a challenge. And he also felt an unanticipated need to prove to Lucy Sweet that he wasn't the devil.

Just because he wasn't suckered in by her magic chocolate scheme didn't mean he didn't appreciate the cleverness behind it. He admired her savvy. Maybe he could spin it that way. Play up the truth. She'd never believe he was suddenly a romantic convert, but the if-you-help-me-I'll-help-you strategy might be viable.

Decision made, he pulled open the door to the delicate tinkle of chimes.

The crowd had thinned out while he was considering his strategy, and there were only a handful of customers in the shop. The sweet little grandma was helping customers at the far end of the counter, while Lucy Sweet was at the cash register up front. It was tempting to try his hand with the more receptive audience of the grandma, but Lucy had proven to be the one in charge.

And the florist had been nothing if not clear. Lucy was the one he had to convince.

He pretended to be examining the chocolates in the nearest display while he covertly watched her. Her thick hair was pulled up in a ponytail today that swung gently as she talked. He could tell the moment she noticed him, her full mouth tightening and her shoulders going stiff, even though her attention never wavered from the girl in front of her.

"Do they really make people fall in love with you?"

Lucy flicked a glance at him beneath her lashes,

so quick he wouldn't have noticed it if he hadn't been watching her so closely. He could practically feel the discomfort pulsing off her in waves.

"The legend is that eating one of the Cupids on Valentine's will help you find your true love," she explained, "but they don't make people do anything. It's more about throwing an opportunity into your path. It's your choice if you take it."

It was a neat little sidestep and Dean felt his lips curve in a small, admiring smile.

"You're back!"

Dean nearly jumped out of his skin at the overly bright voice. He'd been so fixated on Lucy, he hadn't noticed the departure of the other customers, or Lucy's grandmother approaching.

Without missing a beat, he put on his most charming smile and turned it toward the Sweet grandma. "I couldn't stay away. I had to find out what that chocolate you gave me yesterday was."

"You liked it, did you?" Edda Sweet said with a pleased smile. "Vanilla cream. One of our specialties." She cocked her head, studying him. "But if you really want to be blown away, you should try our Mexican hot cocoa. It's my own special recipe. You've never had anything like it. The spice brings out the richness. Of course, you have to be all right with a little heat."

"I'm not afraid of spicy," he assured her.

"Excellent." She beamed. "Coming right up."

Nana Edda vanished through the door to the back of the shop, and Dean turned to watch Lucy finish ringing up the girl who had been asking about the chocolates. When the customer departed with a ring of chimes, the store had emptied out again, and it was just the two of them.

Lucy made a show of tucking the receipt into the antique cash register, closing it with a clang, and then finally turned toward him, folding her arms across her chest.

"You know, we reserve the right to refuse service to pesky reporters."

Dean felt his practiced smile turning into something genuine. He did love a challenge.

Of course he'd come back. After last night's research session, Lucy should have known he wouldn't just stay away. A man didn't get a reputation like Dean Chase's without a healthy dose of determination.

And with the way her morning had been going, it was practically inevitable. Bad news always came in clusters.

In Lucy's experience, there wasn't much in life that chocolate couldn't fix. But unfortunately, even chocolate couldn't do a thing about rent increases. Or fancy, well-funded competitors opening up locations right across the street. Or dogged reporters intent on taking her down.

The email about the rent increase had come just this morning. Lena had called, complaining that their mutual landlord had upped the florists' rent too. Watson Corners was growing, the retail space becoming more valuable, and the property taxes going up. The increase had been inevitable. Lucy had figured it was coming, but why did it have to come *now*?

If she was inclined to believe in omens—which, okay, yes, she absolutely was—then she had to acknowledge there had been some definite portents of doom over the last few days. All seeming to hit at the exact same time.

The Doom Parade had already done a number on her concentration this morning.

And then Dean Chase had walked through the door.

She'd felt his presence, felt him watching her, though she tried to pretend she didn't, even as she became instantly more self-conscious about the usual customer questions about the Cupids. The shop had been bustling all morning and she'd fielded the questions so many times, her responses should have been automatic, but as soon as she'd felt him standing there, watching her, her tongue had seemed to swell, and she had no idea what she'd actually said.

And of course, the shop was suddenly quiet. Right when she wished she had customers to hide behind.

She had no excuse but to face him when the last customer left. She was just lucky she'd made the right change, as fractured as her attention had been since he'd walked in. And now even Nana Edda had abandoned her, rushing off to the kitchen to make the reporter some Mexican hot cocoa.

Her grandmother must have decided he wasn't such a snake, after all, if she was going to the effort of making the spicy hot chocolate. It was a time-consuming recipe that Nana Edda rarely bothered with, one that left Lucy with far too much time alone with Dean Chase.

Where was a parade of hungry customers when she needed them?

He lifted his hands in surrender. "I come in peace. I promise."

She raised a brow skeptically. "Really."

"I know I didn't make the best impression yesterday, but hear me out. I feel like this can be a real win-win situation."

"Why should I hear you out when you decided what we were before you even walked in the door?"

"Okay, I might have done that," Dean admitted. "But come on. Can you blame me? Magic chocolates?"

She frowned at him, and the tinge of scorn on his face melted into an earnestness that was entirely too endearing.

"Look, I'm a skeptic. It's kind of my thing. I'm not going to lie to you and tell you I believe in true love spells when I don't, but it's a nice story. The kind of story our viewers will love, especially around Valentine's. You have my word that anything we put on the air would only be positive. Glowing, even."

"Yesterday, you called me a mercenary con artist."

He had the grace to cringe. "Okay, not my best moment. I know I said some things yesterday that may have crossed a line, but you have to understand where I was coming from. I have a reputation. I'm the defender of the little guy."

"Oh, I know all about your reputation. I looked you up." She refused to blush when she admitted that. She would have looked up any snake who was trying to bring down How Sweet It Is. "But who exactly are you defending here? Who are we hurting?"

"The romantically gullible?" he said, but the answer sounded more like a question.

Lucy folded her arms. "Look around. What do you see?"

He glanced left and right, frowning. "Your shop? It's cute."

"Do you see us advertising magic? Do you see us promising love?"

"Well, you have the photos...and if the legend is verbal..."

"It's a *legend*. A story. Do you get mad at people who believe in wishing wells?"

"Wishing wells aren't promising love for your coin."

"Neither are we. We're promising *chocolate*," she reminded him. "And like I said before, *who is it hurting*? You can call yourself the defender of the little guy, but we are the little guy, and people like our shop. And the legend of the Cupids gives our customers hope."

"So let me do a story on you. On your chocolates. On your hope. That's why I'm here."

It was almost tempting. She could hear Lena's voice in her head telling her to take the chance, but Lucy couldn't quite bring herself to say yes. She was already shaking her head when the door to the kitchens swung open and her grandmother appeared bearing a steaming cup of hot chocolate.

"Here we are! One Mexican hot chocolate!"

Lucy didn't know how Dean had won her grandmother over again so quickly, but Nana Edda was practically simpering as she extended the mug to him.

"Careful." Nana Edda fluttered her lashes. "It's hot. In more ways than one."

"I'm sure I can handle it." Dean accepted the mug with one of his seemingly endless variety of charming smiles.

No wonder he was so great at exposing fraud. He probably just *smiled* at people, and they spilled all their secrets.

Dean lifted the mug to his lips and inhaled the aroma before taking a mouthful. Lucy knew exactly what he'd be experiencing. The rich thickness of the chocolate. The hint of cinnamon, and then that kick of heat, the finish of the chili peppers that built on the tongue and enhanced all the other flavors. Mexican hot chocolate had been one of her favorite additions to the menu when her grandparents had finally convinced her great-grandmother to expand beyond the traditional Belgian delicacies. She'd been drinking it since she was six.

And her face had never turned as red as Dean's did after that first taste.

"Whoa." His eyes watered, and he held the mug at arm's length in an instinctive attempt to get the cocoa as far away from his tongue as he could. He blew out a breath, and Lucy frowned, taking the cup from his hands as he began to sweat.

"Are you okay?"

"Fine," he wheezed, bending at the waist.

"Are you allergic to anything?" They didn't keep an EpiPen on hand. They really should, with all the pralines. She'd never been afraid a customer would go into anaphylactic shock before, but now she was realizing what an oversight that was.

"No, that's just..." He waved at the mug in her hands, still wheezing. "It's got a kick."

Lucy frowned at the mug, lifting it to her nose. It smelled normal. The expected blend of chocolate and spice.

She took a tentative sip.

Immediately, her sinuses began to burn.

She gasped, her gaze flying to collide with her grandmother's. "Nana!"

"Did I make it too spicy?" Nana Edda asked with exaggerated innocence. "This is why I should leave the recipes to you, sweetheart. I'm always putting in tablespoons rather than teaspoons."

Lucy sucked in a breath, fire spreading across her tongue even faster with the exposure to air, and set down the mug as tears began to leak from her eyes. "I'll get you some milk," she told Dean, grabbing her grandmother's arm and pulling her along as she rushed back to the kitchen.

"What did you do?" she hissed as soon as the kitchen door had swung shut behind them. She dropped her grandmother's arm and made a beeline for the fridge and the milk.

"I just wanted to get rid of him."

Lucy pulled out the milk and grabbed two more of the mugs they used for cocoa, filling one for her and one for Dean. "Yesterday, you wanted me to do the TV interview!"

"I did, but that was before I knew he was a nonbeliever. He wants to tell everyone we're fraudsters!"

"That doesn't mean we try to burn off his taste buds!"

Nana Edda sniffed. "We don't need that kind of negative energy around here."

"Next time, warn me before you start doling out

chili pepper overdoses." Lucy grabbed the mugs of milk and returned to the front of the shop where Dean was standing with his head back and his cheeks puffed out, inhaling through his nose.

He immediately reached for the milk, then paused with the mug an inch from his lips.

"It's just milk," she assured him, lifting her own mug. "You want mine instead?"

"No, I trust you," he said, in an obvious lie, and visibly willed himself to take a drink.

Lucy followed suit. She hadn't gotten as big a dose as he had, but the milk was still a welcome relief. "Nana, can you run upstairs to the apartment and see if we have any bread?"

Her grandmother looked like she would protest, but she left, grumbling about snakes and nonbelievers under her breath.

"Did I do something to her?" Dean asked, his face slowly resuming a less alarming shade. "She seemed so nice yesterday."

"I may have told her you called us con artists and threatened to expose our allegedly fraudulent ways," Lucy admitted. "But before that, she really loved the idea of being on television, so I thought she must have forgiven you when she offered you the cocoa."

He shook his head, eyes still watering. "That chocolate yesterday was heaven. It lulled me into a false sense of security. I never suspected your sweet little grandma would try to kill me with chili peppers."

Lucy tried to ignore the little thrill of pleasure she got when he praised her chocolate. She did *not* care what this man thought of her skills. "Never judge a book by its cover. The sweet little grandmas are the ones you have to watch out for."

"I'll keep that in mind." He took another long drink of milk. "So now that I've lost all feeling in my mouth, do you feel sorry enough for me to let me do a story on your shop?"

A soft laugh slipped out before Lucy could catch it. She shook her head, impressed in spite of herself at his tenacity. "You don't give up, do you?"

"Stubbornness is my superpower. Is that a yes?"

"No," she said, but she was smiling. She had to keep reminding herself that this man was the enemy. That he was out to expose them. She was almost starting to like him.

"You can trust me," he assured her. "Once you've survived chili pepper poisoning with a person, there's a bond there."

She chuckled, still shaking her head but feeling herself weakening, finding it harder and harder to resist the more he made her smile. "Dean..."

"I'm not in the business of ruining lives—or cute little chocolate shops. I really am the good guy."

She met his eyes, the rich chocolate brown of them glinting with sincerity. "Why do you want this so badly?"

"Honestly?" Something very real shifted in his gaze, and she was suddenly certain that whatever he was about to tell her would be the pure, unvarnished truth. Involuntarily, she held her breath, her focus narrowing to only him.

Then the door to the kitchen flew open and Georgie rushed through, words spilling out of her mouth. "Sorry I'm late! I lost track of time in the lab—" The words slammed to a halt and so did her forward motion when she caught sight of Dean. Her face drained of color. *"Dean?"*

Lucy's gaze swung back to the reporter in time to see matching shock spread across his face. *"Georgie?"*

Chapter Eleven

"WHAT ARE YOU DOING HERE?"

His sister—his sweet, naive sister who was supposed to be in class right now, studying to get her PhD in hard, reliable science and not *magic*—stood on the other side of the counter. Wearing a bright red apron emblazoned with the How Sweet It Is logo. Looking for all the world like she worked here.

"I got a job," she confirmed. "What are you doing here?"

"A story on the Valentine's chocolates."

Georgie's eyes flared wide, and her attention swung to Lucy. "I didn't say anything to him, I swear. I would never go behind your back after you said you didn't want to be on the news."

"It's okay," Lucy reassured his sister. "With Lena's post going viral, I think the cat's out of the bag. How do you two know each other?"

"He's my brother," Georgie admitted, sounding almost reluctant to acknowledge the connection. Dean frowned at her. He'd once been her *beloved, favorite* brother. Admittedly, he was her only brother, but still.

Lucy closed her eyes on a wince and muttered under her breath, "Chase. Of *course* he is." She opened her eyes, seeming to collect herself, and said more brightly, "I should have caught the resemblance." Her gaze flicked back and forth between Georgie and Dean.

He'd been so sure she was softening toward him right before Georgie burst in. He'd had her smiling, talking to him like he was a person and not an adversary. He'd been about to tell her that he needed this story so he could get the anchor position—an opportunity he hadn't confided to anyone about yet—when Georgie burst the little bubble that had been oh-so-slowly growing around them. And now, unless he was mistaken, Lucy was about to take any excuse to run away again.

"I'll just go check on my grandmother and that bread," she said, proving he'd read her right.

"That's okay," he started to protest, though the burn in his esophagus hadn't fully gone away, but Lucy was already through the swinging door.

"Bread?" Georgie asked.

The Mug of Doom was still on the counter and Dean nodded toward it. "Mexican hot chocolate. *Don't* drink it. Sweet little Edda snowed me. She acted like she was making me a treat and then tried to burn a hole through my tongue with chili peppers to scare me off."

Georgie's eyebrows arched high as she took the mug and, holding it away from her like it was radioactive, carried it to a small ledge behind the counter where it was out of the reach of any customers who might come in. "I see you've made quite an impression."

He wanted to enlist her help to rehabilitate that impression, but his concern for her had always eclipsed everything else, and he couldn't wait another second before asking, "How long have you worked here?" Worry pinched as another, even more horrifying thought struck. *Please don't let her have dropped out of school.*

"Just about a week. It's still new. I was going to tell you..." She hesitated, and they both heard the unspoken *eventually.* "You're just always so big on focusing on my studies and not letting anything distract me from my potential. I was worried you'd tell me to quit, and I really like it here. It's so different from anything I've ever done before. It's *fun.*"

Panic splashed through him. "You aren't going to—"

"Give up biomedical engineering to become a chocolatier? No. Relax, big brother. I'm still going to save the world one scientific breakthrough at a time. I just really needed something like this, too. Something completely different so my brain can be in a different mode for a while. I was burning out. Mentally exhausting myself by fixating on the same thing all the time. I'm actually doing better with my research since I started working here. And I love it. So please don't screw this up for me."

The idea that he would ever do anything to hurt her, even a little, stung. "When have I ever screwed anything up for you?" He looked after her. Stability hadn't always been easy to come by in their home life growing up, but Dean had *always* been there for Georgie. Always.

"Never," she confirmed, soothing feathers she didn't appear to realize she'd ruffled. "But you've never had to choose between me and a story before, either."

"You know I would always choose you," he reminded her. "But I don't think that's going to be a problem here. Lucy's on the verge of agreeing to let me do the story." He smiled his most winning smile. "If you could put in a good word for me, you might put me over the top."

She groaned.

The chimes over the door sounded, and Dean elected for a strategic retreat. "You have customers. Just tell Lucy I'll be back, okay?"

"Welcome to How Sweet It Is!" Georgie called out, before leaning across the counter and lowering her voice just for him. "Dean, I love it here, and Lucy is awesome, and she cares so much about this place, about what it means for her family and the community. Just...be nice, okay?"

"I'm always nice." Her vision of him as the aggressive reporter who would steamroll anyone for a story rankled—even though that was exactly the image he'd been projecting for the last few years. Do anything to get the story. That was Dean. But when Georgie thought she couldn't trust him, it didn't sit well. "And I would never hurt you. Or Lucy. Or this shop. You trust me, don't you?"

"Of course I do."

"Could you tell Lucy that?" He flashed an overly smarmy smile and Georgie groaned again, chucking a tiny napkin from the stack next to her hand at his face.

"Get out of here. I'm working."

"I'll be back," he promised, backing away. "Try the Mexican hot chocolate," he called over to the custom-

ers currently considering the fudge. "It's unforget-
table."

Chapter Twelve

*D*EAN CHASE WAS GEORGIE'S BROTHER. Lucy felt foolish for not realizing it before. But somehow, the fact that Dean was on TV had made him seem like he came from another world.

She knew she should go in search of that bread that her grandmother had apparently decided not to bring down for them, but instead, she found herself lurking just on the other side of the swinging door, eavesdropping on Georgie and Dean.

They were so easy with one another, and there was such obvious affection and protectiveness in Dean's voice that Lucy felt her lingering resistance to him weakening. The fact that he was Georgie's brother shouldn't change anything, but somehow it did. It made him more real somehow. A person and not just an obstacle she had to overcome.

Georgie's *brother.* Now that she was looking for them, the physical similarities stared her in the face. The same dark hair with a slight curl. The same deep brown eyes with a sparkle when they smiled. Georgie was lean and angular where her brother had the broad-shouldered build that would fill out a suit jacket as he sat behind an anchor desk, but they were obviously cut from the same cloth.

He wanted Lucy to trust him. Could she?

She heard his departure and Georgie chatting with the customers and gathered herself to go back out there to see if Georgie needed help. Georgie seemed to have things well in hand with the young mother and her two kids picking out treats, so Lucy busied herself disposing of the five-alarm hot chocolate and tidying up the milk mugs.

That could have gone very badly.

He could have been angry or, even worse, litigious. He'd actually surprised her with how quickly he'd gone from wheezing to laughing. He'd made the moment sort of...*fun.* If he wasn't the enemy, she might actually have started to like him.

And she wasn't so sure he was the enemy anymore.

The last thing she wanted was to let anything threaten the shop, especially a local television reporter looking to make his name by debunking the romantic myth of the Cupids. But was that who he was? Was that what he was after? He claimed he wasn't looking to hurt the shop. Could she believe him? Because she was starting to want to.

"I'm sorry. I should have told you." Georgie's words called her attention to the fact that the shop was quiet again, the customers having left with chocolate and smiles.

Lucy pulled herself out of her thoughts and tried to figure out what Georgie was apologizing for. "You mean that Dean Chase is your brother?"

"I didn't even tell him I was working here."

"Georgie, it's okay. I'm not mad. You said you knew someone who worked for the news. And after Lena's post, if Dean Chase hadn't shown up to check out the story, it would have been someone else. I'm just trying to decide if we should let your brother do a story on us after all."

"He wanted me to put in a good word for him," Georgie confessed.

Lucy had heard as much, but she appreciated that Georgie told her. Dean Chase struck her as the kind of man who would press any advantage. But this could be an advantage for Lucy as well. Georgie was in a position to help her figure out whether she could trust him. "What's he like? You haven't talked about your family."

Georgie cocked her head, her curls shifting around her shoulders as she searched for the right words. "He's...steady. At least, that's what he's always been to me. Protective. Sometimes overly protective, but that's big brothers for you. Ambitious, for sure. He wants to be the best at everything, but he's not the kind of guy who would hurt someone to get to the top. He's a good guy, even if he doesn't know when to give up sometimes." She grimaced. "He asked me to tell you he'd be back. He's always been stubborn."

Which wasn't always a bad thing. Lucy had her share of stubbornness, too. "But you think we can trust him?"

"I know we can." There was absolute confidence in those words.

But Lucy still wasn't sure. It was hard to get past her initial impression of him as a walking threat to her shop's very existence. She bit her lip, nodding. "Thanks, Georgie."

"Thank *you*," her employee gushed. "This job... it's been great for me. I really needed this to keep from burning out. I think that's one of the things my brother doesn't get. We can't be all work and no play."

Lucy frowned, the words *all work and no play* hitting a little too close to home, but Georgie was already smiling and moving toward the customers who had just walked in, leaving Lucy with her thoughts circling those last words.

She'd only been twenty when she took over the chocolate shop. Ever since, How Sweet It Is had been her sole focus. Taking business classes at night to learn how to run it better. Spending endless hours in the kitchen, trying out new recipes. She'd dated on occasion, but the relationships had always ended with the guy saying he wanted someone who cared more about him than her work, and Lucy had never been able to do that. She had a girls' night with some of her friends from time to time, but her life was this shop. Making chocolates, chatting with customers, worrying about the finances.

She'd thought eventually she would get to a point where she didn't feel like every second of every day had to be about the shop, where she would find her feet and feel steady and stable and ready to focus on herself for a change, but that point never seemed to come. Would she ever stop feeling like she was spinning plates, frantically trying to keep everything together?

Lucy was all work and no play, and was that really

so wrong? The shop had come first for so long, and it still needed to. At least for now.

The door chimes sounded again. Dean Chase walked in holding a package shaped like a loaf of bread. Georgie was busy with the customers, but Dean didn't even look toward his sister. His gaze landed instantly on Lucy, and he smiled, lifting the loaf. "Peace offering?"

Her heart gave an unsteady lurch at that smile. Nerves. That was all that was. She couldn't actually be happy he was back. And she certainly didn't find his tenacity attractive. That kind of distraction was the last thing she needed.

Chapter Thirteen

"WHERE DID YOU GET THE bread?"

"From the market a few blocks away," Dean explained.

They were seated on opposite stools in the How Sweet It Is kitchen, each with a large slice of the bread in front of them, along with a sweet, creamy butter Lucy had produced from one of the massive refrigerators. The kitchen was impressive. He hadn't been sure what to expect when she'd invited him through the swinging door, but the back area dwarfed the public portion of the shop. And it gleamed, everything in it sparklingly clean though obviously well-used. *This* was Lucy Sweet. He could see her love for this place on every surface.

"I tried the place across the street first, but I guess it isn't open yet," he commented, his gaze catching on a corkboard in the corner that was cluttered with recipes. "This kitchen is amazing."

"Thank you." Lucy flushed with pleasure, ducking her head and tucking a lock of hair behind her ear.

Flattering her shop would apparently get him everywhere, but for some reason he wasn't in a hurry to push his advantage. He was just curious. About this place. About her.

"The shop's been in your family a long time?" he asked.

She met his eyes, something wry flickering in the pale grayish blue with a darker sapphire ring around the edge of the iris. "Off the record?"

He grimaced ruefully. "What can I do to make you more comfortable with the story? I can't offer you final approval—even I don't have that—but I will promise not to hurt your shop. I'm not a bad guy. I can give you references—other people I've done stories with—if that would help."

She pinched off a piece of bread but didn't lift it to her mouth, studying him. "Right before Georgie came in, you were about to tell me the real reason you want to do this story so badly."

Dean rocked back on his stool. "You're right. I was." He nodded to himself as he realized he was going to have to show his cards to get this interview.

"Well?" Lucy prompted when he didn't immediately explain.

He sighed, nervous to say it out loud, as if he might jinx it just by telling another soul—though somehow, he trusted Lucy. She felt...safe. "There's a job. *The* job. I haven't told anyone this. Not even Georgie." He glanced toward the swinging door, through which his sister was shilling chocolates when she should be studying organic chemistry or whatever ridiculously advanced science-he-couldn't-begin-to-understand she was studying now.

"And this job means you have to interview me?"

"It's the morning anchor position," he explained. "Lots of warm, fuzzy, human-interest stuff."

Understanding dawned on her face and she nodded. "You need to soften your image."

"I do," he agreed, some tension unknotting in him with the realization that she understood without him having to explain. "And you need exposure for your shop. It's free publicity. We can both benefit here."

"I don't know." She bit her lip nervously, and his gaze lingered on her mouth.

"What is it?" he asked, his voice a low rasp.

"The exposure. I don't feel comfortable..." She trailed off. He realized he was leaning forward, dying to know *why* she didn't feel comfortable with him telling her story.

"Is it the story? Or is it me? Is there no getting past the whole mercenary, stock photo thing?"

She flushed. "It isn't that."

"Then what? Help me understand."

"Don't make fun, okay?" she pleaded, taking a breath before admitting, "It's superstition. My great-grandmother made the Cupids, but she never sold them. She didn't think we should. She was afraid if we tried to profit off the magic that it would, I don't know, backfire."

"And you believe that."

"It's safer than not believing."

And Lucy Sweet liked safe. He was starting to figure her out.

Her comment earlier, when she'd said they weren't hurting anyone, whispered in the back of his mind. "What did you mean when you said you were the little guy? Is your shop in trouble?"

"Not trouble, just..." She sighed. "It's not easy being the small, family-owned shop on the corner when the big, fancy places start moving in across the street."

Dean nodded. He could easily read between the lines. He'd seen the shiny new developments around Watson Corners, the blend of old and new. The town was going upscale, which meant the rents would increase, and the little places might get edged out. The chocolate shop had been busy since the viral post, but he'd bet they relied on the Valentine's boost they got every year, and this year more than others with that new French bakery-type-place moving in across the street.

His Champion-of-the-Little-Guy instincts activated, making him even more motivated to get this story and to do it right. This shop meant a lot to Lucy, and to Georgie, and he didn't like to think about the possibility of it closing. For either of their sakes.

"The buzz from yesterday's post isn't going to last forever," he reminded her gently. "I can help you keep the momentum going. Keep riding this wave right into the holiday." He'd already figured out that Lucy didn't like risks, so he just had to show her that the risk of not doing the story was greater than the risk of doing it. "It would be good for the shop," he urged. "Build interest." He met her eyes, those pools of blue. "Trust me. I don't promise what I can't deliver."

Lucy opened her mouth and he cued up another argument, ready to rebut whatever she was about to say.

"Okay."

"Okay?" A grin spread across his face, and a reluctant answering one curved her lips.

"Okay." Her lashes veiled her eyes as she glanced down, still smiling.

He nodded, grinning broadly. "Okay."

Chapter Fourteen

"*I* HAVE TO BE HONEST: PART of me expected you to change your mind."

Dean crouched in the empty public area of How Sweet It Is, setting up lights to film his segment with Lucy. They'd agreed he would interview her in front of the so-called "Wall of Love" and then get footage of her making a batch of chocolates while the shop was closed. Tomorrow, he would come back during business hours to interview a few customers and film some additional B-roll of her doling out the sweets.

"Truthfully? I almost did," Lucy admitted, watching him from a safe distance on the other side of the display cases. She'd been skittish ever since he'd arrived with the equipment, watching him hook up electrical cables as if they were vipers that might strike at any moment.

"Would you mind coming over here so I can check the angle?" he asked casually as he settled the camera on the tripod, more to put Lucy at ease than because he really needed to adjust things.

She looked like she wanted nothing more than to make a break for the nearest exit, but she rounded the counter and came to stand on the mark he indicated. She smoothed her hands down her skirt before clasping them in front of her, white-knuckled, and his jaded heart gave a sympathetic tug.

Some people were more comfortable on camera without others hanging around watching them, but he had the feeling Lucy was the other kind, the ones who needed a cheering section to bolster their courage. Unfortunately, they were alone in the shop, but luckily, he was a master at putting people at ease. He'd simply chat with her until her stiffness eased. And if he happened to enjoy chatting with her, with her quick wit and ready smile...well, that was just a perk of the job.

"Right here?" Lucy asked, the words clipped and short. Nervous.

"That's perfect," he murmured, making a show of looking through the ocular and adjusting the framing. He hadn't quite managed to capture the blue of her eyes, but it would have to do. He'd already clipped a microphone to her lapel. They were ready to go, but she looked like she was about to face the executioner. The only cheerful thing about her was her outfit.

The other times he'd come to the shop, she'd been in soft sweaters and jeans beneath her How Sweet It Is apron, but today she wore a white dress with little red hearts on it; the perfect Valentine's look. Nora would eat it up—provided he could get Lucy to loosen up enough for him to use any of the footage.

"You ready to get started?"

Lucy took a deep breath, bracing for battle. "As I'll ever be."

He needed something to distract her. To get her out of her head. "Don't worry. You'll be great. But before we start rolling, just between you and me, how many of these are stock photos?" He jerked his chin at the wall behind her.

Lucy's eyes flared with outrage. "None of them! I thought you'd given up on the con artist angle."

He pulled his face away from the camera. "I have. Mostly," he teased. "But are you sure about those pictures? That one in the corner looks awfully familiar. I'm positive that's an actress."

"She is," Lucy admitted. "She's also my mother."

Dean's attention sharpened on the words, and he momentarily forgot he was only trying to goad her out of her nerves. "Wait, your *mother* is one of the success stories?"

"It started as a family recipe. I told you my great-grandmother never meant to sell them."

He casually pressed the record button without taking his eyes off Lucy. "So these people really all fell in love because of chocolate?"

She glanced up at the photos on the wall behind her, a small, fond smile touching her lips, and the tension that had been tightening her face eased. "I don't know if they fell in love because of the chocolates, but they all met or were reunited because of them."

"So how did the legend start?"

She glanced back at him, lifting one eyebrow. "What if I told you I come from a long line of witches?"

His eyebrows flew up. "Do you?"

She grinned, that lopsided grin that made him want to smile, too. "No. I come from a long line of chocolatiers." She pointed to the oldest photo, the vintage black-and-white portrait, faded with age, of a young couple beaming into the camera. "My great-grandmother always loved to tell the story of how she and my great-grandfather fell in love. Her family owned a little chocolate shop in Bruges, and he lived across the street. She'd always liked him, but he was a few years older and never really noticed her. Then one Valentine's Day, she and her sisters were making chocolates, and they found this old recipe, tucked into the back of their recipe book—one they knew had never been there before. It was like magic. They decided to make these special chocolates, just for him. They weren't called Cupids then. Gigi, my great-grandmother, made the chocolates and delivered them to him personally. He took one bite, and they were madly in love for fifty-two years before he passed away."

"Very romantic," Dean acknowledged. "But a boy falling in love with a girl who brings him delicious chocolate on Valentine's Day doesn't exactly sound like it requires magical intervention. I've tried some of your family's recipes. Marrying the source of that just seems like good sense on great-grandpa's part."

"No one said it was magic—not then, anyway. But in the years that followed, my great-grandmother made the chocolates for her sisters and their friends, and each one found true love. And the legend grew. But it was still just a family story." Her gaze went back to the top photo. "My great-grandparents came to this country with just her chocolate recipes and opened How Sweet It Is. And as far as I know, she only made those special chocolates one other time, when my grandfather met my grandmother. She never sold them, never taught me how to make them. I never even saw the recipe until a couple years after I'd taken over the shop. It was tucked into the back of her recipe box, along with a note. She said she wanted me to be able to make them for myself when the time was right. But I didn't need them."

His attention sharpened involuntarily. Was she with someone? Was that why she hadn't needed them? It wasn't like he'd been flirting with her, or her with him, but he was inexplicably disappointed, though he didn't let on as he fired off his next question. "So you sold them?"

"Not right away. My dad passed away when I was little—cancer—and when my mom was ready to date again, all she seemed to find were an endless string of Mr. Wrongs. I knew how lonely she was. She had never tried the Cupids. Gigi had been planning to make them for my dad, but my parents met in the summertime and were married by Christmas, so they never had a chance to test the magic, but we all knew the legend and that Valentine's Day, my mom wanted to give them a try. I made my first batch for her. I don't know that I really expected them to work, but then she met Gary."

Lucy gestured to the picture he'd noticed before, with an attractive older couple smiling and holding hands.

"Then she told her friend Claire about the legend," Lucy went on, gesturing to the next photo. "Claire had also been widowed, and she'd had such a hard year, so I thought, what's the harm in making a few more batches? It was my mom's idea to call them Cupid chocolates and sell them on Valentine's Day. Then more of our customers found one another, and the legend started to spread. We gave them a permanent space in the display case and started the Wall of Love. Every year, we have a few more success stories.

People finding love and attributing it to the chocolates."

"Yeah, but can you name them all? To prove they aren't stock photos?"

She narrowed her eyes briefly at his challenge, but she was smiling as she snatched up the gauntlet he'd thrown down. "Claire and Malcolm. Pablo and Mark. Evelyn and Janelle," she said, pointing to each photo as she spoke the names. "Tyler and Lena—whom you might know from her infamous social media presence."

She continued rattling off names, elaborating a little more on each love story as she went. She seemed to have forgotten about the camera and her nerves. A small smile curved her lips as she told each story.

"Renee and Michael were supposed to meet two years earlier when her best friend married his cousin, but a hurricane kept him from reaching the destination wedding, and they never even laid eyes on each other until the Valentine's Day when they both came into the shop. His mom had heard about the Cupids and asked him to pick one up for her. Renee was one of our regulars, but she'd never tried the Cupids before. But that day, she just suddenly wanted one, and he decided to try one while he got another for his mom—and the rest was fate."

"Fate? Or coincidence?"

"It could be coincidence," Lucy acknowledged. "It could be just a pretty story. But all these people were open to love and they found it. That feels pretty magical."

Dean found himself smiling as he watched her. She almost got hearts in her eyes when she talked about this stuff, and it was...it was charming. "You really love it, don't you? That they fell in love here."

She blushed, shrugging. "I guess I do."

Her smile was a little crooked but all the more engaging for that asymmetry. It was real. Unpracticed. And Dean fell silent for a little too long, studying her. He could almost feel himself, hardened cynic that he was, getting caught up in that smile. Was Lucy Sweet for real? Could she actually be as sweet as her name implied?

Lucy's gaze flicked to the camera, and she seemed to remember she was being taped, her smile shifting into something a little less natural.

"What do you think your great-grandmother would think of her legacy?" he asked abruptly, after the silence had stretched too long.

"I think she'd be happy to know her chocolates are making so many people happy." Lucy glanced over her shoulder at the photos on the wall, her eyes soft, and Dean felt the strangest feeling in his throat—almost like he was getting choked up. Which was impossible. He wasn't *moved*. That wasn't him.

He roughly cleared his throat to get rid of the inexplicable blockage. "And you don't think people are too eager to believe in magic love chocolates rather than put in the actual work to make a relationship last?"

Lucy's eyebrows flew up as she turned back to face him. "You're planning to put that question in your fluffy Valentine's piece?"

He grimaced, tapping the button to stop recording. "Sorry. A little of my personal bias poking through. Shall we reset in the kitchen, and you can show me how you make the chocolates while we do the rest of the interview?"

Chapter Fifteen

$\mathcal{H}$E WAS EASY TO TALK to. Easy to confide in.

Of course he was. That was his job. But Lucy reminded herself to be more careful what she said around him, especially when that little red light on the camera was on. She always tried to be so careful, always conscious of the image the shop was projecting, but there she'd been blathering on and not being cautious with her words.

She didn't know how he'd gotten her to be so unguarded. So comfortable. The man was good.

"Would you like a hand with any of that?" she asked as he gathered up the gear to move it into the kitchen.

He caught her eye, his grin making her heart skip as he gave a little nod. "Sure, I'll put you to work. Grab that tripod."

She had a feeling he'd given her the lightest thing, but she wasn't complaining as they moved into the kitchen. The tripod wasn't heavy, but it was a little awkward in her arms, especially since Lena had talked her into the heart dress and heels. She felt like she was wearing a costume, but Lena had convinced her she was representing the shop and it was important to project a certain image. Something she needed to focus on. But right now the cameras weren't rolling, and she could relax a little.

"So you don't believe in love at first sight?"

Dean glanced over at her as he began reassembling his gear in the kitchen. "Did I say that?"

"Only seven or eight times."

He raked her with a look. "I take it you're a big-romantic-gestures person, what with the chocolate."

"As the owner of a chocolate shop, I do have a vested interest in romantic gestures of the edible variety, yes," she admitted. "But that's not all chocolate is. Yes, it can be a way of showing someone you care about them, but even then it can be a celebration or a consolation. Chocolate is a natural pick-me-up, and we try to be the kind of place where when you come in here. Whether you're looking for a treat to celebrate something wonderful, edible comfort to make you feel better when things aren't so good, or just a bit of chocolate for no reason at all, we're always going to be here to make all of life's moments a little sweeter."

"Dang."

She realized he was staring at her and blushed at the appreciation in his eyes. "What?"

"I didn't have the camera on. Can you repeat that in about thirty seconds?"

She glanced down at the ingredients she'd laid out before he arrived, her face still warm. Focus. *This is about the shop.* "Do you want me to be making a batch of chocolates?"

"Can you make the Cupids?"

"I thought I'd make a praline instead of a Cupid. I can't show you all the family secrets on camera."

He clicked the camera into place. "Deal."

Lucy busied herself rearranging the ingredients she'd already arranged on the counter so she didn't gawk at him while Dean finished setting up, moving the lights around and making little noises of frustration in his throat when it didn't look the way he wanted it to.

"Do you have any idea how many reflective surfaces there are in here? It's all stainless steel," he complained, and she smothered a smile without looking up. She was fidgeting with the chocolate thermometer when he spoke again. "So why did you say you didn't need the Cupids for yourself?" he asked casually. "Before. When you said your great-grandmother left you the recipe, but you didn't need them."

"I didn't have time for a relationship." At least, that was the excuse she'd always given herself. Lucy straightened the palate knife, so her tools and ingredients lined up in a neat little row. "I make all the chocolates and run the shop. We've always been family-owned and operated. My great-grandparents did it together. Then my grandparents helped out. But when I took over, my mom and my grandma would help some, but I was the one who wanted to take this on. I was the one making all the calls on marketing and supply orders. The neighborhood has been changing, growing—and now our rent has gone up..." She trailed off, looking up to find Dean watching her attentively, that red light blinking again. "Why do I keep *telling* you things?"

He grinned. "I'm very easy to talk to."

"You are," she grumbled, not entirely sure that was a good thing for her. Or for the shop.

"You were talking earlier about what's so wonderful about chocolates?" he prompted.

"Right," she murmured, staring at her hands, which seemed to have stopped moving. She had no idea what she'd just been doing. Had she already measured out the dark chocolate nibs? What was she supposed to be saying?

He seemed to sense her hesitation, because he did what he always did when she was flailing: he distracted her. "Is that what you usually wear to make chocolates?"

She smoothed a hand over the hip of her dress, which she'd covered with a red How Sweet It Is apron. "It was Lena's idea," she admitted. "Don't you like it?"

"Oh, I love it. And my boss is going to want to kiss you, it's so perfect."

She met his eyes, her brain snagging for some reason on the word kiss. Her gaze fell to his lips as the moment seemed to unfurl. Not that she should be thinking about kissing. And not that he would have any reason to think of kissing. He was here for his anchor job. To soften his image.

Suddenly, an idea that seemed entirely too brilliant popped into her mind. "You should help me make these."

Dean blinked, shaking his head. "Oh no. I'm good right here."

"Come on, Dean." She grinned, liking the idea more and more. She wouldn't have to be the sole focus, and it would be easier to remember that all his smiles were just for the home viewers if he was smiling toward the camera. "You're the one who wants to land the morning anchor job. Come get some practice for those cooking segments." She patted the counter beside her. "I'll even give you your own apron."

He raked a hand through his hair, eyes uncertain. "I don't know."

She put on her most mulish face. "I'm not doing this alone."

Chapter Sixteen

*D*EAN HAD NEVER DONE A cooking segment in his life.

But a man had to do what a man had to do.

He set up the camera with a wide shot, which would hopefully catch everything, attached a mic to his own lapel, washed his hands, and joined Lucy at the counter.

She handed him the promised apron, her fingertips brushing against his, and he cleared his throat to cover the little tingle of sensation that traveled up his arm from that glancing touch.

She issued instructions like a drill sergeant, seeming to have reclaimed her confidence on camera now that he was standing beside her, but he couldn't let her distract him from doing his job. This was still an interview.

"Did you always want to be a chocolatier?"

"Ever since I was little." She adjusted the heat on what looked like an oversized fondue pot, stirring the chocolate melting inside. "I would stand on a stool at this very counter, and my great-grandmother would teach me how to make ganache and chocolate shells and creams."

"You actually knew her? Your great-grandmother."

"She lived to be ninety-two and made chocolates with her son—my grandfather—until her dying day. I used to come stay here with them, sometimes for weeks at a time. It was my favorite place in the world. Everything made sense to me in this kitchen. There's something so peaceful about it. So calm. And it always made me feel like no matter what, I could control the outcomes here. No matter how crazy the rest of life gets, with enough skill and patience, you can always make a delicious chocolate that will make someone else happy."

His attention snagged on her words, catching on something all too familiar. That desire to control something when it felt like the rest of the world was out of your control. He knew that feeling well. But they were on camera, so he kept his reply impersonal.

"You really love it here."

"I do. I always knew this was what I wanted to do with my life. When I was twelve, Gigi took me to Belgium because she said every great chocolatier needed to go at least once, and she believed I was going to be one of the greats." Lucy's smile was small and fond. "Now I'm just following in her footsteps, trying not to screw up her legacy."

"I bet she'd be incredibly proud of you."

"I hope so. Here." She handed him a ladle and picked up a chocolate mold. "Scoop some tempered chocolate on here, fill every hole." He started to scoop, and she studied him with a critical eye. "Don't be stingy—you really want to coat it."

He grinned, ladling up a massive scoop and drizzling it onto the mold until each little cup was full to the brim.

"Perfect," she praised. "Now we scrape." She picked up a large, flat scraper that looked like it could have belonged on a construction site, though it gleamed sparklingly clean. She deftly wielded it, scraping the excess chocolate from the mold. "And then we tap."

She set the chocolate mold on the edge of the counter and rattled it back and forth quickly, the rapid-fire sound echoing in the stainless-steel kitchen like a drumroll.

"I see what you mean. The peace," Dean marveled sarcastically. "The calm."

Lucy grinned. "We have to tap out the air bubbles. Here, you try."

He set down the ladle he hadn't realized he was still holding and accepted the mold, gently knocking it against the edge of the counter.

"You call that a tap?" she teased. "Really get those bubbles out!"

He didn't want to send chocolate flying, but he tapped a little more vigorously, until Lucy took pity on him and took the mold from his hands. She gave it one more machine-gun-fire rattle, then lifted it above the fondue pot thing which held all the melted chocolate he'd scooped onto the mold.

And tipped it upside down. The chocolate drained out in long, thin streams.

"Whoa, did I really do so badly that we have to start over?"

Lucy grinned, shaking her head as the chocolate

continued to drizzle down. "We're pouring out the excess, so what's left when it's cooled and hardened is just the outer shell that we can put ganache or cream or caramel inside. Then we scrape, tap, and drain again until they're perfect."

She showed him the tray, which did indeed look tempting—and smelled even better. "Perfect is right. When do we get to eat them?"

"Don't be so impatient. The outer shell hasn't even set yet. Chocolate is a process."

"So you're saying it takes longer to make the chocolates than it does to fall in love with someone when you eat one?"

She laughed. "For some people, yeah." She slid the tray onto a rack, removing another already-set tray and turning back to him. "Now, the filling."

She was so at ease in the kitchen. Her confidence in this space was incredibly appealing, that steady, unwavering competence. And even though his hands were sticky with chocolate, and he was sure he had smudges everywhere, she didn't have a single spot on that heart-pattern dress.

"How do you not have chocolate everywhere?" he demanded.

"Practice. Lots of practice." She filled a piping bag with deft motions and extended it to him. "This one's yours."

"Oh no." He held up his hands in surrender. "I think I'm better as an observer from here on out."

Lucy gasped with mock shock, her eyes twinkling at him. "Is Dean Chase, Champion of the Little Guy, Defender of the Downtrodden, afraid of a little chocolate?"

"I fear nothing," he announced with false bravado. "But I am man enough to admit when I have no idea what I'm doing."

"I'll show you. Come on." She wagged the filling-filled piping bag at him, and he tentatively reached for it. "Grip it firmly with one hand, here, and then guide with the other."

She put her hands over his, positioning them correctly on the bag, and he glanced down right as she looked up, abruptly realizing how close they were to one another.

He could see that dark blue ring on the edge of her iris from here. The slight parting of her lips as she drew in a breath. The shadow of a dimple that would deepen when she smiled. His heart thudded loud enough he was certain the lapel mic must be picking it up, and the moment seemed to hang, stretching a little too long.

"Um, good," Lucy murmured, a little breathlessly, color rising to her cheeks as she released his hands and reached for a second piping bag. His hands felt strangely cold in the absence of her touch. She swiftly twisted her piping bag and gripped it as she'd shown him, demonstrating as she spoke. "Just fill each chocolate cup, leaving about a quarter inch at the top so we can close the shell. Like so."

Dean cleared his throat, focusing his gaze on his work and trying to remember the rest of the questions he'd planned to ask her. "When do you, ah, when do you make all the chocolates?"

"If someone is manning the shop, I'll make them during the day." Her hands never stopped moving, rapidly filling two rows of the chocolate shells while he was still working on his second little cup—his first one had overflowed. "But usually I make them at night. Like I said, it's a process, and I love the uninterrupted quiet."

"That doesn't leave much time for a social life. Is the purveyor of the magic Cupid chocolates actually single?"

He had not intended to ask that.

Lucy looked up at him, a flush on her cheeks and her eyes a little wide. "Sorry, too personal," he said quickly. "I'll, uh, I'll edit that out."

"No, it's okay. I mean, they're the love chocolates. Of course you would ask that. But like I said before, um, no time. Busy with the shop."

"I'm married to my job, too," he said, and then silently kicked himself. Why had he brought up his love life, or lack thereof, on camera? Where was his head? He cleared his throat, gathering his thoughts, and his gaze caught on the catastrophe of his chocolates. "I don't think I did this right."

She looked at his work, and humor lit her eyes. "You might have been a little generous. Let's see if we can salvage them."

She took over, moving to save the chocolates—and he moved to save the interview. He asked her about presales and online orders, making sure the viewers would know how they could order the chocolates to be delivered on Valentine's. He coaxed her into talking about the magic of chocolate again, this time on camera, as she worked.

She chatted easily about the atmosphere in the shop on Valentine's Day, everyone coming for love and how magical that felt—though he noticed she always talked about the magical atmosphere and never actually promised magic results.

Before he knew it, she was removing a finished batch of the chocolates from the mold with a quick twist-and-tap. Perfect little chocolates tumbled onto the pristine towel she'd laid on top of the choco-late-smudged countertop.

"And now we quality test." She separated a couple of the chocolates, pointing to the tiny spots on the tops. "See the flaws? That's from the air bubbles. We won't sell these because you can see the imperfec-tions."

"Those are mine, aren't they? The imperfect ones."

"No comment. But they still taste good." She held them up to him and he plucked one off the palm of her hand.

His plan was to sample it for the camera and make a show of how delicious it was no matter how it tast-ed, but as soon as the chocolate passed his lips, the taste made him groan with genuine appreciation.

"Oh wow. Is that one of the Cupids? Because this chocolate might be able to make even a skeptic like me believe in the power of love."

"Nope." Lucy grinned. "Just a mocha cream."

"*Just*, she says. *Just* a mocha cream. That thing just changed my life."

Lucy laughed softly. "I'm glad to hear it. Please feel free to leave a testimonial on our website."

"Oh, I will," he promised, meeting her gaze for a moment that seemed to snag him, her eyes sparkling into his. Fortunately, he caught himself staring and turned abruptly to speak straight to the camera. "But in the meantime, I'll just remind our viewers that they can try the magical Cupid chocolates themselves at How Sweet It Is in downtown Watson Corners. Preorder now to beat the rush on Valentine's Day and have them delivered right to your door—though it sounds like being here in person on the day is half the fun. Thank you so much for teaching me the ways of chocolate, Lucy. For Channel Five News, I'm Dean Chase."

They both waited for a beat, smiling and posed, after he delivered the sign-off, and then he moved, breaking that suspended tension.

"That was great," he said automatically as he rounded the counter to shut off the camera. He always assured his subjects they'd been great, even if the interview was a disaster, but this time it really had been great. And fun. He hadn't expected to laugh so much. Or to like her so much. Or to feel...whatever it was that he'd felt there for a moment.

If he was honest, Lucy hadn't been what he'd expected at all.

When Nora had handed him this assignment, he'd expected to find a mystic or a con artist, but instead he'd found a driven, clever, funny young woman determined to keep her family chocolate shop afloat for another generation. She was passionate about what she did—and obviously very, *very* good at it.

"You're really good at this," she said, echoing his thoughts.

Realizing his hands were too sticky to break down the equipment, he moved quickly to the sink to wash up so he could get out of here without getting into any more personal territory. "It's easy when I'm working with the best," he said lightly.

"Just accept the compliment, Dean."

He met her eyes and felt a self-deprecating grimace tug at his lips. "Thank you," he forced out. He was always better at praise when it was joking or exaggerated. Her simple sincerity was disarming. And his defenses were already low enough.

He flicked off the water, and Lucy moved around the kitchen behind him, tidying up the materials they'd used.

"Did you always want to be a journalist?" she asked.

"I always wanted to be a news anchor," he admitted. "They knew everything and were always poised in a crisis. I liked that. They always seemed to be in control."

They had that in common, he realized, remembering how she'd talked about the shop. She seemed to feel the same way about this kitchen as he did about an anchor's desk. It was her oasis of peace. Both of them looking for the calm at the eye of the storm.

Though he didn't feel very calm and in control at the moment.

He remembered what she'd said about her childhood, about the time she'd spent with her great-grandmother and her grandparents, and something about it started to nag at him.

"Where was your mom?" he heard his curiosity asking without any input from the logical should-you-be-asking-this portion of his brain as he dried his hands and moved back to pack up the equipment. "When you were staying here for weeks at a time."

She glanced at him in surprise, and he verbally backpedaled.

"Sorry, I shouldn't have—"

"No, it's okay. My mother's amazing, but she's not exactly a fixed point. More of a force of nature. We moved around a lot when I was a kid, and in between, we came back here. My mom was always very proactive about making sure I knew my dad's side of the family. Though I always wondered, when I was kid, what it would have been like if he'd lived." She cocked her head at him, and he realized he'd stopped moving. "Are your parents still together?"

"No." The word came out like a bullet, too fast, and he pushed himself back into motion to cover the outburst, going through the familiar steps of putting the equipment away. "Not since I was nine. Georgie was a baby."

"No wonder you're protective of her."

"Did she say that?"

Lucy grimaced, arranging the chocolates they'd completed on a tray. "She might have said overprotective."

"Of course she did." He watched Lucy's hands, the smooth, steady movements. "Hold on. Let me get a shot of that." The tripod had been folded up, but Dean put the camera on his shoulder and zoomed in close on the chocolates. "Keep going," he coached. "I need some B-roll."

"B-roll?"

"Action footage to put behind narration and intercut with the interview segments," he explained. "I'll take some more tomorrow—customers in the shop, slow pans of the chocolates on display—but I want to get some of you in action. Just keep doing what you were doing." Her hands hovered in the air, uncertain.

"You can talk to me," he said to put her at ease. "I'm not recording audio right now."

"Right." She hesitated, but then went back to work, moving a bit more slowly. "So how did you get the gig as the champion of the little guy?"

"I sort of fell into it. It was a natural fit. Georgie would tell you it's because I'm so cynical." He sidestepped to get a better angle. "When you're first starting out as a cub reporter, you take any assignment you can get and chase down leads that no one else wants. There was this one tip that no one else wanted to follow up because it was about possible corruption in a wholesome kids' cookie fundraiser. But I've never been taken in by fairy tales and the pretty surface of things, so I dug in, the story broke, and other people started coming to me with their stories. I became that guy. Exposing fraud and corruption where everyone else just sees a feel-good piece."

"The protector."

"I guess."

"Well, I'm glad you're making an exception and doing a warm, fuzzy, feel-good piece now." She lifted an eyebrow. "You *are* doing a feel-good piece, right?"

He grinned. "I am. My boss insisted. Though I have to be honest, if you'd been bilking the customers, I might have had to convince her to let me take you down."

"I'm flattered you've decided we aren't a danger to the community."

He lowered the camera, having gotten enough footage for now. "I've noticed you're always very careful never to promise that it works." She'd never once insisted that the magic was real, though she seemed determined to protect the right of those around her to believe in the legend. "You don't really believe in it, do you?"

When she looked pointedly at the camera, he had to admit he appreciated her skepticism. "Off the record," he assured her. "Here. Give me your microphone. Nothing is recording. Do you really believe it's magic?"

"Honestly?" He thought she would hedge, or evade the question, but she met his eyes and something uncertain shone in those blue-on-blue depths. "I don't know. I guess I want to? But how do you tell the difference between a magic chocolate and a bunch of people who really want to find love all coming in to How Sweet It Is on the same day with their hearts wide open? I like the legend. I like how it makes people feel. I love that everyone who walks through my door on Valentine's Day is optimistic—thinking their life could change in a second. And if people believing in the Cupids makes them a little more willing to open up their hearts, is that really so terrible? Love could always use a little push."

"Love has more than enough pushes already," Dean argued. "The whole romantic love, Valentine's Day, billion-dollar wedding industry—it's so forced. A million love songs and rom-coms—all of pop culture pushing people into believing if they just find 'the one,' all their problems will be solved. Cue the orchestra for the happy ending and who cares if the hard part is all still to come?"

"Wow." Her eyes were wide. "I think I struck a nerve."

He grimaced. "You know it isn't all happily-ever-afters."

"I do," she agreed. "But that doesn't mean I don't believe in love."

"Then why haven't you dosed yourself with a Cupid chocolate and ridden off into the sunset? Physician, heal thyself."

Those blue-on-blue eyes narrowed. "Just because I haven't eaten a Cupid on Valentine's Day doesn't mean I think all love is a construct of the greeting card companies like you seem to. I have a whole wall of success stories. People whose lives were made better by love."

"So you say."

"I do say. And so do they. Go talk to them if you don't believe me."

"Maybe I will." The words sounded strangely threatening as they hung in the air, and he realized he was glaring across the center island at Lucy who stood with her hands flat on the stainless steel, glaring right back.

Until his lips twitched. Something about the moment struck him as funny. And then Lucy was shaking her head, smiling, visibly trying not to laugh as he started to chuckle.

"You're the worst," she accused, folding her arms, and his grin just got broader.

"I know."

"Stay away from my shiny, happy success stories with your cynicism."

"I will," he promised.

She sighed, still smiling. "Are we done here?"

"Yeah. But can I ask you just one last question?"

"Is it about magic or love?"

"Neither. I promise." He held up a hand in a salute. "Scout's honor."

"Okay..."

"Is your name really Lucy Sweet?"

She laughed. "Van Suyt."

"What?"

"My great-grandparents had their name legally changed to Sweet after they emigrated to this country. Dietz and Genivee Van Suyt became Des and Gigi Sweet. So yes, it's my real name."

"Huh."

"Not what you expected?"

"No." He held those blue-on-blue eyes, his lips curling involuntarily. "You, Lucy Sweet, are not what I expected at all."

Chapter Seventeen

"*LUCY SWEET HAS THE MAGIC touch when it comes to love. At least that's what everyone who comes to the How Sweet It Is chocolate shop every February 14th believes. The Watson Corners institu-tion has become a Valentine's Day mecca ever since the rumor started to spread that eating one of their special Cupid chocolates on that most romantic of days will lead you to meet your one true love.*"

Nora stabbed a button and the screen froze on a shot of Lucy's hands stirring melted chocolate. "I love it," she declared, her voice as firm and strong as always. "You did a great job, Dean. It's perfect."

"It was a fun assignment," he admitted.

"I'm glad you enjoyed it," Nora folded her hands on her desk. "Because we want you to keep going."

Dean blinked. "Excuse me?"

"This is great." Nora waved a hand at the screen. "The cute grandma, the hopeful customers, the adorable chocolate maker. But I want you to go deeper. Talk to some of those Wall of Love couples who met at the shop. Get their stories. We'll make it a multi-part series leading up to Valentine's."

Dean rocked back in his chair. A multi-part series would be great for his chances to make anchor. And if he was honest, a little part of him had been disappointed that the chocolate story was over because he wouldn't be seeing Lucy anymore.

But he was still reluctant to dive back in. He felt almost like he'd dodged a bullet—though what he would have been dodging, he had no idea. He wasn't susceptible to the love stuff. His romantic defenses were titanium. No sweet, smiling chocolatier could get past them so easily. No matter how cozy the other night had felt.

"Don't tell me you still think it's a scam," Nora said when he didn't respond.

"No, they really believe it," he said—and then he realized he was sabotaging his best excuse to get out of the story. "Or at least they seem to. But there's a lot of coincidence, and one of the success stories is her mother. I don't know if you want me to go digging. The whole house of cards might collapse."

"You're a true skeptic, Dean." Nora chuckled. "You think you can hide that long enough to get the story? Or should I assign someone else?"

"No, it's my story," Dean protested instantly. He wanted that anchor job. Even if it meant a little romantic bullet-dodging.

"All right." Nora settled back into her chair. "Then go get it."

"It's on!" Lena squealed, grabbing Lucy's arm.

Lucy barely resisted the urge to hide behind the sofa.

Dean had texted her that the story would air for the first time tonight, and she'd made the mistake of telling Lena, who had shown up with Tyler and a bottle of champagne at the little apartment above the shop that Lucy shared with her grandmother. They closed early on Fridays, so she couldn't even use manning the shop as an excuse to sneak out. Georgie had stuck around after her shift, and a couple of the other success-story couples had dropped by, and somehow, it had turned into a watch party.

Lucy hadn't wanted to make a big deal of this. She was too nervous to really enjoy it. But everyone else was so excited, she'd let them pour her a glass of champagne and drag her in front of the television.

A decision she was now regretting.

The news had just started, and their segment wasn't up yet, but Lucy's stomach was already in knots.

Dean had sent her a sneak peek this morning, a link to the video of the piece that would be going live on the website after it aired, so she already knew what was coming. She knew it was good. Really good. Optimistic and cheerful. He'd made the shop look great, just like he'd said he would, and never once had anything to do with magic been promised or guaranteed.

But she was still a mess.

The anchor was delivering the top stories of the day, and Lucy distracted herself wondering if the piece had helped Dean toward getting the morning anchor spot. She knew he'd be great at it. He was good at his job. Insightful, disarming.

She'd had fun during their interview. He'd made her laugh, and had somehow known exactly what to ask and when to ask it to get her to open up. Like the way he'd honed in on how unsteady things always felt with her mom, and the way How Sweet It Is had become her sanctuary, meaning so much more to her than just a business to be run.

Her mom had always been chasing something— the next acting gig, the next shiny new project to help her cope with the loss of the love of her life—and Lucy had been along for the ride, never really settled in one place. But How Sweet It Is had always been her home. Home in a way she wasn't sure she'd even realized herself until Dean was asking her about it.

This had to work. She couldn't let the business fail.

"Lucy Sweet has the magic touch when it comes to love..."

Dean's smooth voice broke into her thoughts, and everyone in the room squealed so loudly that they lost the next several words in all the commotion. Then they all shushed one another frantically and fell silent to watch, hanging on every word.

"The shop looks really good. You, too. I love that dress on you," Lena whispered about halfway through the piece, and Lucy smiled though her throat was so tight, she couldn't form a verbal response.

The entire piece was only four minutes long, but it felt like a lifetime before Dean was sampling the chocolates they'd made together, groaning in bliss, and promising to leave a testimonial on their website.

"That looked *friendly*," Lena murmured, a speculative lilt to her voice, while, on screen, Dean was turning to face the camera and sign off.

Lucy felt her face heat and avoided meeting her best friend's eyes, pretending to be absorbed in the television. "He's very good at his job. Good at putting people at ease." That was all it was. At least, that was what she'd been telling herself ever since the interview.

"Uh-huh."

"That was amazing!" Nana Edda saved her from Lena's all-too-perceptive eyes by rushing over to hug her.

Someone muted the television, and suddenly everyone was talking over one another, toasting and praising their favorite parts of the piece.

"You looked so good, Lucy!"

"We all did!" her grandmother cheered, without an ounce of false modesty. "But you and Dean really stole the show. You two have such a natural, what's the word...?"

"Chemistry?" Lena suggested, and Lucy shot her a death glare.

Nana Edda snapped her fingers. "Banter!"

"You should post the story on your website," said Mark, one of the Cupid success stories, who stood with his arm around his husband's waist.

"Oh, I don't know," Lucy said, as the rest of the room cheered the idea.

"I need to share this." Lena's thumbs were flying across her phone.

"I almost forgot!" Nana Edda exclaimed, darting out of the room only to return a moment later showing off a large picture frame like a champion holding up a trophy. "I had this framed today so we can put it up on the Wall of Love."

Lucy's chest tightened with the sudden feeling that she'd been strapped into a rollercoaster and they were about to reach the first drop. "You framed Lena's post?"

"Of course! I've thought for a long time that we needed a written explanation why we have the pictures hanging on the Wall of Love," she continued. "People come in, they see the smiling lovebirds, but they don't necessarily know the Cupids are responsible for all of it. This way, they'll know. Even the customers who might never have asked about the pictures."

"Nana, we talked about this. I don't want to advertise the Cupids."

Nana Edda flapped a hand at her. "Superstition. How is this any different than putting up the photos of our success stories? Or appearing on the news talking about them?"

"It makes it look like we're guaranteeing it works," Lucy argued.

"*We* aren't saying it works. Lena is saying it works."

"And we would be advertising that Lena said it. I don't want to go down that road."

Lucy's phone pinged from its place on the coffee table, and Lena scooped it up, glancing down at the screen as she handed it over. "I think that ship may have sailed," Lena said.

For a fraction of a second, Lucy thought it must be Dean, checking in now that the piece had aired, but instead an order alert lit up her screen. Just this week Lena had coaxed Lucy into putting an online order form up on the website and raising the online price of the Cupids. She'd set it up so the system sent a notification to her phone every time an order was placed.

"It's an order," she confirmed to everyone watching her. While she was staring at the first order, her phone pinged again. And again. "Several orders."

"It's starting!" Nana Edda squealed.

Nerves flashed brightly inside her as her phone continued to buzz. Dean had explained to her that the story would likely air multiple times. Would they get a response like this every time it did? What about when it went up on the Channel Five website?

Everyone seemed to be talking at once. Her grandmother was trying to figure out how to hang a television on the Wall of Love that only showed the story on repeat. Lena and Mark were speculating that more news organizations were sure to call, and discussing what they would wear if they were interviewed on a nationally televised talk show.

Lucy just wanted to run and hide.

"I'm going to get a start on these orders," Lucy said, edging toward the door and away from the champagne toasts in progress.

"You aren't leaving!" Lena exclaimed.

"We're running low on several of our best sellers already, and I'm barely keeping up with the demand for Cupids. I really should make several batches tonight."

Lena looked like she would protest, but luckily, Nana Edda pulled her into a discussion about whether they should email the national morning shows or wait for the producers to come to them, and Lucy was able to make her escape.

After the hubbub of the apartment, the quiet of the kitchens was even more stark.

Normally, Lucy loved the hush of evening, when she could experiment on new recipes or get a jump on fresh batches of chocolates for the next day, but tonight the silence felt too heavy, and she didn't want to be alone with her thoughts. She turned off her notifications and pulled up a French jazz station on her phone, filling the room with the smooth sounds of Duo Gadjo. She'd only learned a little French, so the lyrics floated right on the edge of comprehension, more mood than meaning without the complications of specifics. She didn't need any more complications right now.

She knew she was worrying too much. Borrowing trouble, her mother would call it. But then, her mother never seemed to notice trouble whether it was borrowed, bought, or sold. And she was halfway around the world with her new husband. She couldn't tell Lucy that her panic was silly in her usual blithe, confident way. The yin to Lucy's worrywart yang.

Lucy fell into the routine of making the chocolates, letting the soft music weave its spell around her as her hands went through the familiar motions and her thoughts circled back to Dean's piece. And Dean.

She'd been thinking of him a lot.

All afternoon, she'd been trying to think of which chocolates to send him as a thank-you present. The Cupids would send the wrong message—and likely be unwelcome given his anti-love stance—but nothing else felt special enough.

It was strange to think that it was over. That she probably wasn't going to see him again, unless he came into the shop to see Georgie. She'd had a lot of fun doing the story, way more than she'd ever expected—but he probably made sure all his subjects felt that way. There wasn't anything else there. Even if she'd had the time to pursue it.

He was good at his job, and that was all there was to it.

And she had her own job to do. A job that was going to keep her even busier, thanks to this new rush of orders. Lucy pushed away the thoughts of Dean and concentrated on chocolate.

Chapter Eighteen

*H*ow Sweet It Is was dark, and Dean kicked himself for not checking the Friday hours before coming down here on impulse. He needed the contact information for Lucy's success stories to arrange the follow-up series, but he could have called. Should have, probably. Somehow, it had just seemed more convenient to drop by.

Or maybe, if he was honest, he'd wanted to see her. By visiting the shop, he could find out how she'd liked the story, get the information he needed, and pick up a few chocolates at the same time.

But the lights were off, and the doors locked. And she hadn't responded to his text.

He was already here, so he headed down the alleyway to the kitchen door, just to check. She'd said she often made chocolates at night. He'd knock on the door and if she didn't answer, he'd call it a night.

But before he even reached the door, it swung open, spilling light—and Lena and Tyler—into the alley.

"Dean!" Lena exclaimed when she saw him. "Fancy seeing you here."

"I was just dropping by to talk to Lucy about a potential follow-up piece," he said, uneasy in the face of Lena's knowing smile. "Including you two as well, if you're interested. I'm looking to interview some of the success stories, do some additional features about your personal experiences with the chocolates."

"Oh, we'd love that, wouldn't we, babe?" Lena asked her fiancé, hooking her arm through his. Dean had met the man when he'd gone by the flower shop to get Lena's quotes for the piece, but he wasn't sure he'd heard him say more than five words. Tyler made an agreeable noise now, and Lena tipped her head back toward the shop.

"Go on in. She's in the kitchen."

Dean nodded his thanks as Lena and Tyler headed off down the alleyway. He pulled open the door and stepped into the small back hallway. To his right was a stairway leading up to the apartment above, and to the left was an open door to a tiny, cluttered office, but straight ahead, from the direction of the kitchens, came the faint sound of a guitar and a silky woman's voice singing in a foreign language.

Dean followed the sound, pausing where the hallway opened into the kitchen when he saw her.

Lucy stood at the counter, swaying gently and humming along to the music, ever so slightly off tune. His lips curved automatically in a faint smile at the sight of her. He knew he should announce his presence, but for a moment he found himself just watching her. She was making chocolates. Her hands moved with that same assured confidence that had captured his attention the other night. Steady with skill and years of practice.

She wasn't all done up like she had been for their on-camera chocolate-making session. Her thick hair was twisted into a sloppy knot on top of her head, a few stray strands trailing against her temples and the nape of her neck. The cute little heart dress had been exchanged for jeans and a simple long-sleeved white shirt with the sleeves shoved up to her elbows, but the How Sweet It Is apron remained the same, along with the scrap of a towel tucked into her apron strings.

She looked...warm. Like just the sight of her was a welcome.

He didn't know why he stood there in the shadows of the hallway, but he waited until the song ended to speak into the silence.

"Did you like the piece?" he asked, his voice deep and raspy.

Lucy's head snapped up and her eyes widened, her hands stilling. "Dean. You're back."

Then she smiled, and something inside him he hadn't realized he was holding onto unclenched. Anxiety about not being able to get the rest of the story, he told himself, and stepped into the kitchen.

Chapter Nineteen

*L*UCY HAD BEEN DISTANTLY AWARE of her friends leaving, some part of her brain processing their calls of "Good night" and the clang of the alley door, but she'd been lost in her work, lost in the hypnotizing pattern of piping filling into tiny chocolate shells. Her face heated as she wondered how long Dean had been standing there while she was so far in the zone she'd lost all sense of her surroundings.

He was back.

"Lena let me in," he said as he moved fully into the light of the kitchen. "Is that okay?"

"Yeah, yes. Of course." She was happy to see him. A little too happy, if she was honest with herself. She'd thought she might never see him again after the story was over and she'd been a little...well, a little sad about that, but that was just because he'd turned out to be a good guy. And fun to talk to.

He'd make a good friend. Nothing more than that, obviously. She still wasn't looking to jump off the Love Cliff and Dean had made his position on the entire prospect of romance very clear. But that didn't mean they couldn't be friends.

"You didn't answer my question." His low voice brushed across her senses.

He'd asked a question? "About...?"

"Did you like the piece?"

She smiled softly. "I already told you I did." She'd texted her reply as soon as she'd finished watching it the first time that morning, hiding in the storeroom as the video played on her phone so no one would see her nerves.

"Yeah, but that was a text. I wanted to see your face when you said it. See if you meant it." He indicated the half-filled trays of chocolate shells in front of her. "Are you making more Cupids?"

"As a matter of fact, I am." And the filling wouldn't stay the right temperature forever. She bent back to her task, quickly piping ganache into the centers, one by one.

"So this is my chance to see the secret ingredient?"

"Not on your life." She smiled and flicked a glance up at him without pausing her work. "Is that why you came back? To steal all my secrets?"

"No. Not this time," he joked. "My boss loved the story."

She looked up, catching him watching her. "I meant to ask. Did you get the anchor job? Do you know?"

"No news yet. But my chances definitely look better than they did a week ago. And there's one more thing you could help me with that might improve my odds even more, if you're willing."

His smile made her feel all fluttery and she likely would have started fidgeting with her hair like a lovesick teenager if she hadn't had her hands full with the chocolates. *Get it together, Lucy.* "I'd be happy to help," she assured him. *There. See? Professionalism.* "Though I don't know what I could do."

"Nora wants me to continue the piece. Film testimonial interviews with some of your success stories. We'd extend it into a series, run new pieces every couple of days for the week leading up to Valentine's Day. It'd be great for the shop—keep you in people's thoughts and catch viewers who might have missed the first story."

Something that could have been disappointment whispered through her, though she didn't care to examine why. Of course he was here for professional reasons. Finishing the piping, she slid the trays onto a rack to set, and turned back, picking up her phone. It was still playing her French jazz station, but the screen was cluttered with the silenced notifications. The online orders were still pouring in.

La Vie Douce—which, it turned out, was a French bistro, bakery, and patisserie—had opened on Tuesday, but business at How Sweet It Is had been so good, she'd barely noticed. If things kept up like this, they might actually be able to survive the competition. How Sweet It Is could thrive, and finally become something that didn't require all of her time and energy. She might even be able to afford to hire some more help.

Dean apparently took her silence as reluctance, because he kept persuading. "It wouldn't be an imposition. Lena and Tyler are already on board. All I need from you is the contact information of your other success stories."

Lucy frowned as a new concern popped up. "I

don't know. Our customers trust us not to give out their information. I don't want to bother them." What if they didn't like the publicity? What if they told her to take their photos off the Wall of Love?

"So we don't bother them. We just make them aware of the opportunity to tell their stories. You could reach out to them yourself. Give them my number if they're interested."

Pablo and Mark would probably love it. And Lucy could already think of a few other couples who would enjoy the spotlight. She didn't know why she was hesitating.

"Can I go with you?" she blurted, the words more impulse than thought, but as soon as she said them, they felt right.

Dean blinked. "What?"

"I'd like to go with you when you interview the couples."

"I'm not going to try to poke holes in the legend," Dean assured her.

"Yes, you will. At least in your head." She was smiling as she spoke to soften the impact of her words, but she knew him. He wouldn't be able to help himself, the incurable cynic. And she didn't want him unraveling her legacy, even unintentionally.

"Okay, yes," he admitted, "I will, in my head, but that won't be the story. You saw the piece we aired tonight. I managed to keep my cynicism entirely to myself, didn't I? Trust me, this is totally on the up-and-up."

"It's not about trust. It's still my shop, my chocolates. Do you not want me there? Are you worried

I'll coach answers out of the stock-photo models I'm paying to lie about their magic romances?"

He snorted. "No, you're welcome to come. Having someone they already know and trust in the room will only make my job easier. It's a good idea. Put everyone at ease." Then his smile quirked. "And I'm sure I can work out a blink-twice-if-you're-being-coerced-by-the-crazy-chocolate-lady signal."

She rolled her eyes and grabbed one of the less-than-perfect, not-for-purchase chocolates off the tray where she kept them before they were donated to local charities. She flicked it at him, and he caught it one-handed, grinning as he popped it into his mouth.

"Get out of here." She shooed him toward the door. "I have chocolates to make." And he was entirely too distracting. "I'll reach out to our happy couples tonight and see who's interested in being on camera."

They already had a group chat. She'd set it up last week when she'd wanted to warn them all that there would be a television story and their photos might be included. They'd all been excited—and no doubt the texts had been flying fast and furious all night since the piece aired. She surely would have seen them if she hadn't turned off her notifications.

Dean grinned. "That sounds perfect. Thank you."

"How many do you need?"

"Three or four pairs? We won't have time for any more segments than that. Valentine's is coming up fast."

"Don't I know it. Now get out of here so I can work."

"Lots of orders?" He picked up his coat, his smile cocky. "Did my story save the family chocolate shop?"

"We'll see. We still have to make it past Valentine's."

"You aren't still worried about that bakery across the street, are you? They're open now. Why don't you go over there? Scope out the competition. Maybe you're worrying about nothing, and they don't even sell chocolates."

"A French bakery that doesn't sell *pan chocolat?*"

He shrugged into his coat. "It could happen." He started toward the door but nodded to the tray of imperfect chocolates. "I think that one was my favorite yet."

"They're all your favorite," she said—rather than tell him he'd just eaten one of the defective Cupids.

"True," he agreed.

She trailed him toward the door so she could lock it behind him.

"You should go over there," he said, circling the conversation back to the bakery as he turned to face her in the alley. "You'll just bury yourself in dread until you do. Better to see what you're up against."

She leaned against the doorjamb. "I'll think about it."

"Do. I give excellent advice. I'm very wise."

She laughed. "And modest, too."

"So many virtues in such a handsome package. I know. It's a lot to take in."

She shook her head, still smiling uncontrollably. "All right, egomaniac. Get out of here so I can work."

"Yes ma'am." He tipped an imaginary hat. "Let me know what your happy couples say?"

"I will. Good night, Dean."

"Good night, Chocolate Siren, luring men to their doom with your delicious treats."

She closed the door in his ridiculous face.

And was still smiling half an hour later.

Chapter Twenty

THE FARMHOUSE WAS ONLY FIFTEEN minutes away from How Sweet It Is, but it felt like a different world.

There were peacocks, for one thing.

And Dean was discovering he was not a peacock person.

He'd expected their first Happy Couple Interview would be with Lena and Tyler, since he'd already talked to them and they were right down the street, but Lucy had surprised him when he'd shown up at the shop tonight with camera gear in hand. Apparently another of their success stories, Claire and Malcolm, were having a celebration with their entire blended family that night, and they thought it would make the perfect backdrop to the piece, showing how the chocolates had brought them all together.

So to the farmhouse they'd gone. To be bombarded by peacocks as soon as he parked the car.

He stepped out, and a giant bird was suddenly squawking loudly in his face. Dean backed up until he was pinned against the side of the car.

"That's Humphrey. Don't worry. He's harmless. He just doesn't respect boundaries." Lucy was visibly amused by his discomfort, but since she was helping him with the camera gear, he decided not to take umbrage at her grin.

"Do all of the Happy Couples have guard peacocks?" he asked as he sidled away from the bird and unlocked the trunk.

Lucy laughed. The sound was like a sparkler setting off inside his chest. "Not that I know of." She nodded toward the large, wraparound front porch. "Come on. I think I see some curious eyes watching us already."

Every light in the house seemed to be on, casting a warm glow out into the twilight, and he could see crowds of people moving around inside. And some of the younger ones were definitely peeking out the windows

Dean didn't know much about tonight's couple. Lucy had refused to prep him on Claire and Malcolm's "love story" on the fifteen-minute drive into the country. She'd merely said that they were one of the earlier couples—Claire was an old friend of the family—and that she wanted him to get the rest straight from the source.

Normally, he liked getting the story from those personally involved, but he also didn't like not getting the chance to do advance research. And yes, it was just a puff piece, but that didn't mean he didn't want to control the narrative.

From the photo on the Wall of Love he knew that, like all the other Happy Couples, Claire and Malcolm looked picture-perfect happy: a handsome Black couple in their mid-sixties with radiant smiles. Arms linked, heads tipped together.

And when they opened the front door after Lucy rang the bell, that was exactly who he saw.

"Lucy!" The couple hugged Lucy like she was a long-lost daughter, asking after her mother and her grandmother.

Lucy handed Claire the box of chocolates she'd brought from the shop, then seemed to remember Dean was standing behind her. "Oh! Claire, Malcolm. This is Dean Chase, Channel Five News."

"Oh, we know. We loved your piece on the Cupids!" Claire exclaimed.

"And that fake charity story," Malcolm added, extending his hand for Dean to shake, then seeming to realize Dean had his hands full. He took the case containing the sound equipment off his hands instead. "You do good work, young man. Everyone's excited to meet you."

"Come in, come in," Claire urged. "Put all that stuff down. Where would you like to set up? We weren't sure if you would want to be in the thick of things or if somewhere quiet would be better."

"Quiet would be good for the actual interview with the two of you," Dean explained, "but I'd love to take some B-roll of the party. Just observe in the background, if that's okay."

"Absolutely. Whatever you need," Claire assured him. "Why don't we do the interview up here, in the sitting room? Sound won't carry quite so much."

"Perfect. Thanks."

"I think Humphrey got out," Lucy told Claire as they all shuffled into the front hall and set down the equipment in a sitting room that was closed off from the rest of the open concept downstairs. "He startled Dean when we arrived."

"That bird." Claire shook her head. She linked her arm with Lucy's as they headed toward the great room where the rest of the family was gathered, raising her voice to call out, "Jamie, did you let that peacock out again?"

"It's kind of a zoo around here," Malcolm said, hanging back with Dean while he unpacked the camera. "Claire's never met an animal she didn't want to adopt. When she moved out here to the farm, she was like a kid in a candy store. All this space to fill." He nodded toward the rest of the gear. "You need a hand with any of that?"

"I'm good for now, but thank you." Dean settled the camera on his shoulder. "What are you celebrating tonight?"

A proud smile filled Malcolm's face. "New grandbaby on the way. Our fifth, if you can believe it. Come on. Meet the family. We can sit down for the interview when the little 'uns have bedtime."

It was a good plan, but Dean still felt like he didn't know what story he was telling, like he was still searching for his angle as he trailed Malcolm to the party in progress.

There were over a dozen people of varying ages in the living room. Most were close to his and Lucy's ages—Claire and Malcolm's children, no doubt—but there was a toddler and a couple little kids running around. Everyone was moving—laughing, talking, eating—and he didn't have a prayer of figuring out who belonged to who. Until Lucy sidled up to him and murmured under her breath. "Claire had two kids from her first marriage, and Malcolm had four. All but two are married and two—soon to be three— have kids of their own."

"Big, happy family."

"Exactly," Lucy agreed, as a new voice spoke from his other side.

"Big, happy family *now*."

The camera on his shoulder had given him a blind spot so he hadn't seen the young woman approaching. Buoyant curls shifted around her ears as she cocked her head to study him.

"Dean, this is Sierra," Lucy introduced.

"Claire's youngest," Sierra explained.

"So it wasn't always a big, happy family?" Dean probed, always on the scent for the truth beneath the shiny surface. Lucy shot him a look, but Sierra just shook her head.

"Always happy, just not always so big. It was just Mom and Owen and me for a long time. She always seemed so happy, I'm not sure either of us kids realized how much happier she *could* be. Then she met Malcolm, and now..." Sierra waved a hand that encompassed the loud, laughing group.

"So you didn't mind sharing her?"

"Mom's always had a big heart. We knew there was room in there for a lot more than just us. Have you seen the menagerie yet?"

Dean admitted he hadn't, and one of the younger generation bounded up. "Can I show him, Aunt Sierra?" the boy asked, bouncing in place.

"If Grandma says it's okay."

When he darted away to get permission, a little

girl of about four marched up to Sierra and thrust her arms imperiously into the air. Sierra laughed and picked her up, settling her on her hip. "My niece, Farah," Sierra explained.

"My mom says you're here about the magic chocolates," the little girl declared, staring at Dean with unnerving intensity.

"I am," he admitted. "I'm a reporter, and I'm doing a story on them."

"That's how my grandma and grandpa fell in love," Farah declared, with the absolute conviction of someone who hadn't yet discovered life wasn't always black and white. "I'm gonna have one too, but my mom says I'm not big enough yet."

"Your mom sounds smart," Dean said. "Wait until you're thirty, at least."

Farah seemed unimpressed by his reasoning, and Sierra smiled. "Come on. Maybe we can talk your mom into having one of the non-magical chocolates Lucy brought." She winked at Lucy and jerked her chin toward Dean. "Good luck with that one."

When they walked away, he found Lucy watching him with a slight, amused smile. "What?" he asked.

"Careful, Mr. Anchor. Your cynicism is showing."

"Thirty is a very reasonable age for falling in love. Any younger than that and your brain is still developing and you're ruled by irrational hormones."

"Because love is always so rational." Her blue eyes twinkled at him.

"It should be. If it's going to last."

"So you're the expert on lasting love?"

"No. I'm the expert on the kind that goes up in smoke in six months," he admitted, not bothering to hide his bitterness. This was Lucy, after all. She already knew what she was getting with him. "And I don't think we can rely on magic chocolates to solve all our problems."

"Hmm."

"*Hmm?*" He feigned shock. "Is that all the rebuttal I get from the purveyor of magic love chocolates?"

"No comment," she said, with a pointed look at the camera.

Something about the wry way she said it tugged at his investigative spidey senses. "I can never quite figure out if you believe in the magic or not. Off the record. Do I detect a kindred skeptic?"

"You don't detect anything," she informed him. "How could I not I believe in the Cupids? I've seen firsthand what they can do." She gestured to the room.

Dean let that declaration linger, taking a moment to pan the room with the camera before he met her eyes. "You still didn't say you truly believe."

She smiled at the challenge in the words, but whatever she was about to say was cut off by the arrival of the five-year-old on a mission to show Dean the "menagerie," and the little bubble that seemed to have formed around them popped.

Dean let himself be pulled away to meet *all* the animals, including a proper introduction to the obnoxious peacock named Humphrey, but he cast one last look over his shoulder at Lucy.

He still felt like he wasn't quite seeing the whole picture yet with her. She was optimistic, so hopeful, and yet so cautious. So quick to worry. She was a puzzle. And he'd never been able to let one of those go unsolved. That must be why he couldn't stop thinking of her.

Chapter Twenty One

" *I*T WAS LOVE AT FIRST sight."

Dean schooled his features so his overdeveloped sense of skepticism didn't show and asked, "And this was five years ago?"

"Oh no," Malcolm laughed, his fingers interlaced with Claire's. "More like fifty. We were high school sweethearts. I remember thinking, when I was maybe seventeen, 'I'm gonna marry that girl.' Course I never suspected it would be when we each had a grandbaby on the way." His deep chuckle reverberated in the small sitting room.

"We fell out of touch after graduation," Claire said, seamlessly picking up the story. "I married Reggie. He married Marie. We each had kids and went about our lives. I'd think about him from time to time, but it was always just as a fond memory. Someone I used to know." She glanced at her husband with a smile. "Then, about six years after Reggie passed, I heard this story about magic chocolates that make you fall in love. My youngest had just gone off to college, and I was looking around my empty nest, thinking, 'Is this it?' So on Valentine's Day, I let my good friend Helen talk me into going in to How Sweet It Is. She credited those magic chocolates with helping her meet her husband. I don't know if I really believed in magic, but I took one bite of that Cupid, and there he was."

"I didn't know anything about any magic chocolates," Malcolm admitted. "My son was in the doghouse with his pregnant wife because he'd forgotten Valentine's Day, and he had to pull a double shift so he couldn't even come up with anything on the fly. I'd just retired and happened to be driving through Watson Corners when I saw the chocolate shop and thought I'd arrange a little delivery to help my boy out. I walked through that door and *bam*. Magic."

"So you didn't actually eat the chocolate?" Dean prompted.

"Oh, I did," Malcolm corrected. "I saw Claire and recognized her straight off. She hadn't spotted me yet. She'd just taken a bite of a chocolate and her eyes were closed, so I walked right up to the counter and said, 'I'll have what she's having.' I thought I was being funny, but that chocolate changed my life. I remember biting into it and looking at her and thinking, 'This is it. This is why you're here.' I wasn't really looking to meet someone when I was already on the back nine of life, but then I saw Claire, and I felt like I was seventeen again. Like there was a whole lifetime of possibility in front of us—even if it doesn't have quite the same shape it did when we were kids."

"It's never too late," his wife said, squeezing his hand.

"Never," he agreed.

"And what did your families think about you instantly falling in love?"

"Oh, there were bumps," Claire said wryly, "but they could all see how happy we were."

"They thought we were moving too fast, but there's no point wasting time when you know. The kids always want to protect us—like now that they think they're all grown, we've suddenly become the ones who need parenting. But they came around pretty quick. Now I can't imagine our family as anything other than a big noisy combination of hers and mine."

"Ours," Claire agreed. "I moved out to the farm right away, and now every day is filled with pets and grandchildren."

"Never realized how quiet things had gotten around here until Claire showed up and brought everything to life."

The couple shared a fond smile. Dean was pretty sure this was exactly the kind of story Nora had been hoping for: so sweet it could give you tooth decay. But something kept scratching at the back of Dean's mind. He kept his smile steady and his questions neutral as he encouraged them to talk more about their life together and how the chocolates had played a part. Apparently, they ordered two Cupids every Valentine's Day just to remember the day they met, which was a cute tradition. Dean barely stopped himself from interrogating them, from challenging every syllable of their supposedly perfect love story.

After the interview, he broke down the equipment, thanked the family, and loaded everything into the car. And the entire time, that need to poke holes in the story and inject some reality into all that fairy-tale nonsense burned in his gut. He made it until about two seconds after Lucy had closed the passenger door before the question that had been needling at him for the last hour burst out of his mouth.

"You can't honestly claim they fell in love because of the chocolates."

Okay. Not so much a question. More of an accusation. But he'd meant it to be a question.

Lucy glanced over at him from the passenger seat, a slight smile on her lips and her eyebrows raised in a high arch. "I can't?"

They were still rolling slowly down the driveway, away from the farm, and Dean shot her a look. "They were already in love in high school. And Malcolm didn't even eat the chocolate before he saw Claire. He was already flirting with her when he ordered his Cupid. That isn't a magic love chocolate. That's history—and a man who sees what he wants and goes after it."

Lucy smiled, unfazed by his argument. "Just because they had history doesn't mean they would have fallen right back in love. Lots of people see their exes and nothing comes of it."

"But they'd already loved one another once. It's just a coincidence that they saw one another again on a day when they ate your chocolate."

"Isn't that what falling in love is? A coincidence? A random meeting with someone that somehow turns into so much more? A happily-ever-after isn't just about liking the look of someone—it's about timing and commitment and your lives fitting together. Claire and Malcolm found one another again at exactly the right time. They were both ready to love again."

"But you're saying eating the Cupid chocolate makes it the right time."

"I'm not saying anything. Claire and Malcolm are."

"And there you go again. Never saying whether you believe in the magic."

He could feel her studying him as he drove. "Why is it so important to you to know whether I believe or not?" she asked lightly.

Why *was* it so important? Why couldn't he let it go? "I'm just trying to figure you out."

"Are you sure that's all you're doing?" she challenged, a note he couldn't quite identify in her voice. Did she think he was still trying to prove fraud? He wasn't, but he also wasn't sure why it mattered to him so much to figure out the puzzle of Lucy. He wanted to *know* her. But why?

"Do you believe in it?" he asked again, that question he couldn't seem to stop asking.

As he made his way back to the interstate, she said, "Some things are...they're hard to explain. Like how I found the recipe, exactly when I needed it." Her words gained strength as she spoke, becoming more sure as she went.

"How Sweet It Is was in trouble. Financially. The last few years before I took over, my grandpa was starting to get confused, and the books were a mess. Our costs were going up, but business was just the same steady trickle it had always been, and it was getting harder and harder to make ends meet. I was starting to think I'd made a huge mistake—that we were going to lose the shop. I thought I was letting my family down. And then one night, I was making chocolates, and I decided to go through my great-

grandmother's recipe book, looking for something...
magic. Something to save us."

"And you found the Cupids."

"You have to understand," she said earnestly. "We
thought the recipe had been lost. No one had seen
it in decades. My entire life, it had just been a story.
I knew the legend, but Gigi hadn't made them since
before I was born. And that night, it was just *there*.
Like it had been there all along. Not even stuck to
another page or hidden behind anything. Just right
there, with a note from Gigi. And seeing how that
recipe has changed things for the shop—how is that
anything other than magic?"

He wanted to argue, but when he glanced over the
light on her face stopped him. She seemed to glow
with uniquely Lucy radiance as she spoke.

"It isn't even the money, though, yes, we are doing better now that I'm selling them. It was like I'd
found, I don't know...hope. The whole atmosphere of
the shop changed."

Because Lucy had changed it. Because her enthusiasm was infectious, and when she believed, it
was impossible not to believe with her. Something
tightened in his chest, and Dean spoke to diffuse that
feeling. To remind himself this was a story and nothing more.

"I really need to start recording everything you
say," he murmured, his voice a little too raspy. "I
keep missing all the good sound bites."

Chapter Twenty Two

*L*UCY TWISTED IN HER SEAT, turning to face Dean so she could study his face as he drove. "You aren't starting to believe?" she asked. "Even a little?"

"My cynicism was ingrained at too early an age. You'll never crack it."

She heard the wry, I'm-too-jaded-to-be-moved-by-your-magic tone in his voice, but she also heard something else underneath it. Almost like he was protesting too much. Or like his resistance was personal.

He'd told her that his parents split when he was a kid. From what she'd gleaned from him and Georgie, their childhood had made Dean feel like he needed to protect everyone from the dangers of gullibility, especially in the love department. Not unlike the way losing her father had made Lucy want to cling to her family legacy. It didn't take a therapist to see they'd both grown up feeling like the big things in life were out of their control. So they found order where they could. Dean with his stories, and Lucy with her chocolates.

If they weren't both so dead set against letting themselves fall in love, they'd almost be perfect for one another, she thought wryly.

"The idea of the magic offends you, doesn't it?" she asked. "The idea that some force outside of you—fate or magic—could determine the course of your life."

"It's just a cop-out," he argued. "People throw around *fate* and *meant to be* when they don't want to take responsibility for their actions. Oh, my marriage fell apart? She must not have been 'the one.' It couldn't possibly be because I had unrealistic expectations. Overblown romanticism, the belief that there's this one magical person who will complete you, and once you find them, having a good relationship will never be work, you'll never go through rough patches, you'll always be as blissfully happy as you could possibly desire to be because you've found your *fated soulmate*—it's all a way of shirking responsibility. There's so much pressure on relationships nowadays. Historically, marriage was about property or procreation. Now it's true love and the weight of that, the burden of having to find your one person and be truly happy *forever*...how can any relationship hold up under that strain?"

"Maybe 'the one' is just the person you choose to go through thick and thin with."

"But people don't choose that. They bail as soon as things start looking thin. I know people who've gotten divorced not because they were unhappy, but just because they thought there might be a world in which they could be happier. It's this grass-is-greener mentality when, in reality..."

"Love is what you make of it?" she asked softly.

He grunted a vague agreement.

"You just need to find someone who believes like you do," she said. "That tending your own grass will make it just as green."

He flicked a glance at her, catching her eye briefly before returning his gaze to the road. "I guess, maybe." His tone was careful, gentle as he reminded her, "But not everyone is built for forever, and no magic chocolate is going to change that."

Lucy glanced out the window, grateful for the darkness hiding her blush. She hadn't meant that *she* was the one who would tend metaphorical relationship grass with him. Not really. They seemed to keep falling into these philosophical conversations about love and magic, and it wasn't always clear where the line between the philosophical and the personal fell. But he was here for work, and he obviously didn't want her getting any ideas.

Not that she was. He was just fun to talk to. Fun to argue with. She'd been so wrapped up in work it had been a while since she'd met anyone new that she could talk to like this. That was all this was. Novelty. And a challenge to meet his every verbal sally.

She might like his intelligence and his tenacity— even his cynicism seemed to be an extension of his desire to protect people—but liking him wasn't going to change the fact that he didn't want love. She knew that.

"Did you go over to that bakery yet?" Dean asked as he slowed to cruise down Main Street, the sign for La Vie Douce looming ahead.

"Not yet," she admitted, eyeing the darkened windows of the competition.

"What are you waiting for? A sign from fate?"

She threw a narrow-eyed glance across the car at him, but he didn't notice in the darkness. "I have been a little busy," she reminded him. "Someone did a television story about my shop and, believe it or not, business has been booming."

He pulled into the alleyway beside How Sweet It Is, parking behind her car. "Don't you feel silly now for putting up such a fight about doing the story?"

"You mean when I said no to the man who called me a mercenary and a con artist?"

"I think I just *implied* you were a con artist. Let's not get carried away."

She laughed. "Oh, forgive me. That makes all the difference."

He grinned. "It's all about the details."

"I'll keep that in mind next time someone implies I'm running a scam."

"See that you do."

Lucy's cheeks hurt from smiling, and she shook her head, unhooking her seatbelt and reaching for her purse. "Do you know when this one is going to air?"

"Probably in the next couple days. My boss is going to eat it up."

"Good news for the future anchor."

He lifted a hand in a stop sign. "Don't jinx me."

Her eyebrows flew up. "So you believe in jinxes, just not in fate?"

"I believe it's dangerous to want anything as badly as I want this." His voice was low.

Lucy's heart squeezed at the words, recognizing a

familiar truth in them. "Then I'll just say good luck and leave it at that."

"Thank you. Tuesday night for filming the next couple?"

"Yes. Pablo and Mark. You're going to love them."

He nodded. "Sounds good."

There was a finality in his voice. Her cue to leave—and she realized she would have lingered, would have stayed too long, just to talk to him. She opened the car door, stepping out into the chill of the February night. She was just about to close the door when Dean's voice froze her in place.

"Lucy?"

Her heart beat inexplicably faster as she bent down to peer into the car. "Yeah?"

"Go to the bakery. It's not this Goliath you're building it up to be in your head. It's just a store."

She ignored the little flicker of disappointment that tried to rise up. What had she expected him to say? That he wanted her to stay? That he wanted to talk about love some more? This was Dean. "We'll see. G'night, Dean."

"Goodnight, Chocolate Siren."

She bit her lip on her smile, the nickname sending a shaft of sunlight right through her heart. Then she shut the door and watched him drive away.

Chapter Twenty Three

"*T*HAT CAME TOGETHER WELL. THE big, happy family is a nice touch."

Dean jerked and turned at the sound of Nora's voice. He'd been standing in the newsroom watching his own segment air and feeling smug about how it had turned out, and she'd caught him in the act.

"It was a fun interview," he acknowledged. And it had been fun debating the dubious merits of love with Lucy afterward. He continued to enjoy this assignment far more than he'd thought he would. "We have our second Happy Couple interview tonight."

"Excellent." Nora nodded, satisfied. "Do you have anything scheduled for tomorrow?"

"Not yet. Should I? Do you want me to increase how many Happy Couples we're interviewing? We only scheduled three, but Lucy said there were others who were willing."

"No, I just wanted to make sure you're free. There's an event, hosted by our parent company—standard networking thing, cocktails and schmoozing with advertisers. The anchors often get trotted out at those things as the face of the news to smile and press the flesh. Some of the brass thought it might be useful to see how our short list for the morning slot handle themselves around the sponsors, and since this Valentine's series has put you on that short list..."

"Seriously?" Dean didn't fight the smile spreading across his face.

"Don't get too excited. Nothing is decided yet. This is still an audition. I'll email you the invitation." She watched the television in front of them for a moment as a recorded Dean laughed with Claire and Malcolm's family. Nora nodded slightly, approvingly, and Dean resisted the urge to fist pump. She started to move away but turned back after only one step. "Oh, and Dean? Bring a date."

Her gaze flicked to the TV screen beside him, where Lucy was holding one of Claire and Malcolm's grandchildren and smiling. Dean had seen the shot a dozen times—he'd edited the piece himself—but something about it this time made his mouth go dry.

He turned back to say something to Nora, but his boss was already gone. Leaving him with an opportunity to further his case for morning anchor...and a need to find a date for tomorrow night.

Lucy stared at the box of chocolates with her shop's logo emblazoned on top. "This might be a terrible idea. Is this a terrible idea? Who takes sweets to a bakery?"

"It's neighborly," Nana Edda assured her. "Every-one loves free chocolate. And it's the perfect chance to scope out the competition. Clever of Dean to think of it. I always liked that boy."

Lucy diplomatically refrained from mentioning the Mexican cocoa incident. "Hopefully they won't be competition. We can be partners in providing delicacies to the residents of Watson Corners."

And if not, at least she would know what she was up against.

Dean was right. She'd been driving herself crazy imaging the worst. Much better to rip the Band-Aid off and know what she was dealing with.

"Okay. Here we go." She sealed the box, her palms suddenly clammy.

"Good luck!" her grandmother encouraged. She'd be manning the shop while Lucy headed across the street on her welcome mission.

But before Lucy made it out the door, the frosted glass opened and a cell phone on a selfie stick thrust through, nearly smacking Lucy in the face. She dodged the stick and the woman wielding it as the tall blonde stepped into the store, never missing a beat in the narration she was providing to her phone, and evidently unaware she'd nearly taken someone's eye out with her entrance.

"I'm walking into *the* How Sweet It Is chocolate shop in Watson Corners, your one-stop shop for true love this Valentine's Day. *If* the rumors are to be believed. Can a chocolate really make you fall in love? Don't worry, Kate-lings, Kate Kelly is on the case, and I am going to get to the bottom of this for you."

When she finished her intro, her gaze finally left

the camera she was holding on a stick, and she became aware of the chocolate shop. "The scene: How Sweet It Is chocolate shop. It really is just as *charming* as everyone has said."

She spun in a slow circle, spinning with the camera extended so she stayed in the shot even as she panned to show the shop in the background—a maneuver that made Lucy grateful the shop was empty at the moment because she probably would have taken down three customers otherwise.

Then Kate Kelly, the blonde with the Selfie Stick of Doom, went alert, her gaze locking on Lucy like a tractor beam. "Do my eyes deceive me? Is the actual magical chocolatier here before me?" She swung the selfie stick to one side, rushing up to Lucy and grabbing her arm, and somehow catching it all on the little camera. Lucy would be impressed by the hand-eye coordination if she weren't so busy trying to disappear.

"*The* Lucy Sweet, Kate-lings. The woman herself."

Lucy instinctively retreated a step, nervousness making her throat close and her face flush. "Uh..." She stared at the camera, probably doing an excellent deer-in-headlights impression.

"Kate Kelly," the woman introduced herself, evidently undeterred by the naked panic on Lucy's face. "Of the award-winning investigative web series, Kate Investigates. Here to get to the truth behind the chocolates that have *everyone* talking."

"I, um, could you not film this?" Lucy had been on her way across the street and so she was wearing makeup and not covered in chocolate, but she hadn't been prepared for an ambush interview.

She suddenly felt self-conscious in her jeans. Was she projecting the right image for the shop? Lena had told her that she needed a stylist. At least when Dean had done his piece, he'd given her some warning, arranged things with her in advance. This felt like a sneak attack.

There had been other reporters. Other inquiries. Mostly local TV or radio talk shows or podcasts interested in the story, but they'd all called or emailed. No one else had just shown up in the shop, camera rolling.

Kate Kelly's brassy smile vanished in a blink, and her eyes narrowed slightly as she lowered the Selfie Stick of Doom. "Do you have an exclusivity agreement with Channel Five?" she asked, in a normal tone that was in sharp contrast with the breathless, this-just-in voice she'd been using on camera. "Because you should look at the terms closely. Since the story has already aired, you may be free to talk to other news outlets."

Lucy shook her head. She didn't have an exclusivity agreement with Dean. She'd very carefully read each of the releases he'd had her sign before doing the story, and not one of them had featured anything about restrictions on her ability to tell her story to anyone else. But she trusted Dean. They felt like a team. They were working together: him to get his promotion, and her to promote the shop. It felt wrong somehow to talk to another reporter. Like she was cheating on him. Which was ridiculous.

"Even if we film today," Kate bulldozed over Lucy's hesitation, "I can hold the footage until you're released from exclusivity, provided it's before Valentine's. Obviously, it's no good to either of us to post it after that."

Indecision swallowed Lucy. More publicity could be a good thing. The shop had been on Dean's station, and lightning hadn't struck. No curse had been unleashed that she could see. No sudden conflagration that swallowed her shop in a fiery inferno. Wouldn't more press just mean more customers? More free advertising?

But it came back to that trust. She knew Dean wouldn't paraphrase or exaggerate. She knew he respected her caution when it came to the reputation of How Sweet It Is, the Cupids, and the couples on the Wall of Love. She didn't know this woman, who seemed like a hybrid between a reporter and social media influencer, and she wasn't ready to trust her.

"I'm sorry," Lucy said, steeling her spine. "This really isn't a good time. Perhaps if you'd called ahead—"

"I tried emailing this morning, but no one replied," she said, with a note of irritation in her voice.

Lucy flushed. Maybe she shouldn't have been ignoring the calls and emails from other reporters, but the head-in-the-sand approach had been her comfort zone for so long. "I'm sorry. We've been very busy."

It wasn't an empty excuse. Every single one of her Cupid molds was filled and needed time to set right now or she wouldn't even be taking the time to head across the street.

The internet orders had exploded after Claire and Malcolm's piece aired this morning. Most of the walk-in customers also placed advanced orders for Valentine's Day—all including the Cupids though many also ordered other decadent treats to go with them—but it was the online order form that had really gone crazy.

Lucy had been afraid the website was going to crash. They'd never had traffic like this.

She was going to need to make Cupids nonstop until Valentine's just to keep up. And the shop was busier than ever. Georgie had already offered to work more shifts than she'd originally been hired for, and her grandmother was there at all times, but Lucy was starting to wonder if she needed to hire even more help, both out front and in the kitchens. Maybe just until Valentine's.

"I'll try to get back to you as soon as possible," she told the reporter, "but right now..." She needed to go across the street with a welcome basket? Except she didn't, really. She could easily put that off and do this interview. Get it over with. But some instinct stopped her.

"We'll see if I'm willing to come all the way out here again," the ambush reporter said, with a distinct lack of good grace, as she thrust a card at Lucy. She turned on her heel and flounced out.

Lucy felt only relief when she was gone. She was just glad there hadn't been a flock of customers watching the little standoff.

"Are we exclusive with Dean?" Nana Edda asked, her eyes wide from where she'd watched the whole thing from behind the counter.

"No," Lucy admitted. "Something about the way she waltzed in here, already filming, and nearly smacked me in the face with her camera, didn't really feel like she was going to be careful with our reputation."

"Pushy," her grandmother agreed.

"It's probably in her job description to be pushy." Lucy knew that. She respected the hustle. But she would always be cautious when it came to How Sweet It Is.

Nana Edda grunted and began arranging a tray of cocoa bombs.

Dean was pushy, too, even if it was couched in charm. And he was stubborn, coming back again and again until he'd worn her down. But somewhere along the way, she really had started to trust him. And even if she didn't need his permission to film an interview with someone else, she kind of wanted his advice. He knew that world.

She knew she shouldn't ask a reporter for advice about other reporters—he was bound to be biased— but somewhere in the last couple of weeks, Dean had stopped being just a reporter. He was a friend.

A good friend.

Lucy glanced down at the box of chocolates still in her hands. She and Dean were meeting after the shop closed tonight to head over to interview Pablo and Mark for the next segment. Maybe she would talk to him about the other interview offers when they did. But right now, she had a welcome basket to deliver.

Chapter Twenty Four

"*I* WENT TO THE BAKERY." LUCY barely managed to wait until Dean had backed out of the parking area before the words burst out of her mouth.

He glanced over at her, his grin bright in the dark interior of the car. "And? How was it?"

"*Awful.*" She groan-laughed, admitting, "And wonderful. Awful because it was so wonderful. Seriously, the place is *gorgeous.* It's all rustic and atmospheric and if they weren't going to put me out of business, I would probably eat there every day."

"They aren't going to put you out of business," Dean said with absolute conviction. "How Sweet It Is is special."

Her heart skipped, surprised by the certainty in the words—and more than a little touched.

"On the plus side," she said, ignoring the lingering warmth in her cheeks as he steered them through the slow turns of downtown Watson Corners, "they seem to be less chocolate-focused and more bistro-ish. Lots of soups and gourmet croissant sandwiches and fancy French dishes. But they *definitely* have a bakery counter, and it's longer than my entire store. Breads and pastries and tarts—oh my word, the *tarts*. Fruit and lemon and chocolate mousse. *Chocolate mousse,* Dean."

"I'm sure their mousse has nothing on yours."

"I think I might have offended the owner," Lucy confessed, finally circling around to the root of her anxiety. "I was trying to be neighborly and brought a few chocolates to welcome them to the neighborhood, but then one of the servers tried one and started gushing about how amazing it was and asking if it was one of the magic ones, and I think the owner might have been a little put out that this server hadn't gushed about how amazing her desserts were. She got this sort of frozen look on her face and then said, 'You mean that little awning across the street is actually a real shop?'"

Dean glanced over at her as he drove, frowning. "What's that supposed to mean?"

"She thought we were a prop or a photo backdrop or something. Like a publicity stunt by the town so tourists would have a cute window to take pictures in front of. I guess she got the idea because so many people have been taking pictures in front of How Sweet It Is since the story of the Cupids broke. But then when I said, no, we were a real chocolaterie, she started talking about how adorably old-fashioned that was and how she couldn't even fathom how we could make a profit *only* selling chocolates."

Dean tapped a finger on the steering wheel. "So what I'm hearing is that she's jealous because your chocolate is better, jealous because you have people who are so excited about your place they're taking pictures in front of it, and jealous because your choc-olates are so good you can make a living selling *only* chocolates when she has to do soups and sandwiches and breads and everything else."

"Except I'm barely making a living," Lucy pro-tested. "And when the Valentine's furor dies down, what then? Another reporter came by the shop today, trying to get in on the story, and I was so flustered that she just showed up unannounced that I didn't give her an interview, but now I'm thinking I should have. That I need as much free press as possible be-fore Valentine's because people are going to discover La Vie Douce and once they do, we may lose some of our customer base, and we really can't afford to lose any."

Dean glanced over at her as he drove. "Do you mind my asking who it was? The reporter?"

"Someone with a web series? I have her card. I actually wanted to ask your advice. I've gotten a few other requests—everything from the local newspaper to podcasters—and I've been avoiding responding be-cause I don't really have time to do a full press tour when I need to be making the Cupids so we actually have them to sell."

"It's not all or nothing," he said, pulling onto the freeway toward downtown where Pablo and Mark lived and worked. "You don't have to say yes to ev-ery single interview request just because you say yes to one. What you need to do is evaluate each offer to select the ones that will help How Sweet It Is the most. Which ones give you access to a new, desir-able audience. Which are going to build your brand in a way that helps your business. For example, you don't need a podcast where most of the listeners are in Australia, because you don't ship that far. Yet."

She smiled at his confidence that she would one day ship to Australia. When had Dean Chase become her biggest cheerleader? "There are just so many."

"If you want, I can go through them with you, give you my thoughts on each one. But you can do this. The most important thing to remember is that all these opportunities are about you and your business. Giving interviews isn't about pleasing the people who are asking you for things."

She arched a brow, even though he was focused on the road and didn't see it. "Are you implying I would say yes just because I don't want to disappoint people?"

"I'm *implying* that I've noticed you like to help people—and anyone who hasn't ambushed you in your shop or *accidentally* called you a fraud gets the benefit of the doubt, so you end up bending over backwards for them."

"Accidentally?"

He slanted her a sheepish look. "Have I mentioned how sorry I am about that?"

She grinned. "Once or twice."

"I may not know much, but I know the media feeding frenzy can be overwhelming if you let it control you. So you need to be in control. Don't work yourself to death giving a press tour you don't want to give. But don't feel like it's all or nothing, either. Just remember, if *Good Morning, America* calls, you might want to pick up the phone."

She bit her lip, nerves spiking. "I don't know. I'm

not sure I'm going to be able to keep up with orders as it is."

"I'd be happy to help out, but my chocolates would probably have air bubbles." He tossed a smile at her. "And, of course, you'd have to tell me your secret ingredient."

"Never," she swore, overdramatically. "I trust you, but not that much."

He chuckled, changing lanes. "I always knew you were smart."

"But thank you for offering to be my chocolate minion."

"Anytime."

She glanced out the window, and they rode in a cocoon of comfortable silence for a couple minutes until Lucy realized she'd started talking his ear off as soon as she got in the car. "I kind of hijacked the conversation, didn't I?"

"I don't mind. I like listening to you."

"Even when the cameras aren't rolling?" she teased.

"Especially then."

She didn't know why that simple statement should make her blush, but suddenly her cheeks felt warm and her voice was a little too breathy as she asked, "So how was your day?"

"You really want to hear about the thrilling world of legislative sessions?"

"Don't you usually do a report on those sessions on the evening broadcast?" She glanced at the dashboard clock. "You aren't missing that for this, are you?"

"Already filed. I recorded it in advance—and

they'll probably replay it on the eleven o'clock broadcast if you don't want to miss any of the bureaucratic excitement."

"We've actually been recording all your shows, so I can just check my DVR."

Dean flicked a glance across the car at her. "Checking up on me to make sure I don't sneak in any extra Cupid-related content?"

She blushed. "Something like that." There was no way she was going to admit she just liked watching his pieces, even when they were about legislative sessions. "Any word yet on the anchor position?"

"Some developments this morning. They're being very hush-hush about the whole thing, but Nora invited me to some corporate cocktail thing tomorrow night to meet a few of our sponsors. Apparently, it's an audition for the people on the short list."

"Which means you're on the short list! Dean! Congratulations!"

"Thank you. I'm pretty sure I wouldn't be on it without your help. I wouldn't even know I was up for the job if Nora hadn't—" He broke off.

Lucy studied his profile, and she could swear he looked embarrassed. "If Nora hadn't what?"

He winced, but admitted, "She only told me about the possible promotion to anchor to get me to stop pitching her a takedown piece on How Sweet It Is. Sorry."

Lucy almost laughed. "I'm not remotely surprised. Once a cynic, always a cynic."

"People say 'cynic' like it's a bad thing. A little skepticism is just good sense."

"Well, thank you for not doing a takedown piece on my livelihood."

"I wouldn't have gone through with it," he assured her. "Not once I figured out there's no nefarious intent—just a bunch of people indulging in the collective delusion of love and magic."

"You're still so certain it's a delusion?" she asked. She wasn't remotely offended by his doubt. Not now. There was something almost comforting about it. It was who he was, and she knew she could rely on him to question everything...so maybe she didn't have to. They balanced one another.

He tossed her a wry glance, as if she should already know the answer. "Ask me again after tonight. Maybe these two will finally convince me."

Chapter Twenty Five

"*I*F WE HAD MET ANY other way, I never would have given him a chance."

"Our first date was an absolute disaster," Mark confirmed.

The couple sat on the couch in their downtown condo, the lights of the city behind them as they faced the camera. They were both in their late thirties or early forties, but Mark had a genial, round face and a boyishness to his smile, while Pablo was all serious intensity, with silver starting to appear at his temples and lines of concentration around his eyes.

"We had nothing in common," Pablo continued. "He wasn't at all what I thought I was looking for."

Mark rested his hand on his husband's knee, smiling fondly. "He had an actual physical list of requirements. It was about as romantic as a job interview—for which I was woefully underqualified. No Ivy League education. No big career goals."

"I didn't think someone could possibly be perfect for me if they didn't understand my drive. And how could he understand my ambitions if he didn't have any of his own? I'd always envisioned myself as one half of a power couple. I thought the only way someone could be understanding about my schedule and the demands of my job would be if they had their own demanding job and a similar lifestyle."

"He would have been miserable," Mark said with absolute conviction. "Did you ever see Carrie Fisher's one woman show? She said she and Paul Simon were two flowers in search of a gardener. I always loved that. Someone has to tend the garden." He grinned. "And who better than an actual gardener?"

"The neurosurgeon and the gardener." Pablo shook his head. "He wasn't at all what I pictured when I imagined my ideal, but now I can't imagine life without him."

Dean let the moment hold for a long beat—recording that shared smile between the happy couple—before he prompted them with his next question. "So how did the chocolates play a part?"

"Well, we met at the shop. How Sweet It is," Mark explained his gaze flicking over to Lucy with a whisper of a smile on his face. "We'd both heard about the magic love chocolates and thought, 'Why not?' Pablo made a plan—of course—to pick one up after his shift, but he was barely going to get there before the shop closed. I'd lost track of time, and got stuck in traffic, and I didn't think I was going to make it, so I was rushing."

"I bought my chocolate, took a bite, and nothing happened," Pablo picked up the story. "I thought, 'Oh, well, it's a nice idea, but it's just a silly superstition.' One of the nurses had goaded me into coming, and I was a little skeptical to begin with. And then I'm turning to go when this guy comes racing through the door and knocks me off my feet."

"Literally." Mark laughed. "It was so cliché. I ran right into him, and we both went crashing to the floor. Total romcom scenario." He grinned. "And then I asked him out."

"He didn't even let me get up first." Pablo rolled his eyes.

Mark shrugged. "When you know, you know."

"But wait." Dean frowned. "Had you bought your chocolate yet?" he asked Mark.

"I bought it right after," he explained. "But I didn't eat it right away. I talked Pablo into being my Valentine and having our first date right away, so I brought the chocolate with me for dessert, and we walked down the street to the trattoria."

Pablo looked at his husband, and their eyes met, humor kindling at the shared memory. "By the time the appetizers arrived, I think we were both pretty sure we'd made a mistake."

"He was so uptight," Mark confirmed.

"And he was so directionless," Pablo added.

"He couldn't understand why I didn't want to invent some new rose or redesign the gardens at the White House. The idea that I only wanted to go to the greenhouse each day and nurture plants that my customers would buy and love was a totally foreign concept."

"I didn't want to understand," Pablo admitted. "I wanted to be the best at everything, and I couldn't imagine I would be well-suited to someone who didn't even see being the best as a goal. I was convinced I would have to change myself, be somehow less, if I settled for someone who wasn't as manically type-A as I was."

"And how are your big, important ambitions now?" Mark asked, a glint in his eyes as he challenged his husband.

"Bigger. Better." Pablo took his hand, linking their fingers together before turning back to the camera. "I never would have gone on *Jeopardy!* without him."

Mark smiled, eagerly explaining, "He used to record it every night, come home from work, and shout all the correct answers at the screen. I kept saying, 'You should go on the show.' And he would pretend not to hear me. Or say he didn't have the time. Or that it was a distraction."

Pablo shook his head fondly. "So he started sending me emails and text messages at random hours throughout the day. 'Here's the link to register for the test to be on the show.' 'Look, Pablo, the test is Tuesday night and you're not working then.' 'We should order salmon for dinner Tuesday since it's brain food, so you'll be ready for the test.' It became a whole thing. And the more he encouraged it, the more I had to admit I'd always wanted to be a *Jeopardy!* champion."

"Did you win?"

Irritation twisted Pablo's face. "It's the buzzer! I knew all the answers, but I only managed to ring in first a few times and there's no way to learn the system since they won't tell you whether you're a fraction too early or a fraction too late."

"He's still bitter about the buzzer." Mark patted his knee.

"But I'm so glad I did it. It was so much fun—

and made me realize that you have to prioritize fun. That's what Mark gave me. He helped me gain that perspective I'd always thought I didn't need. We joined a pub trivia league after we got back from the show. And then I got into a vendetta with the quizmaster."

"Pablo has very strong feelings about trivia."

"He was *wrong*," the neurosurgeon insisted. "Anyway, he quit after that—*not* related to me—and I volunteered to take over as quizmaster. Turns out I like that even more than being on a team."

"He loves being the Answer Dictator," Mark teased. "Getting to decide what's right and what's wrong."

"We have a quiz starting soon, actually," Pablo said, glancing at the clock. "Lucy said you might want to take some footage there? We cleared it with the bar owner, just in case."

"That would be great, if you don't mind."

"Of course not. Anything for Lucy." They both looked at her fondly.

Two weeks ago, Dean's cynical spidey-senses would have perked up at the sentence, latching onto it as evidence that they were lying for Lucy about the chocolates. But now he was starting to understand why so many people loved the shop—and its owner.

Still, the evidence for the chocolates here was pretty thin. He would have expected her to bring him to the clients with the most convincing chocolate + Valentine's = Love stories, but Mark apparently hadn't even eaten one.

"You never said what happened after the first date," Dean prompted. "If it was such a disaster, why do you think the chocolates brought you together?"

The couple exchanged an amused glance, and Mark picked up the story.

"By the time we were done with dinner, all I could think was that I couldn't imagine spending the rest of my life with someone who organized the sugar packets while we were waiting for our entrees—"

"And I could not stop thinking about how he'd ordered the special without even asking what it was—"

"So by the end of dinner, we were both just done. We wished one another luck and he started walking back toward his car. I was standing there, in front of the trattoria, watching him go, when I remembered I still had the Cupid chocolate. And I thought, of course he wasn't the guy! I didn't eat my chocolate yet! The magic hasn't started! But then I popped it into my mouth and I'm chewing and it's delicious... and suddenly all I could think was what if? What if the person you think is absolutely wrong for you is absolutely right? What if that's what's been missing all this time? What if this is my happily-ever-after, and I let it walk away from me because I wasn't willing to take a chance?"

"Mark has never met a chance he didn't want to take," Pablo said affectionately.

"So I chased him down the street. Again, very romcom dramatic. I wanted a soundtrack to swell in the background. But then I caught up to him and I took his hand and there was this *zing*."

"Static electricity," Pablo said dryly, but he was smiling.

"And I said, 'What if we give the chocolates one more chance?' I thought for sure he was going to turn me down flat."

"I almost did. I never like admitting I don't know everything, and I was so sure I knew what I wanted. But there was this moment...I don't know, I can't explain it, but I thought, What if I'm wrong about this? What if I'm wrong about him? And I said okay. Just okay. But after that, it was like everything changed. When I looked at him, I no longer saw the stereotype of the guy I'd always thought would be wrong for me. I saw Mark. Messy and pushy but also fun and supportive and sweet."

"And now?" Dean prompted gently.

"Happily ever after." Pablo squeezed his husband's hand.

"And it turns out I had ambition I never even knew about," Mark said with a smile. "I ended up cultivating a new species of rose, after all. I call it the Cupid's Kiss."

They shared a smile so intimate and affectionate that Dean cleared his throat, feeling awkward in the face of the couple's happiness. He glanced at his watch. "What time do we need to head to the trivia night?"

Chapter Twenty Six

"**H**OW MUCH DO WE WANT to risk on the last question? All of it? Go big or go home?"

Lucy grinned at Dean's intensity as he sat with his pencil poised above the answer sheet, his gaze locked on hers.

They hadn't planned on participating in the trivia night; they both had early mornings and Lucy still had Cupid chocolates to make. When Dean was setting up to get his footage, Pablo asked them if they wanted to play a few rounds and Dean refused, claiming he would be too distracted trying to get the B-roll he needed, but Lucy and Mark decided to form an impromptu team to entertain themselves until Dean and Lucy had to go.

They'd dubbed themselves The Cupid Coalition and settled in to give it their best try. Neither of them was particularly passionate about trivia, but as soon as the first question was asked, it was immediately apparent that Dean *was*.

He'd nearly dropped the camera in his haste to rush to their table to make sure that Lucy and Mark submitted the right answer. By the end of the first round, Dean was seated at their table, answer pad in hand, brow furrowed in concentration. By the third round, Mark was calling him Captain Cupid, having declared him the leader of their team.

They'd laughed and argued over answers, heads bent together, voices lowered so the other teams wouldn't hear them. Dean had only filmed the activity in the room when they'd already turned in their answers, taking fair play very seriously, but he'd declared he had enough footage after round three and had dedicated himself fully to the trivia questions after that.

It had been incredibly fun, seeing this new ultracompetitive side of him, his dark eyes flashing with intensity and concentration, and by the time the final round started, they were ahead by two points.

Mark had spotted someone he knew and left to greet them, leaving Lucy and Dean to decide how many of their accumulated points to risk on the final question.

"If we risk the maximum, no one can catch us," Dean urged, his face close to hers. He was sitting so close, she could feel the warmth of him all along her left side, their arms brushing every time either of them moved. They *had* to sit this close, their heads bent together, so the other teams wouldn't overhear their strategy.

"You're assuming everyone is going to get the final question," she pointed out. "Mark did say sometimes Pablo throws in a stumper to keep the teams on their toes, and then the people who risk the most finish last. Maybe the best strategy is not to risk anything at all. Just hold our position."

Dean groaned dramatically. "And let the teams with more guts pass us? We have been owning this game. We can't let up on the throttle now."

Lucy grinned at his theatrics. She should have guessed they'd be on opposite sides of this decision. They seemed to be on opposite sides of everything from magic to movie taste—they'd discovered tonight that she loved romcoms and he was all about political thrillers—but somehow their differences just made it more fun.

Dean was good at trivia, but it wasn't the fact that he knew all the answers that made her heart beat a little faster. It was the light of enthusiasm in his eyes. The quick smile. The way he leaned forward whenever she or Mark had a suggestion, eager for them to be a team, to put their heads together...and she'd found herself leaning in, too, smiling a little brighter. Every cell in her body had felt like it was sparkling with energy all night. She should have been tired, but she felt more awake, more alive, than she had in ages.

"What if Mark doesn't make it back for the final question? Are you sure you want to risk it all if we're going to be down a team member?"

"You think we can't handle one question without Mark?" Dean asked with mock affront. Then he tipped his head even closer to hers, his smile catching her right in the chest and making her go breathless. "It's you and me, Chocolate Siren. We've got this."

And suddenly it felt like he was talking about so much more than just trivia.

Everything seemed to slow, from the music playing

in between rounds to the heavy thud of her heartbeat. He was asking her to take a leap, and she couldn't look away from his eyes—or think of a single reason to say no.

A chair scraped loudly as Mark flung himself back into his spot. "What's the verdict? Did you guys agree on how much to risk?"

Lucy still didn't look away from Dean's eyes as a smile spread across her face. "Let's go for it."

Dean's grin grew impossibly wider. "*All* of it?"

Lucy felt a laugh bubbling up inside her, but she didn't release it, as if she was too happy for the joy to escape her body. "All of it."

Dean whooped, and Mark cheered, and Lucy's joy escaped in a laugh.

Dean quickly turned in their wager. The moment didn't feel broken when he jumped up from the table and rushed to drop off the little piece of paper; it was more like the feeling had stretched, changing into something new but no less wonderful.

"All right, team," Dean announced when he returned, taking up his pencil again. "We've got this."

Lucy and Mark exchanged exaggeratedly fierce competitive faces, which Dean didn't notice because he was too deep into his unexaggerated competition mode, his attention sharpening on Pablo as the microphone crackled over the PA.

Time for the final question.

Pablo looked all around the room, reminding them of the rules and the scores one last time, before requesting, "Drumroll, please."

Everyone in the bar drummed their hands on their tables, and Lucy giggled, joining in with Mark and Dean. Then Pablo held up his fist, silence reigned,

187

and the last challenge was finally revealed: a multi-part question about famous movie quotes.

Dean's eyes lit and locked on Lucy's. "Oh, we are *winning*," he announced with absolute confidence. "I know this one."

Lucy could only smile. Maybe a little risk wasn't so horrible.

With the right person...

"I don't understand how someone who prides himself on being right can be so incredibly *wrong*."

Lucy sat in the passenger seat of Dean's car and pressed her lips together so he wouldn't catch her smiling. He'd been ranting about the *injustice* of their trivia loss for the last fifteen minutes and there was no sign he was close to stopping.

Their victory had been cruelly snatched away when their team was knocked out of the top three by what Dean felt was a technicality. His certainty that he had been done a grievous injustice shouldn't have been nearly as endearing as she found it, but tonight, she seemed to find everything about Dean endearing.

"It's not like there's another movie called *Terminator 2*," Dean ranted. "He knew we knew the right answer. It would have been different if we'd picked any of the other Terminator movies, but we *obviously* knew the right one and to count us off just because we didn't include the *subtitle* is ridiculous. No one is going to ask, 'Oh, which *Terminator 2* did you mean?

Judgement Day? Or the other one that *doesn't exist?*'"

Lucy fought the urge to laugh. It was very clear that Dean did not think this was a laughing matter.

"He was harder on us because he didn't want anyone to accuse him of favoritism toward his husband's team," Dean grumbled.

"It's not like we could have accepted any of the prizes, anyway, with Mark on our team," Lucy reminded him. "And this way, the winning teams don't feel like they got it by default because we had to forfeit."

"That's not the point. We should all be held to the same standard."

Lucy tactfully refrained from mentioning that the winning team had written the full title. "I had no idea you were so serious about trivia."

Dean glanced over at her, and some of the fight went out of his eyes as he seemed to realize he'd been venting for fifteen minutes. "Sorry. Neither did I. I've never gone to anything like that before. It was fun."

"Have you always been competitive?"

"I like to win," he admitted. "And I've always been pretty intense about fairness."

"Defender of the little guy," she teased, smiling softly.

"You know it."

Her heart squeezed. "You'll be good anchor."

He glanced over at her. "You think?"

"Absolutely. You have that thing. That presence. That sense of fairness. And the compassion, even if you don't always let people see the softy inside."

He grimaced as they drove though the quiet night.

"I still have to get through tomorrow night. And I have to—" He broke off, flicking her another quick glance. "Actually, do you think you might want to come to the cocktail party with me? I'm only getting this chance because of you, and Nora told me to bring someone. I bet she'd love it—and I'm sure our sponsors would love it—if you came. I know you're really busy right now, so I understand—"

"No, I'd love to. That sounds fun."

She shouldn't go. She should stay home and make more Cupids, especially after the time she'd lost tonight, but she couldn't help thinking about what Georgie had said about all work and no play. And she *really* wanted to go.

Dean looked over at her long enough to smile. "Yeah?"

"Of course. With all you're doing to help the shop, it's the least I can do."

"Well. I am benefiting from these stories, too. It's not purely altruistic."

"Dean. I'm happy to help you schmooze the higher-ups," she insisted.

"Thank you. I'll text you the details. And if I can ever return the favor..."

"I'll take you up on that," Lucy assured him.

Because this was a *favor*. Just something between friends. Not a date. Even if her heart picked up a bit at the thought of spending another evening with Dean before the story was over and they went their separate ways. She liked him. As a *friend*. That was all.

Though maybe...maybe it could be more?

Chapter Twenty Seven

" *You* AND DEAN ARE SPENDING a lot of time together."

Lucy fought a blush at Georgie's oh-so-innocent statement, and the speculative look that accompanied it, the next afternoon. They were both in the kitchen, Lucy making another batch of Cupids and Georgie boxing them up so they'd be ready for delivery while Nana Edda manned the front of the shop and called out for help when it got too busy. It was a good routine, but it did make it hard for Lucy to avoid Georgie's speculative looks.

"We're doing Valentine's segments for his show," Lucy reminded her, keeping her attention on the chocolate she was tempering and strategically not mentioning tonight's cocktail party. She'd been thinking about it all day, and trying to avoid thinking about why she couldn't stop thinking about it.

Georgie said nothing, and when Lucy glanced up, she caught Dean's sister studying her like she was an experiment in her lab.

"It's not...he doesn't think of me like that," Lucy

insisted, not sure which of them she was trying to convince.

Georgie's brow furrowed, and her hands paused on the delivery orders she was packaging. "I know he seems like he's all tough and cynical, but be careful with him, okay? Dean's a lot more sensitive than he seems."

"I know," Lucy murmured. "But honestly, nothing's going on. We mostly argue about the chocolates, and I'm pretty sure he enjoys the arguments."

"That sounds like Dean," Georgie agreed with a fond smile that Lucy matched.

Two weeks ago, she'd disliked him intensely, but now he was real. He was a person, not a caricature of an evil newsman out to destroy her business. He was considerate and kind, always looking out for others, and *fun*. She'd found herself looking forward to every moment she would see him. Like tonight.

A little bubble of anticipation had been building in her all day, no matter how many times she told herself it was silly. He didn't want love. He'd been *very* clear about that. And about his skepticism. Though she hadn't actually remembered to ask him if he was still a skeptic after Pablo and Mark's interview last night. They'd been too caught up in trivia drama.

Dean might be coming around. Or was that just wishful thinking? Was he really softening toward the idea of love, or was she only seeing what she wanted to see?

He seemed so dead set against love when they met, and against magic, whereas his sister couldn't be more different. Or at least, she'd always seemed that way.

"Do you believe in the Cupids?" Lucy asked Georgie. "In the idea of magic and falling in love because of a chocolate?"

"I think it's fun to believe," Georgie said, glancing up from the ribbon she was tying on one of the embossed boxes. "And why couldn't it be true? There are a lot of things we still don't understand. Whether it's causal or coincidental, psychological or chemical, it's still a really nice story and there's no harm in it."

"So you aren't anti-love?"

"Like Dean, you mean?" Georgie pulled a face. "He isn't *really* anti-love. He just wants to protect everyone from anything that might hurt them. And he's seen that sometimes love hurts. But, to answer your question, no. I'm not anti-love. In fact, I was actually considering trying one of the Cupids myself."

"Really?"

Georgie blushed, smiling. "Why not? I mean, if it's a shot at true love, why wouldn't you take it?"

Because I'm a coward, Lucy thought. She hoped that Georgie wouldn't ask her why she'd never eaten a Cupid on Valentine's.

"Are you going to tell Dean about your Cupid plan?" Lucy asked, guiding the conversation away from her lack of gumption.

"Sure." Georgie picked up another box and another order form, moving to collect the correct chocolates. "He can't be as against them as he's pretending to be, or he would never do a whole series of segments on them."

"I'm pretty sure he's only doing them because he wants that morning anchor slot."

Georgie looked up, her brow wrinkled. "What morning anchor slot?"

Oh no.

Dean hadn't told his sister. Lucy's mouth worked as she tried to figure out how to put the cat back in the bag. "I thought there was...I probably misunderstood."

Georgie snorted. "I'm sure you didn't. Knowing Dean, he was probably trying to save me from getting my hopes up about him staying in case he didn't get it."

"Staying?"

"He's always wanted more than this," Georgie explained. "Either anchor or something national. I always knew if the right job didn't come along here, he'd eventually go somewhere else where he could be who he wanted to be. I think he only stayed in town this long because of me, because he's ridiculously overprotective and can't imagine that he could possibly support me as well from across the country." She smiled. "I don't actually need the hovering, but I do like having him here, so I let him think I believed him when he said this was all he wanted for now."

"But if he doesn't get this anchor job?"

Georgie shrugged. "I can't imagine he'll stay much longer."

"Right."

Lucy had no idea why that should be such a sobering thought. It wasn't like it mattered to her whether he stayed. He was just a guy doing a story on the shop. And her clerk's brother. She would probably never see him again after they filmed the last segment. So why should it matter to her if he went off to

New York to be the next Walter Cronkite? Why should the thought of him leaving pinch at her heart?

Lucy stared at a box of chocolates beside her on the counter, her gaze absently tracing the logo emblazoned on the top. She would always be here. Always tied to this place. Provided it didn't go under.

Dean was just a temporary distraction.

But even with that reality check in mind, she was still excited to see him tonight. Her stupid heart didn't seem to know a lost cause when it saw one.

Chapter Twenty Eight

*D*EAN PULLED INTO THE TINY employee parking area behind How Sweet It Is, tucking his car beside the one Lucy had pointed out as hers and wondering what on earth he'd been thinking when he'd asked Lucy to be his plus-one for this networking thing.

It wasn't a date, he assured himself. No matter how much it felt like one.

Wednesday was one of the nights the shop closed early, and the front windows were already dark, but all the employee spaces were full, and the scooter his sister used to get around campus was tucked against the alley wall.

Dean frowned at it as he climbed out of his car, concerned again at how invested Georgie seemed to be in the chocolate shop when she ought to be focused on her studies. He was still wearing his disapproving big-brother frown when the back door to How Sweet It Is opened and Georgie emerged, laughing as the voices inside the shop shouted goodbyes to her.

Her smile was still on her face when the door bounced against the metal doorjamb and she caught sight of him. "Dean! Nice suit. What are you doing here?"

"A better question is what are *you* doing here?" he deflected. "I thought you weren't working evenings so you'd have time to study?"

"Relax, Grumpy. I promise I've already finished my homework like a good girl. I just stuck around to finish boxing up some extra delivery orders and get some free chocolate therapy."

"What do you mean 'therapy'?" Concern surged up, swallowing his rational thinking with insta-worry. "Are you all right? What's wrong? Why didn't you call me?" He'd had his phone silenced most of the afternoon while he was covering a legislative session, but he still checked it frequently, so he knew that he hadn't had any messages or missed calls from her.

"Dean. I'm fine." She grinned, shaking her head. "Not everything is an emergency. I just wanted to talk, and Lucy and Edda are great listeners."

"I'm a good listener. You know you can come to me with anything."

Her eyebrows arched skeptically. "Even dating advice?"

Overprotective big brother mode rose up even more strongly. Love hurt, and if someone hurt Georgie... "You don't need any more distractions. Your studies..."

She rolled her eyes. "Lots of people have relationships and get degrees at the same time."

Lots of people didn't have their family history.

But Dean couldn't bring himself to say that out loud and burst the tentative bubble of hope on his sister's face as she admitted, "There's just someone

I've been thinking about a lot. A girl at the lab. I don't even know if she's queer, but I thought maybe if I ate a Cupid chocolate on Valentine's, fate would give us a little push. If it's meant to be." His little sister glanced over her shoulder back toward the shop, her lips quirking up in a private smile. "I just wanted to make sure I officially reserved one, so I wouldn't miss my shot."

Panic like he'd felt when he watched her fall off her bike for the first time shafted through him. "Georgie..."

She turned back to him, a question in her eyes. "What?"

He didn't have a logical way to express his very illogical level of fear for her. His chest squeezed hard on the protective impulse to wrap his sister in Bubble Wrap so no one could ever break her heart, but all he said was, "You're a scientist. You know the chocolates aren't magic."

Her eyebrows arched up high. "I know there are a lot of things we don't understand in the world. And until we do, magic is one way of trying to make sense of them. Not everything has to be black and white, Dean. Love rarely is."

"You're seriously arguing for the possibility of love chocolates?"

"Why not?" She folded her arms. "Dozens of studies have shown that the components present in chocolate trigger some of the same neurotransmitters in the brain as love. The phenylethylamine stimulates the brain to release dopamine, which produces feelings of pleasure and motivation. Anadamide activates pleasure receptors. Typtophan and serotonin create feelings of relaxation and well-being while the theobromine increases blood flow."

"That isn't love," Dean insisted. "It's just the chemical illusion of it."

Georgie shrugged. "Who's to say that feeling can't make people more receptive to the real thing? Every love story has to start somewhere."

Dean leaned against his car, his arms folded as they argued. "By that logic, why would the Cupids only work on Valentine's Day? And why only the Cupids? Wouldn't any chocolate do?"

"I'm not saying part of it isn't psychological. I'm sure the legend itself plays a part. Belief is a powerful force in the workings of the mind."

"So is self-delusion," he grumbled. "So your theory is that if you didn't know about the legend and believe in the magic, the Cupids would be just another chocolate?"

"I haven't exactly done a double-blind study on the matter, Dean," Georgie drawled.

He shook his head. "You've been spending too much time at this shop. It's corrupting your logic."

"I'm not the only one," Georgie returned, blithely unoffended. "You've sure been hanging out with Lucy a lot."

He narrowed his eyes at her speculative tone. "It's not hanging out. It's work."

"That why you look so spiffy tonight and Lucy's all dressed up? For *work*? 'Cause it sure looks like a date."

"It isn't a date," he snapped, a little too loudly. "I have to attend this network thing, and Nora expressly told me not to come alone. It was just convenient to ask Lucy because bringing the magic chocolate lady will help me soften my image." And if he couldn't imagine taking anyone else, well, that was just a co-incidence.

"Soften your image so you can get the morning anchor position?"

His focus sharpened at the pointed words. He hadn't told Georgie about it, hadn't told anyone. Except... "Lucy told you."

Georgie's dark eyes held his. "She didn't mean to. She thought you already had. But you didn't because, let me guess, you were protecting me from being sad if it doesn't work out?"

"Maybe," he admitted. "Or maybe I'm afraid if I tell people then I'll jinx it, and it won't really happen." He'd never wanted anything this badly and had it be so close to within his grasp while still not quite in his reach.

"But you told Lucy."

"I needed her cooperation. It was a negotiating tactic."

"Are you sure that's all it was?" Georgie asked, her lips quirking with amusement.

"What's that supposed to mean?"

"I'm only saying you seem..." Georgie shrugged. "I don't know. Loose around her."

"*Loose?*"

"You know what I mean. I've watched all the inter-views, and with her, you're relaxed. *Open.*"

"Open," he repeated dubiously.

"You're different with her," Georgie insisted. "You have this facade. This wall. Even I can't always get past your perfect, polished news face. But with Lucy...you're real with her. It's nice."

She wasn't wrong. His smiling, unflappable facade was his armor. And Lucy had somehow gotten past it. He'd always been willing to do whatever it took to get the story, and this time, somehow that had meant letting his guard down. That was the only explanation he had for it.

That, plus the fact that he'd put his foot in it so hard when they first met, there had been no point in putting on his "news face," as Georgie called it. Lucy had already seen behind it. She'd slipped past his polished image right from the start, and he'd had to be real to get her to trust him, but he hadn't realized it would make him trust her, too.

He'd been honest with her about his ambitions in a way he rarely was with anyone else. He might joke around with his coworkers about wanting an anchor job, but Lucy knew how much it meant to him.

Lucy knew a lot of things he didn't tell anyone else.

How had that happened? How had her sunshine and optimism, mixed with caution and constant worrying, somehow worked its way past all his titanium defenses?

"Don't get any ideas," he grumbled. "We're just friends."

"Of course you are," Georgie said, with a cheeky agreeability that was incredibly annoying. "It's just nice to see you making friends."

He narrowed his eyes. "Don't you have groundbreaking research to conduct or something?"

She just laughed as she headed toward her scooter. "Have fun on your playdate tonight!"

"It's work. I'm working."

It certainly wasn't a date.

Except it kind of felt like one.

What was he doing? He'd just needed a plus-one. He could have invited anyone. A colleague. His sister. Inviting Lucy was complicated, and he liked his life simple. He preferred his heart safe...right up until the moment the chocolate shop door opened, Lucy stepped into the lot, and his breath whooshed out.

She looks like chocolate.

He knew, in the rational part of his brain, that the thought didn't make any sense, but it popped into his head and refused to leave. Her dress was the exact shades of white and dark chocolate swirled together, the way they drizzled on the chocolate-covered strawberries she sold. Her hair was swept up on top of her head in some sort of complicated twist, and her lips were a deep, luscious red as she flashed him a bright smile while he just stood there, dumbfounded.

"I thought I heard someone out here," she said cheerfully, and he realized the door to the shop hadn't closed all the way when Georgie came out. "Are you ready to go?"

"Uh, yeah." His voice was a little too deep, and he cleared his throat, pulling himself back together. "Ready when you are."

"I'll just grab my coat." Lucy disappeared back inside.

Georgie waited until she was out of sight. "Oh, yeah, this isn't a date at all."

He shot his little sister a glare. "Stop. It's work. She's helping me get this anchor position."

"If you say so," Georgie called, snapping her helmet on as Lucy swept back into the back alley, claiming all of his attention.

"All set?" she asked, her smile making the dark alley feel suddenly brighter. She looked like she was glowing from the inside out, the beam of that smile shining right on him.

Dean had rounded the car while talking to Georgie, so he was already standing next to the passenger side. He opened the door for Lucy. "Always," he murmured as she brushed close to him to climb in.

"Don't do anything I wouldn't do!" Georgie singsonged, as Dean closed the door. He could only hope Lucy hadn't heard that. He sent his little sister his most ominous look—which had never worked, anyway.

Georgie just laughed and started her moped, the roar of the engine cutting off any response.

Chapter Twenty Nine

THE VENUE FOR THE EVENING was the ballroom of a historic hotel, all lush wood paneling and antique crystal chandeliers. And it was already packed.

Lucy gripped Dean's arm, suddenly nervous she was going to say the wrong thing to the wrong big-ticket sponsor and ruin everything for Dean. She'd never been to anything like this before. There weren't a lot of fancy industry networking events in the independent chocolatier world.

According to the sign at the door, the ostensible reason for the gathering was a commendation for excellence in journalism being awarded to one of Dean's colleagues, but for now, everyone was mingling with cocktails, and Lucy knew *this* was the part of the evening that could make or break things for Dean.

Dean guided her into the room, nodding to a few of his colleagues and pausing to introduce her and chat for thirty seconds at a time—quick, light, leaving a cheerful impression and moving on.

He had his polished "news face" on. Oddly, it wasn't until she saw him in smooth, flawless professional mode that she realized she'd started to see a different, more relaxed side of him over these last several days. A side she was coming to like a little too much.

He guided her toward the bar, and they both ordered the signature drink of the evening, a "chocolate kiss" martini.

"Thank you for doing this," he murmured when they had a private moment as they waited for the drinks. "Have I mentioned you look fantastic?"

Lucy blushed, reminding herself that she'd overheard him talking to Georgie, insisting that he just needed a plus-one and that she was convenient. "So do you. And I'm not sure I'm actually doing much. I don't think I've said anything beyond 'nice to meet you.' I should have brought chocolate bribes so at least I'd be useful."

He looked down at her, his gaze warm as he brushed his fingers over hers where they rested on the bar. "You're perfect just the way you are. No chocolate bribes necessary."

Her heart stuttered. She could still feel that contact zipping along her nerve endings as she dropped her gaze. "Well, it's the least I could do for you after all you've done for me." *Keep it professional. Businesslike.* "I took a look at the books last night after we got back from trivia, and I think if I can actually make as many chocolates as people are ordering, How Sweet It Is might be on solid financial ground. I had to rush order more raspberries today to keep up with demand for the Cupids."

"That's wonderful." Their drinks arrived, and he

slid her one before lifting his own glass to clink gently against hers. "To success."

"Thank you." She took a sip of the decadent martini, the sweetness of the chocolate a familiar comfort on her tongue. "It feels kind of surreal. I've been working toward financial security for all this time, and all at once, I might just have it."

She still wasn't sure it would continue after the initial furor died down and Valentine's Day passed, but so far, the interest in the Cupids seemed to only be building, if the orders coming in were anything to go by. The online order form was on fire.

She'd even gotten past her fear that it was all going to blow up in her face.

Well. Almost.

Somehow arguing with Dean about love had made her fear of the curse and lawsuits feel as silly as his objections to love. What was it Pablo had said about perspective? Something about Mark showing him things he hadn't even known he needed?

"You deserve it," Dean insisted.

"It's kind of mind-boggling," Lucy admitted. "All that financial stress just *gone*." She made a *poof* gesture with the hand that wasn't holding her cocktail. "Thanks to you."

He grinned and wagged his eyebrows, all over-the-top arrogance. "Well. I *am* pretty amazing."

She giggled, entirely too entertained. She felt all bubbly and light, and she wasn't sure whether it was the newfound financial security or Dean or the chocolate martini in her hand.

She needed to remember he was anti-love. Even if tonight, it felt like anything was possible, the only possibility that mattered to him was landing him that job.

"So what do we need to do tonight to make sure the Big Bosses see how amazing you are?" she asked.

Dean flashed his camera-ready smile. "Smile for the higher-ups, don't let on that I'm secretly a cynic, and make sure all the sponsors think I'm the perfect face for the morning show." His voice was low, for her ears alone.

She scanned the room, all the gorgeous people in their gorgeous clothes mingling and smiling. "Do you know who the competition is?"

"I've been trying not to think about it. I can't control what they do—only the impression I make." He grimaced, his eyes catching on someone across the room. "Honestly, at this point, my biggest obstacle may be Anna."

"Anna?"

"Anna Robinson," Dean explained. "The morning co-anchor." He nodded toward a small group across the room, and Lucy followed his gaze to a tall, gorgeous Black woman with a brilliant smile. "Whoever gets the job is going to need her seal of approval—or at least, her reluctant acceptance."

Lucy snuck a glance at Dean's pained expression. "She doesn't like you?"

He grimaced. "Unfortunately, she has good reason."

"Did you accuse her of running a fraud ring out of a chocolate shop?"

She startled a laugh out of him and got him to stop staring morosely across the room. He met her eyes, shaking his head. "I'm never going to live that down, am I?"

"Probably not," she teased, glad she'd gotten the desired result and lightened the doom-and-gloom expression on his face. Beneath the charm and banter, he took things so seriously. Cared about people so much. Sometimes she just wanted to make things lighter for him. "So what happened with Anna?"

He cringed. "When I heard that she'd gotten engaged, I might have been a little too honest about my thoughts on love and marriage and happily-ever-after. I inadvertently implied that she was on a course headed straight for divorce. And she might have been standing right behind me when I said it."

Lucy winced sympathetically. "Not your finest hour."

"No," he agreed. "And now she's very professional, but I have a feeling I'm the last person she wants to be saddled with at the anchor desk."

"Have you tried making amends?"

"I apologized. Right after I said it. As soon as I saw her there."

"She probably thinks you only apologized because you got caught, not because you're actually sorry. Have you tried explaining?"

"Explaining what?"

Lucy hesitated, trying to find a tactful way of saying *that you have enough baggage to fill a jumbo jet and more hang-ups about love and romance than anyone I've ever met.* "Explaining that it wasn't about her or her marriage."

Realization lit in his eyes. "It's not you, it's me?"

She smiled. "Something like that."

"You think that would make a difference?"

Lucy shrugged. "It couldn't hurt."

Dean glanced back across the room. "Maybe. I'll think about it."

Lucy let the subject drop as another couple approached them and they were sucked back into hobnobbing.

Chapter Thirty

THE NIGHT WAS GOING WELL. Lucy was a triumph. At first, she'd been nervous and quiet, but after their conversation at the bar, Dean started introducing her as the best chocolatier in the city and chocolate, it turned out, was a natural icebreaker.

She still gripped his arm like a lifeline, but he kind of liked being the one she leaned on. He liked that he could read through her body language when she needed him to rescue her with a quip and steer the conversation in another direction. He'd always been good at buttering up the sponsors, but it was somehow even more fun when Lucy was gently teasing him and smiling shyly at his side. He couldn't seem to stop brushing her fingers where they rested on his arm.

Nora beamed at him like a proud parent whenever she caught his eye across the room. He had a strong feeling that he was doing *very well* on this anchor audition.

But he still hadn't worked up the gumption to approach Anna yet.

His potential co-anchor was attending with her fiancé, which added an extra layer of cringe to his shame.

He wasn't *avoiding* her, but he certainly wasn't trying to bump into her—which made it all the more surprising when he literally did, his shoulder crashing into hers.

"Anna! Sorry!" Dean reached out a hand automatically to steady her when they collided in passing. Lucy was still on his other arm, while Anna's fiancé moved to her side.

"Dean." Anna's tone was civil, without an ounce of extra warmth.

His tongue tangled in his mouth, and for once, Dean found himself speechless. Thank goodness for Lucy.

"Ms. Robinson, I'm a huge fan," she said with a soft smile.

Right. Introductions. "Uh, Anna, I'd like to introduce Lucy Sweet. She owns the How Sweet It Is chocolate shop we've been featuring lately."

"Of course." Anna's smile warmed the second her gaze moved from Dean to Lucy. "It's nice to meet you."

"You, too. And I understand congratulations are in order?" Lucy's smile drew the tall man at Anna's side into the conversation.

"Ah, yes. Thank you." Anna's gaze flicked back to Dean for a fraction of a second, and he barely stopped himself from visibly wincing. "This is my fiancé, Dorian."

"Anna, do you think I could have a word with you in private?" Dean blurted, the request tumbling out of his mouth in a rush.

Reluctance instantly washed over his coworker's face, and Dean added softly, "Please."

It was tempting to just beg forgiveness where they stood, to lean on Lucy and hide behind her ability to smooth things over, but he wanted to be man enough to do this himself. And he was the one who needed to make things right.

"I suppose," Anna agreed hesitantly.

"Thank you."

"I'll be right here," her fiancé assured her. Anna nodded and moved a couple feet away to the shadow of a large floral arrangement that gave them the illusion of privacy.

Dean swallowed his nerves and his pride. "I just wanted to tell you how sorry I am. About what I said when you—"

"It's fine." She shook her head.

"It isn't," he insisted. "And it wasn't about you or your engagement."

Anna's face was tight, a fortress with thousands of walls he couldn't scale. "Look, I don't know how you found out about Alex, but I would never let my personal feelings affect my work life. You'll get fair consideration. You don't have to do this."

"Yes, I do. I still owe you an explanation." Dean grimaced. "I...my family...we don't have a good track record when it comes to stuff like that. Love and weddings. Forever doesn't really mean forever, in my life. And I, um, I've let myself get really jaded. I was so cynical about this stuff that I thought my assignment to cover the Cupid chocolates was a punishment. When I said what I said, I couldn't see past my own feelings about marriage and love. But it was a lousy thing to say, and I've regretted it ever since. And I just really wanted to apologize, again, and tell you that it was never about you. And I was in the wrong." The words started slow and halting, but by the end, they were pouring out.

Anna's brow furrowed as she studied him. "You really mean that, don't you? You aren't just saying it to butter me up so I'll put in a good word for you."

"I do."

"Huh." Her head cocked as she continued to stare at him until he had to fight the urge to fidget. "You always seemed sort of, I don't know...*surface* to me. The shiny exterior is all I've ever seen you show people. But the stories you're doing now, when you're real...they're *better*, Dean. You're better." She glanced past him. "It's a nice change."

Dean looked over his shoulder, following Anna's gaze straight to Lucy. She stood with Dorian, the pair chatting comfortably, even as they both periodically cast looks at Anna and Dean to check on them.

Lucy glanced over, her eyes locking with Dean's. A single eyebrow lifted, a single dimple appeared. And his heart thudded hard.

Dean tore his gaze away, turning back to Anna. "We aren't... That isn't..."

Anna just smiled. "If you say so."

He did say so.

Lucy was the bright spot in his days, her optimism and hope saturating his life, her determination and skill impressing him at every turn, but he couldn't be feeling more for her than just respect, with a dash of admiration and a friendly affection. Just the thought of more scared him senseless.

No. They were just friends. He didn't do more.

Chapter Thirty One

"*D*O YOU THINK IT WORKED?"

The car slipped through the night, swift in the late-night lack of traffic. Dean had been quiet ever since they left the party—or, to be more accurate, ever since he talked to Anna. He'd said that she'd accepted his apology, but he'd been strangely distant.

He glanced over at her in the cab of the car, his eyes inscrutable in the darkness. "Do I think what worked?"

"The master plan to make you anchor," Lucy said, trying to lighten the mood.

Dean just shook his head, his attention back on the road. "I don't know." He tapped the wheel, that one finger the only evidence of any internal agitation. "I'm glad I apologized to Anna. And explained. Even if I don't get the job."

"You'll get it," she assured him.

"Maybe not." The finger tapped some more. He didn't say anything else for so long that Lucy started to wonder if they would drive the last few minutes to Watson Corners in heavy silence, but then, abruptly, he blurted, "Georgie told me she wanted to try one of the Cupids."

"She does," Lucy confirmed. She studied his profile as he drove, eyeing the tight line of his jaw. "And you don't want her to?" she guessed.

"It's not that I don't want her to. You just have to understand..." He stared out the windshield. "I told you our parents split up when we were young. But then they each remarried, and divorced, and remarried again. And divorced again. For Georgie and me, it was this never-ending cycle of change all through our childhood. All because someone else fell in or out of love. We had each other, but...our family, we don't have a good history with this stuff. I've seen firsthand how love crashes and burns and hurts more people than just the lovebirds involved. So yes, I protect her too much, and I worry too much, but I never want anything to hurt her like I know that stuff can hurt."

Lucy studied his profile.

He wasn't just protecting Georgie. He was protecting himself. All that cynicism, all that doubt—it all made so much sense for a little boy who had grown up feeling like he was being tossed around by the waves of love that were out of his control. No wonder he wanted so badly to control something, anything. And the only way he could control love was to not let it in.

But that sounded so lonely. Lucy wanted to reach out to him, her heart aching with the urge to take his hand. But she wasn't really one to talk. She'd never taken that leap, either. She'd never been in love.

She swallowed the thickness in her throat, focusing on Georgie. "It's her call, isn't it? If she wants to risk her heart?"

"Of course it is. But how do you watch the person you care about most in the world do something you're sure is going to hurt them, down the road?"

"Maybe it won't," she offered lightly.

"But you don't know that. And the odds are terrible, especially in my family. Why set yourself up for failure like that? How can I support that?"

"Because she wants you to? And because sometimes you have to take a chance to get the things that really matter." Now if only she was brave enough to take her own advice.

Dean shook his head, changing lanes for their exit. "There are some things you don't take chances with."

Lucy didn't have a response for that, though she did wonder if he meant his little sister...or his own heart.

She watched him as they rode in silence for a few minutes until they were gliding down the darkened Main Street.

"I never asked you last night," Lucy said, finally.

"Asked me what?"

"You told me to ask you later, if you still think the Cupids are a collective delusion after talking to Mark and Pablo."

Dean slanted her a cynical look across the dark interior of the car as he pulled into the parking area behind How Sweet It Is. "Lucy. You can't honestly think Mark and Pablo reinforce the myth of the chocolates. They said themselves that neither of them was what the other was looking for. If the Cupids are supposed to find you your romantic ideal..."

"The Cupids are supposed to find you true love," Lucy argued, twisting in her seat to face him. "That doesn't mean you're only allowed to fall in love with the kind of person you walked into the shop thinking you wanted."

Dean parked behind her car, but she didn't unfasten her seat belt. She didn't want him to go. Even if this wasn't a date, she wasn't ready for the night to be over.

She glanced toward the shop, wetting her lips. "I told Nora and some of the other producers that I would give you a box of chocolates to bring into the studio. Would you like to come inside for a second while I grab it?"

"Yeah. Of course." He shut off the car and they climbed out. "Thank you again for tonight," he said— and then made it exactly two steps before his need to argue his point overtook him again. "Though I still don't see how you can say the chocolates made Pablo and Mark fall in love."

Lucy ducked her chin so he wouldn't see her fighting a grin as they approached the back door of How Sweet It Is. She secretly loved arguing about love with him.

"It seems more like Pablo and Mark chose to keep giving one another second and third chances, because they both *wanted* the chocolate to be magic, until they eventually got past their own prejudices," Dean insisted, "but that's *them*. That's not the Cupids."

"Love is a choice." Lucy glanced at Dean as she reached the door. "We choose whether to accept it or not. Whether to fight for it. We decide what it means to us. The magic isn't the choice. The magic is..."

She shook her head, pausing in the act of fishing for her keys as she searched for the right words. "Pablo and Mark were both looking for love when they came into the shop. And fortunately, they believed in the chocolate enough to look past their own narrow expectations to find exactly what they needed. We don't always know who will bring out the best in us until that person is right there, staring us in the face."

She looked up at him, his dark hair burnished by the gold light above the door, and her breath caught in her throat. She didn't know what it was. She didn't know what had changed. But all at once, even the air around them felt different.

And suddenly he was right there.

Staring her in the face.

Chapter Thirty Two

ER HEART JUMPED UP TO her throat, so she felt every beat heavy and thick against the pulse at her neck. He had to see it, too—but he wasn't looking away from her eyes. How had she never noticed before that his were the exact shade of dark chocolate? Decadent and just a little bitter, but all the more sinful because of that bite. Would he taste like dark chocolate?

He shifted toward her. Not even a full step. More of a shuffle. A question. Giving her the chance to retreat even as his dark-chocolate eyes dropped down to her lips, indicating his intent. She was staring at his mouth, too. The lower curve was so full and the dip in his upper lip...how had she not noticed that dip? There was a name for it. Cupid's bow. Of course he had a perfect one.

He said her name softly, that Cupid's bow moving, and then there was another shuffled step closer. The look in those dark-chocolate eyes slayed her. She felt herself leaning forward and tipped her chin back, her eyes drifting closed. He was so close now. She could feel the warmth of him, the brush of his breath, like her entire life had been building to this moment—

"Oh! It's you! I thought I heard—never mind! Carry on!"

Her grandmother slammed the back door shut again, but Dean and Lucy had already jerked apart, the moment shattered like chocolate shards when she dropped one of the delicate chocolate eggs.

Dean came to a stop four feet back, everything in his body language leaning away from her when Lucy finally managed to force her gaze off the pavement. She couldn't quite meet his eyes, but she managed somewhere in the vicinity of his left shoulder.

"I should get going," he said, his voice a little rough. With embarrassment? Or something else? "I'll, uh, grab the chocolates some other time. If the offer's still open?"

"Yeah, of course," she stammered, her voice too bright, and a little too breathless. "Any time."

"Great. Good night, Lucy."

"Good night, Dean."

She watched him walk back to the car but turned away before he could catch her watching, shoving open the door. Of course, it hadn't been locked at all. Why had she bothered fishing for her keys before she checked?

She half-expected to find her grandmother waiting just inside, trying to eavesdrop through the thick door, but instead the hallway was empty.

"Nana?" she called, the sound echoing hollowly.

She headed toward the kitchen, in case Nana Edda was lurking there, but everything was as quiet as she'd left it. Several batches of half-finished chocolate shells sat in neat rows, waiting to be filled and sealed.

Her thoughts still a jumble from the aborted I-really-thought-he-was-about-to-kiss-me moment outside, Lucy set down her purse and washed her hands.

Making chocolates always helped her clear her thoughts, and she needed lots of thought-clearing tonight.

She prepared the ganache, her movements more muscle memory than thought, and piped the filling into the shells. Tempering the chocolate and sealing the pralines took time, but tonight, it felt like it was done in a blink. And her thoughts—and emotions— were no clearer.

The chocolate needed to set before she could remove the finished chocolates from their molds. She should just go upstairs. Finish in the morning. But instead she found herself wandering to the front of the shop.

The diagonal yellow beams from the vintage streetlight outside provided the only light and seemed to shine like a spotlight, right on the Wall of Love. Her mother's photo caught her eye. She knew what her mother would tell her if she was here, but her mother always gave the most reckless advice. Never looking before she leaped—but was that what you had to do? Just take that leap of faith? Throw yourself on the mercy of fate?

Lucy stood in the slanted shadows, staring at those photographs, the physical evidence that she'd done something good. Something more lasting than just chocolate. Those photos were tangible proof that love was real. That it was possible.

She didn't know how long she'd stood there when her grandmother spoke from the kitchen doorway. "What are you doing standing here in the dark?"

Lucy didn't take her eyes off the pictures. "Just thinking." She glanced over at her grandmother's dear, familiar face.

"Did Dean go home?"

"Yeah. He didn't come in. He was just dropping me off."

Something about saying it out loud caught at her brain, and she found herself wondering for the first time if he was driving out of his way to pick her up and drop her off when they did the couple interviews. She could easily have driven herself and met him downtown near Pablo and Mark's place. Or driven herself to the venue tonight. Not that she didn't enjoy the time in the car with him. She did. Maybe too much. Talking to Dean had become the highlight of her days.

The lines had been blurring between reluctant partners and friends and...something else. Something she wasn't quite ready to think about.

Her grandmother came fully into the shop.

"I'm sorry, sweetheart. I thought I heard something in the alley, and I worried you might have forgotten your key. I didn't mean to interrupt—"

"You didn't interrupt anything," Lucy insisted, before her grandmother could get any more carried away with her *mea culpa*s.

Nana Edda's face fell. "Are you sure?"

"Positive," Lucy said. "And if, hypothetically, you had interrupted something, I would have been glad you did."

That never should have happened.

Somehow saying the words out loud gave her the clarity the last twenty minutes of chocolate prep hadn't. She'd been too busy feeling, but now she was thinking again, and the answer was clear.

Any kind of romantic involvement with Dean was a terrible idea. She needed to focus on How Sweet It Is. She was glad they hadn't kissed. Ecstatic, even.

"It's okay to like him," her grandmother said gently, carefully.

"I do," Lucy insisted, staring at the wall of photos instead of meeting her grandmother's eyes. "As a collaborator. A person I'm working with to advance the interests of the shop." Her grandmother made a soft huffing sound and Lucy gave her a stern look from the corner of her eye. "No matchmaking. This is business."

Nana Edda released a dissatisfied *tsk*. "As focused on this business as you are, the only way you're going to fall in love is if you meet someone as a *collaborator*. Or if you finally bite into one of the Cupids yourself."

"I have enough to worry about right now without a relationship complicating things. And even if I was going to get involved with someone, it wouldn't be Dean. He doesn't believe in anything. Love. Chocolate. Weren't you the one who said nonbelievers were bad energy to have around?"

Her grandmother studied Lucy's face. "I may be reconsidering my opinion."

"Well, don't. He's been very clear that he is actively against the idea of falling in love." And the last thing she needed was the heartache of throwing her heart at someone who wouldn't love her back.

He was so anti-love. He'd been so adamant with Georgie that this wasn't a date. When he'd started talking about his family tonight, something inside her had softened, but hadn't he just been reinforcing all the reasons he didn't believe in love? Explaining why he would never want that? Making sure she didn't get the wrong idea? Did he think she was falling for him? Was he trying to warn her off?

There might have been a moment when he was dropping her off when things felt different...but that was just a glimmer. A lapse. The real Dean was rock-solid on his aversion to romantic relationships. Moonlit almost-kisses notwithstanding.

Nana Edda *hmmed*, watching her closely. "People don't always know what they need."

Lucy faced her grandmother in the low light of the shop. "It isn't going to happen. Dean doesn't want it to, and even if he did, it would be a conflict of interest."

"So?"

Lucy groaned. "You never see the downsides."

"And you always do. You might be the most cynical hopeless romantic I've ever met."

"I'm not cynical. I'm practical. And I'm not a hopeless romantic."

"No? Then why are you standing here in the dark, staring at the Wall of Love?"

Lucy blushed and turned back toward the wall, grateful her grandmother couldn't see her rosy cheeks in the low light. "I like knowing we had a hand in making people happy. That doesn't mean I'm looking for it myself."

Her grandmother sighed. "I just don't want you to be afraid to feel something real."

"I'm not afraid. I'm busy. The shop is important to me."

Nana Edda arched her eyebrows high. "The shop is important to all of us. Just be careful you don't miss out on the juicy bits of life because you're so busy fixating on what's 'important.' I don't want you to look back and feel like you let your chance go by. That's what the chocolates are all about, aren't they? Seizing the day?"

"And keeping us solvent," Lucy added dryly.

Her grandmother sighed again. "You can pretend all you like. I know you, Lucy Sweet. I know you care about more than our profits. And I know you like that boy. The one I caught getting ready to kiss you."

"He wasn't." Lucy turned away from the Wall of Love and the entire idea of the ill-advised kiss, moving back toward the peaceful quiet of her kitchens. Dean was firmly anti-romance. A relationship wasn't even an option. Thinking anything else was just wishful thinking and Lucy was much too practical for that. "Anything between us is about the shop. That's it."

Her grandmother nodded. "I'll keep that in mind." Then she cocked her head, tapping a finger on her chin. "How many times does the lady have to protest before it becomes protesting too much? I can never remember."

Lucy groaned. *"Good night, Nana."*

Her grandmother's laugh trailed her up the stairs

to her little apartment above the shop. "Good night, Lucy."

Chapter Thirty Three

"*D*EAN. COME IN. CLOSE THE door."

Dean obeyed, entering Nora's office and clicking the door shut behind him. "Everything all right, boss?"

Instead of the nerves he'd felt last time she'd told him to close the door, he felt only anticipation now. After last night, had they made their decision? Was she calling him in here to tell him the job was his?

"Have a seat," she instructed, and he settled himself in the chair opposite her desk, mentally coaching himself not to over-celebrate when she told him.

"I saw you talking to Anna last night," she began. "I seem to recall telling you not to bother her."

Dean barely contained his flinch. Okay. Maybe he wasn't about to be promoted. "I know. But I never mentioned Alex or the job. This had nothing to do with that. I just owed her an apology."

Nora studied him and nodded slowly. "All right." For another long moment, she said nothing, and he resisted the urge to squirm in his chair.

Dean silently pushed down his impatience. *Just tell me the job is mine, already!*

"Lucy was a hit," Nora said finally. "I was a little surprised you brought her."

"It seemed fair. She's the reason I'm even in the running, isn't she?"

"She is," Nora agreed. "And the two of you have quite a rapport."

"Oh?" Dean said, as if he hadn't noticed it.

And as if he hadn't gotten carried away and nearly kissed her last night.

Thank goodness he'd come to his senses. With all the talking they were doing about love and romance, it was almost inevitable that they'd get confused at some point and start thinking they were feeling all the things they were discussing. With a little distance, he'd been able to see what a disaster that would have been.

She was so sweet. So vulnerable. She didn't have his tough hide. If she fell for him, when the love stuff went up in flames, like it inevitably would, she'd get hurt. And he didn't want to do that to her. Or to himself.

No. Much better to keep his distance. Keep it friendly and professional. Which his boss would surely approve of. The new anchor did not run around kissing sources for stories.

"You're almost done with the segments, I understand."

"We're filming the final Happy Couple interview tomorrow night, with the woman who wrote the original post and her fiancé. Figured that sort of brings it full circle, since Valentine's is coming up fast."

"You're getting great material," Nora praised. He braced himself for the announcement that he was about to become the morning anchor, but what she said instead was, "I asked one of the assistants to go through the unused footage, see if we had enough for another segment. There's some good stuff there. I especially loved the part where you and Lucy were debating love. The camera loves her." Nora smiled. Something about that smile made him nervous. "It gave me an idea, actually."

Dean shifted in his chair, uneasy with the direction this was taking—and no longer at all sure he was about to be promoted. "An idea?"

"For the perfect way to end your series. A live feed. On Valentine's Day. From How Sweet It Is. We'll set it up for right after the headlines on the evening broadcast. That's when our viewership is highest." She met his eyes, giving her next words a significant weight. "The perfect way to let all our viewers really get to know you."

Dean's heart started beating fast again. If she wanted more of the viewers to get to know him, then they must be seriously considering him for the anchor position. It was so close.

"That sounds great," Dean said, trying to play it cool. "I'll need to get Lucy on board, but I don't anticipate that being a problem."

"Excellent," Nora beamed. "We'll set it up with a shortened version of the original piece and then throw to you live where you'll eat one of the Cupid chocolates on camera."

"Abso—" The meaning of her words finally caught

up with his brain, breaking off his agreement. "I'm sorry? Eat one of the Cupids?"

"It's perfect. You show the crowds, eat the chocolate, smile for the camera, and then throw back to Kevin and Lee Ann."

"Isn't that—it just seems like—" He tugged at his suddenly too-tight collar. "Do the viewers really want to be voyeurs on my love life?"

Nora snorted. "Yes. They'll eat it up. But don't worry. You're not required to pretend to fall in love on camera."

His face felt like it was on fire. Was that normal? "I just wasn't planning to eat one of the Cupids."

"Don't tell me you're actually starting to believe in the magic chocolates." Nora's eyebrows lifted, and she couldn't quite suppress her grin.

"No. Of course not."

"Then what's the problem? You already ate a chocolate on camera, so I know you aren't allergic."

"I just didn't think that, um..." An excuse. He needed a good excuse. "Wouldn't we be inviting the viewers to speculate on my romantic status? It might actually hurt the chocolate shop if I never, you know, fell in love with anyone when the viewers would all know I ate the chocolate."

"If it becomes a PR problem for How Sweet It Is, you can come out as a nonbeliever and say something about how only people who believe in the magic fall in love." Nora waved away his concern with a flick of her fingers. "But these stories don't have long shelf lives, Dean. People will forget about it until next Valentine's Day, when we do a follow-up and have someone else eat the chocolate on camera." Her eyes met his, heavy with meaning. "Unless you'd rather I send someone else to do it this year?"

A sharply possessive spike stabbed into him at the idea of anyone else eating a Cupid on camera at Lucy's shop—even though he'd encouraged her the other night to consider other press offers.

"No. I'll do it," Dean insisted. "It's my story." And he wasn't giving up the opportunity of that live feed.

"That's what I thought." Nora smiled, the matter decided. "You'll get Lucy's permission for the live feed tonight?"

"Consider it done."

He would set it up. He would eat the chocolate on camera. And he would be *fine*. Because he didn't believe in the sappy hearts-and-flowers stuff. And he knew better than to let himself get caught.

At least, he thought he did.

Chapter Thirty Four

_P_ARISIAN JAZZ FLOATED THROUGH THE kitchen, twining around Lucy as her hands moved rhythmically over the chocolate molds. The piping bag was a familiar shape in her hands as she deftly filled the molds and hummed to herself, the foreign words blurring together in a harmony of feeling, casting a rose-colored glow over the night.

The shop had long since closed for the night. Nana Edda had gone to her book club and wouldn't be back for hours, making the quiet atmosphere of the shop feel that much more complete. Lucy loved this solitude, the peacefulness of it, and the melodies of French jazz tangling around her kept her from thinking too much about Dean.

She'd told herself she was glad they hadn't actually kissed last night. She'd almost completely convinced herself of it. Everything would have changed. She would no longer have been able to deny that she was developing feelings for him. Feelings she couldn't afford to have for someone who would never let himself return them.

But that last whisper of a question kept surfacing in the back of her mind when she least expected it.

What if?

Wasn't that what Mark had said he'd thought right after he'd bitten into his Cupid? What if? What if she took a chance? What if it didn't blow up in her face? What if it worked?

She wanted the love, the partnership. She'd never really let herself admit that she was missing out, that she wanted more. Until now. Until Dean.

A knock at the back door jolted Lucy out of her thoughts—and chocolate smeared as she overfilled one of the chocolate shells.

She set aside the piping bag and started toward the back door, her heart beating a bit too quickly. It was too early for her grandmother to be back, and she had her own key. Lena always used the buzzer, tapping a syncopated rhythm that rang through the kitchen.

Only Dean knocked.

Her nerves jumped as she peered through the peep hole, her heart squeezing tight when she saw him, as if she'd conjured him by thinking about him.

She opened the door and smoothed her hands down her apron. "Hey."

Dean stood in the exact spot he'd nearly kissed her the other night, the golden light above his head gilding his dark hair. His dark-chocolate eyes locked onto her, and she had the brief, crazy thought that he'd come here to finish the job. To kiss her senseless. And her grandmother wasn't even here to interrupt them.

But then he grimaced, and the spell was broken.

"Sorry. I should have called ahead," he said. He lifted the bag in his hands. "Georgie said you don't always remember to eat when you're working, so I grabbed pretzels. I don't even know if you like soft pretzels."

"No, of course. I love them. Come on in."

She pushed the door open wider, making room for him to cross the threshold before turning toward the kitchen. The hallway was small and seemed all the smaller for his presence.

"You don't have to eat them," Dean said as he followed. "I'm not trying to force pretzels on you. I just didn't want to show up empty-handed." They emerged into the wider kitchen, and he spotted the trays arrayed on the counter. "More Cupids?"

"They're in demand. Thanks to you."

"I can't take credit," Dean insisted. "If it hadn't been me, some other reporter would have followed up on Lena's post, and you would have been just as popular."

Lucy knew that might be true in theory, but somehow she couldn't escape the feeling that everything had started to change the moment Dean walked into her shop. Lena's post had started the dominos falling, but the changes Lucy felt weren't from how busy they were but from him.

"Though if you are feeling grateful, I will shamelessly take advantage of that," Dean teased, "because I have a favor to ask. The pretzels were actually kind of a bribe."

"Oh?" He seemed nervous, and Lucy was fascinated by this uncertain side of calm, collected Dean. Melody Gardot still sang softly in the background as

Lucy picked up the piping bag and resumed her work. "I'm intrigued. What's this favor?"

Silence greeted her, and when she looked up from her task, he was watching her, and he looked a million miles away. Her heart skipped.

"Dean?"

Chapter Thirty Five

*D*EAN DIDN'T KNOW WHY HE'D come here in person.
He could've called. He could easily have asked Lucy about the live feed over the phone. She would have said yes. He didn't need the pretzels that were still clutched in the bag in his hand. He didn't need to be here in person, listening to some woman with a sultry voice singing in French while Lucy made chocolates and smiled at him.

What was he doing here?

"Dean?"

He jerked. Right. He had a job to do. "Nora wants me to do a live feed from How Sweet It Is on Valentine's Day," he blurted. "It'd be for the evening broadcast. Nothing fancy. Just me standing with some customers, maybe a shot of you handing out the Cupids..."

"Of course." Lucy's smile brightened. "That's a great idea. But you didn't have to come all the way up here to ask me—in fact, I've been meaning to ask you. Have you been driving hours out of your way to pick me up and drop me off after each interview?"

"Not hours."

She groaned. "So it is out of your way. Why didn't you say something? I could have driven myself."

"I like driving with you," he admitted, a little too truthfully. "Who else am I going to argue with about the nature of love and magic after every interview?"

She looked over at him, and something about her smile went still, almost puzzled. Then it brightened again. "Well, thank you for letting me tag along. It's like I'm watching you learn what love is in real time. Very educational."

"Very funny." He reached out and snagged one of the rejected, imperfect chocolates, rolling it between his fingers. "There is one other thing," he said. "About the live broadcast."

"What's that?"

Just say it. Get it out fast. "Nora wants me to eat one of the Cupids on-air."

The confession came out in such a rush that the words blurred together. Lucy blinked—and he could see the moment she processed the jumbled sentence. "*Oh.*"

"I told her I'd do it."

"Oh." Softly this time.

His throat tightened. "It's great exposure for the shop. That time slot is usually some of our highest viewership. Good exposure for me, too," he admitted. "To build a fan base."

"The anchor position?"

"It's looking good. This could put me over the top."

"Wow. Congratulations." Her hands had gone still when he told her he'd be eating a Cupid on the air—and suddenly they began moving again, filling the molds. "But are you sure you want to risk it?"

"Risk what?"

"Falling in love. I thought you didn't want..."

"I don't," he said too quickly. "And I won't. The legend is cute, but I don't believe in that stuff," he said, as much to himself as her. "Eating a Cupid isn't going to make me feel anything."

"Right," she murmured. She dropped her gaze to the chocolates she was making.

He could have left. He had her agreement. His job was done.

But still he found himself lingering. And asking, "You know what I still don't understand?"

Finishing with one tray, she put them aside to set and moved on to the next. "What?"

"If you really believe all you have to do is eat a chocolate to get true love, why are you single? I know you said you were focused on your work, but I feel like there's got to be more to the story than that."

Lucy looked up and grimaced. "My grandmother called me a cynical hopeless romantic the other day."

"You? Cynical?"

"Skeptical, then."

He shook his head. "I don't buy that one, either."

She bit her lip, her eyes going distant as she searched for the right word, finally settling on, "*Cautious.*"

"Now that I believe." Lucy was not a risk-taker.

She smiled gently. "I know you don't think love can last, that happily-ever-after is just a myth, but I've seen it. I know it's real. My great-grandparents had it. My grandparents, too. But I also watched my mom lose my dad. I saw how lost she was, how long she drifted before she found her way again. I'm not a complete stranger to heartbreak. I know things can end badly."

Dean frowned, something fiercely protective rising up in his chest. "Did someone break your heart?"

"It was ages ago. Before I dropped out of culinary school to take over the shop. And I know it was for the best, though I never would have admitted that at the time. But the heart remembers the hurt, you know?" She flushed, refocusing on her task. "What about you? Ever had your heart broken?"

"My exes would probably tell you I don't have a heart to break." When she gave him a questioning look, he explained, "I'm not good at all the things you're *supposed* to do. Not just the fancy dinners for Valentine's Day or getting the right Christmas present, but the other milestones like when you're supposed to say I love you, or buy a ring. I never thought it was romantic for there to be expectations and time-lines—like you can't possibly care about someone if your feelings don't develop on a schedule preordained by the greeting card companies."

"I don't think greeting card companies actually care when you say 'I love you.'"

"No, but there's this whole industry of love—"

"Which I'm part of," she reminded him.

"Which you're part of," he acknowledged. "And it's all pushing you toward saying something that's only going to turn around and bite you."

"What if it doesn't?" she asked. "What if when it's right, it doesn't feel forced or obligatory and nothing blows up in your face? What if you end up like Pablo and Mark? Or Claire and Malcolm? Or my grandparents or my great-grandparents? What if you're really happy?"

He met her eyes and didn't have an answer.

He didn't know when she'd stopped working on the Cupids, but her hands were still and her gaze didn't waver from his. The scent of chocolate was rich and sweet around them. Music he'd barely noticed was suddenly all he could hear above the beat of his own heart.

"What is that?" he asked, the words barely audible, but Lucy somehow knew what he meant.

"Duo Gadjo. *'Ne me quitte pas,'*" she murmured, identifying the song.

"Do you speak French?"

"Not really."

"Do you always listen to people singing in languages you don't understand?" he asked, but the words didn't matter so much as the unspoken thing that seemed to be winding around both of them, an invisible net drawing tighter, pulling them closer.

"Not always," she whispered. Again, the words felt like nonsense, just sounds, breathless with that other meaning. The one he wasn't ready to think about too closely.

Her hand was resting on the edge of the stainless-steel countertop. It was so easy to brush his fingertips across hers. Her hand lifted just enough for him to slip his hand under hers so his palm was beneath her fingertips and hers was just above where his fingers curled gently to brush against the soft skin.

Her downward-curled and his upward-curled fingers linked, catching and holding, and he gently pulled her forward until she stepped away from the counter—and right in front of him.

He set her hand on his shoulder, his own going to rest ever so softly on her back. He gently clasped her other hand and they swayed as the lyrics neither of them fully understood wove around them like magic.

He didn't know what he was doing.

If he'd been thinking at all, he never would have pulled her into his arms. But now that she was here, he could only look down at her upturned face and sway. All the reasons he shouldn't be doing this seemed so much less important when he was with her, until he started to wonder why he'd ever thought they mattered at all. There was something so inevitable in this moment—as if this was a destination he'd been heading toward without ever knowing it for weeks, maybe even months. Maybe even his entire life.

Her eyes were so open. So trusting. And for the stretch of a song, he forgot. He forgot about his promotion and the live feed and the chocolates and everything else. For the length of that melody, there was only Lucy. Her face. Her smile. Her whole heart shining in her eyes. His throat tightened.

But then the song changed.

Unlike the lingering longing of the last one, this one had a bouncy, jazzy, up-tempo beat. And the mood was broken in an instant.

Dean and Lucy shifted away from each other, and he couldn't meet her eyes as he dropped her hand.

Hadn't he just been thinking this afternoon that he didn't want to hurt her? And what did he think was going to happen if he got involved with her? Lucy believed in true love and happily ever after, and he couldn't give her that. He didn't have that in him.

He knew he should keep his distance, and yet here he was dancing with her while they were alone in her kitchen surrounded by chocolate and French jazz?

What was he *thinking*?

"I should go."

"Right. Of course," Lucy agreed quickly, but there was something in her voice, a catch he didn't want to think about.

"I'll see you tomorrow? For Lena and Tyler's interview?"

"Absolutely!" Too bright. Too shiny and happy. False. "Thanks for the pretzels."

Dean nodded, retreating toward the door. "Anytime."

Lucy groaned and thunked her head against the door as soon as it closed behind Dean.

What had she been *thinking*?

Hadn't she just decided that nothing could ever happen between them and they were better off as friends? So what was she doing dancing with him in her kitchen like they were the only two people in the world?

She blamed the music.

Lucy swiped a finger at the Pandora station, silencing it.

She'd been caught off guard. That was all. She

hadn't expected him to come over here. Hadn't expected him to look at her like that.

Hadn't expected him to tell her he was going to eat one of the Cupids on Valentine's Day.

Her first thought had been that she could be standing right next to him when he did.

She'd had a sudden flash of herself eating one of the Cupid chocolates, too. Of him looking at her, and her looking at him, and the two of them just knowing...

But then she'd remembered that this was Dean. He didn't want to fall in love. If he did, would he resent her for it? Would he be mad if the Cupid worked?

Maybe she could offer him a fake Cupid. One that wasn't magic. Though she wasn't sure how she would make it.

Did it even matter?

He genuinely didn't believe. Even after the last few weeks, he didn't have a shred of faith, to the point where he didn't even feel the need to protect his heart by avoiding the Cupids. He was so certain love couldn't touch him.

And maybe it couldn't.

She really needed to stop falling for the guy who would never fall for her back.

Chapter Thirty Six

THE SHOP WAS STILL OPEN when Dean arrived to meet Lucy the next night. The lights inside glowed warmly onto Main Street as he peered through the frosted windows. He'd parked down the street next to Lena's family's flower shop so he wouldn't have to lug the camera equipment so far to set up for the interview. He always parked by the shop, so this was really his first time just strolling down Main Street at twilight, absorbing the charm of the small town as he made his way toward How Sweet It Is.

Through the window, he saw Lucy's grandmother, who had agreed to man the shop while Lucy joined him for the last Happy Couple interview.

And there was Lucy.

She wore another of her seemingly endless supply of jeans and soft sweaters, this one a pale gray beneath the bright red How Sweet It Is apron. Her hair was pulled up into a ponytail, and she was laughing with the customer across from her as she filled a box with the chocolates the woman pointed to.

His chest tightened. He couldn't be alone with her.

He'd proven that last night. Showing up in person to ask her about the live feed when he could have called, or texted, or done anything more intelligent than dancing with her while surrounded by chocolate. It had been foolish. And on the drive home, he'd made a pact with himself. No more being alone with Lucy.

He'd walk her down to the flower shop for Lena and Tyler's interview—on a public street, with plenty of other pedestrians—and he would conduct the interview with her. But no more blurring the lines between professional interest and *other* interest. He knew better.

Her smile lit up the shop. She looked so happy. For a moment all the stress, all the worry, all the responsibility she carried with her everywhere seemed to have lifted away. Then Dean stepped through the door, and she turned that smile on him.

His own lips curved in automatic response, even as he reminded himself that he was not getting sucked in. He didn't want anyone getting hurt.

"Hello, young man."

Dean eyed Lucy's grandmother warily, remembering his hot pepper overdose. "Hello, Mrs. Sweet," he said, as Lucy finished with a customer.

"Edda, please," her grandmother insisted. "I hear you two are heading over to the flower shop to interview the happy couple."

"As soon as Lucy's ready. Thank you for watching the store so she can supervise me. I know she wants to make sure I don't tarnish the good name of the Cupids."

Edda eyed him. "You really think that's why she's going with you?"

"Ready?" Lucy asked as she appeared at her

grandmother's side, tugging off her apron as her customer left the store.

Dean didn't have the chance to ask Edda what she'd meant—and he wasn't sure he would have wanted to, either way. Better to leave well enough alone. "Ready when you are," he confirmed.

"I won't be late, Nana." Lucy hugged her grandmother quickly and grabbed her coat and purse. She wasn't quite looking at him, and he was almost grateful that he didn't have to meet her eyes. Safer that way. "Let's do this."

He held the door for her, and the night air closed around them, along with a blanket of awkwardness.

"Last interview," she commented as they started down the street, and he got the distinct impression she was just trying to fill the uncomfortable silence.

"Yep."

They'd never been uncomfortable with one another before. Not like this. Things with Lucy had always been light and easy. Too easy, like the way she'd slid into his arms last night. Much better that they kept their distance.

"Are you excited to be done with this fluff piece so you can move back to the exciting world of legislative budgets?"

"Hopefully, I'll be moving to the morning anchor desk instead," he reminded her. "And this isn't the end. We still have the live feed."

"Right. You know, I've been thinking about that," she said abruptly, looking up at him. "I could always make you a fake one."

"A fake one?"

"A fake Cupid." Her face flushed as she explained,

the words rushing together. "One without the magic ingredient. Since you don't want to fall in love."

Something shifted in his chest, something almost—sad? Was he sad that she didn't want him to eat a real chocolate? That was ridiculous. He knew better.

"That's a nice offer. But it doesn't matter if I eat a real Cupid or a fake one. It's not going to work for me."

"Right," she murmured. If she seemed disappointed, that wasn't his concern.

This wasn't love. This was business. Even if it had started to feel like something more.

He liked Lucy. Of course he liked her. She was an extremely likeable person. Hardworking and determined—which he would admire in anyone who displayed those qualities. Cheerful and optimistic—which, admittedly, he hadn't really valued before, but somehow respected in her. Their senses of humor lined up, and he enjoyed her company more than he recalled enjoying anyone in...well, maybe ever.

But that was just friendship. Anything else was out of the question.

And he had an interview to conduct.

Lena was in rare form.

Which was usually a ton of fun, but Lucy was having a hard time appreciating it. She was too intensely, awkwardly *aware* of Dean. Why did last night have to make everything so weird? And why had she offered to make him a fake Cupid? She'd just made everything that much *more* awkward.

Thank goodness it was nearly impossible to be awkward around Lena's overpowering energy.

Her best friend had clearly spent some time considering her wardrobe and arranging the perfect setting for the interview. As soon as Lucy and Dean stepped into The Corner Florist, she saw that a little settee, which was normally *not* in the middle of the flower shop, had been artfully placed so Lena and Tyler could cuddle together in front of a giant bouquet of roses and a carefully placed vase with the name of the shop in elegant cursive on the front.

As product placement went, it was classy. Understated. And Lucy was certain Lena had planned it down to the exact angle of every rosebud. Lena took visuals very seriously.

As soon as Lucy and Dean entered the shop, Lena rushed over to Lucy, looking like pure, old-school Hollywood glamour in her white dress with the splash of embroidered red roses. She'd done her thick, dark hair in victory rolls, and her bright red lipstick completed the 40s screen siren look. She was definitely ready for her close-up.

Lucy knew Lena hadn't originally posted about the Cupids to benefit herself and her shop, but once the publicity took off, there was no way Lena wasn't going to make sure she got her share. She'd always been a better businesswoman than Lucy. Aggressive where Lucy was cautious. Confident when Lucy questioned herself.

And Lena's confidence was shining tonight.

"I'm so excited," she whispered to Lucy, latching

onto her arm as Tyler went to help Dean set up his equipment. "The whole world is about to hear my love story."

"I think the whole world already has, judging by the number of views on your post," Lucy reminded her.

"But this is different," Lena insisted. She watched Dean begin to unpack the gear, explaining the function of each item to Tyler as he set them up. "How long will the setup take?"

"Five minutes? Dean's pretty quick with this stuff."

"Come with me." Lena hauled her toward the back by their linked arms. She pulled Lucy into the refrigerated storeroom where they were surrounded by the heady scent of flowers and blossoms on all sides. As soon as she shut the door, Lena spun to face her. "Okay, now tell me everything."

"Everything?" Lucy shook her head, bewildered.

Lena bounced on her kitten heels. "What's going on with the reporter?"

"Dean?" her voice squeaked.

One of Lena's perfectly penciled brows rose. "Is there another reporter I should know about?"

"No, it's just, there's nothing going on. We're just working together on the story. For the store."

Lena rolled her eyes. "Lucy Sweet. I have known you since we were four years old. Are you honestly trying to tell me you don't have the mother of all crushes on that very cute, very charming, *very interested in you*—if the way he looks at you is any indication—man out there?"

"It isn't like that."

Lena groaned. "Please don't tell me you're playing it safe."

Lucy narrowed her eyes. "Have you been talking to my grandmother?"

"No. But I can probably guess exactly what she's been saying. You've gotta live a little—and this guy lights you up. I've seen the footage! Have you even been watching yourself in these Cupid segments? The *chemistry*." She fanned herself but charged on before Lucy could refute her claims. "You say you're too busy for a relationship, but that's an excuse. You're scared to take the leap. Always so careful."

"What's so terrible about careful?"

"Everything! Adventures aren't careful! It's like you believe in the magic because it's safer than not believing in it, not because you *really* believe it. You like safe. You always have."

Lucy pressed her lips together primly. "I just don't believe in taking unnecessary risks. And Dean has said over and over again that he doesn't want romance. He doesn't want love."

"You've said that, too," Lena reminded her.

"But he means it."

"Are you sure about that?" Lena asked, thankfully not pointing out that Lucy had just admitted she hadn't meant it. "I know you love the shop, but that isn't all there is. You used to work crazy hours because you never wanted to be anywhere else—but now it's like you're so scared of letting the family legacy down that you've cut all the chance out of your life. But with no risk, there's no reward. Don't you want that? To be in love?"

It was exactly the advice she'd given Dean about

Georgie—you had to take the chance to have a chance—but it was harder to follow that advice herself. Especially when caring for someone who might never want her back felt like the biggest risk of all.

"Come on." Lucy reached for the storeroom door. "They're probably set up by now."

Lena caught her hand. "Just try to be a little daring? For me?"

Lucy sighed, saying neither yes nor no, and Lena released her so she could lead the way back to the front of the flower shop.

Tonight wasn't about her love story, anyway.

Chapter Thirty Seven

"VALENTINE'S DAY AFTER A BREAKUP is never fun. Valentine's Day after a breakup when you work in a flower shop arranging bouquets all day for other people who are madly in love is pretty much torture," Lena declared with a well-rehearsed delicate cringe. Tyler's arm curved around her lower back where they sat cuddled together on that artfully arranged settee.

Her words were practiced, maybe even a little over-rehearsed—but Lucy probably only noticed the preparation because she knew Lena so well. Lena would be talking a mile a minute if she were speaking off the cuff, the words tripping over one another in a laughing rush.

"I've always loved love," Lena went on. "I wanted to be in love so badly—and I knew all about the Cupids—but I'd been hurt. I wasn't sure I was ready to open my heart again, but I knew I had to do something to change my luck. So I marched down to How Sweet It Is on Valentine's Day and bought my Cupid. As soon as I ate it..." She paused dramatically.

"You saw Tyler?" Dean prompted.

Lena's smile was wry. "Not quite."

Her fiancé just smiled.

"It turns out," Lena explained, leaning forward as she got into the story, "Tyler had already been into How Sweet It Is earlier in the day. He'd eaten his chocolate, and another woman had asked him out after buying a Cupid of her own. He wasn't even in the shop when I bought mine. So I was standing there, waiting for lightning to strike, and nothing. Nada. No sparks. No fireworks. But then the door opened, and this guy walked in, and I thought, maybe this is him. Maybe this is my guy. I didn't want to miss my shot, so I asked him to dinner."

Dean was frowning. Lucy could already tell she was going to get an argument about how the Cupids worked later.

"It was *awful*," her best friend gushed. "I mean he wasn't horrible—he was a perfectly decent guy—but we had *nothing* in common, and I think I scared him a little. I know I can be a lot, and I'm pretty sure by the time we got to dessert, he couldn't *wait* to get away from me. So we said good night and thanked one another for giving it a shot for the sake of Valentine's Day and went our separate ways."

Dean slanted Lucy a quick look—one she could easily interpret as *how is this possibly magic?*

And she sent him a look which she hoped read as *be patient, you cynic!*

"There I was, on my way home, feeling like a total love failure, like not even the Cupids could redeem me, and I realized I was missing an earring." She grabbed her ear in a dramatic reenactment. "So I go back to the restaurant, and as soon as I walk in the door, I see this guy. Down on one knee beside the table where I'd been sitting, holding something in his hand which I swear looked exactly like an engagement ring in the light."

"It was her earring," Tyler interjected with a fond smile.

"But that moment!" Lena feigned a swoon. "It was like I was flashing forward into the future. It was magic."

"Good thing he was single," Dean muttered.

"But that's what made it so magical," Lena insisted. "He'd gone to the shop and eaten a Cupid, too! His date had been just as much of a bust as mine was. She'd already gone home. And then as he's walking out of the restaurant, he just happens to spot my earring and pick it up at the exact moment I walk back inside? That's fate."

"But what about the other people? The ones you went on dates with? Didn't they eat the Cupids, too? Where are their fairy-tale endings?"

"Dean," Lucy warned in a low voice to remind him that he was supposed to be doing a fluffy puff piece and not debunking the myth.

But Lena was unfazed. "Obviously, they went on to meet their own true loves. We didn't keep in touch with them, but I bet if you tracked them down, that's just what you'd learn."

"Actually, I do touch base with Jessica from time to time," Tyler commented.

Lena's head snapped toward him. "You do?"

"She is seeing someone. Apparently they met a few days later," Tyler confirmed for the camera—oblivious to the way his fiancée's eyes were boring into the side of his head.

Lena's knuckles went white where her hands were clasped in her lap. "I thought your date was a flop. Why did you even have her number?"

"We exchanged numbers that morning when we set up our date," Tyler explained.

"But why would you call her after you met me?"

"Well, she texted me, and I didn't want to be rude."

Lena was off-script now. Dean gently cleared his throat, and she snapped back to attention. "I'm sorry," she smiled brightly. "Where were we?"

Lena rallied quickly, but her poise was slightly off for the rest of the interview. Though again, Lucy wasn't sure anyone would notice but her. Lena's smile was still sunny and her answers still charming, but there was something uncertain in her eyes.

Dean coaxed Lena to talk about her post which had gone viral and about her upcoming wedding plans—and then he let Lena get in a good plug for the florist's Valentine's services before wrapping up the interview.

Dean moved to shake hands with Lena and Tyler, telling them what a wonderful job they'd done, and Lucy hung back, waiting to one side.

She caught Lena's hand as her friend started to move away. "Hey," she said gently. "Are you okay?"

"Of course!" Lena enthused with false cheer. "That was great. I will admit it wasn't exactly as I pictured it when I thought about telling my love story, but it was really fun. Thank you so much."

"Okay. You're welcome," Lucy said softly, not wanting to push when Lena didn't seem to want to talk. Though worry still whispered in the back of her thoughts, especially when Lena didn't even make any more pointed innuendos about Lucy and Dean.

Their goodbye was surprisingly subdued, and before she knew it, she was back at Dean's car, just the two of them as she watched him load the last of his equipment.

"Well?" she prompted, going for a lightness she didn't quite feel. "No arguments about the nature of love or how the Cupids work tonight?"

Dean looked up from the equipment that didn't seem to be sliding into the trunk as easily as usual. Skepticism was written all over his face. "They didn't even see one another in the shop."

"Sometimes love takes a circuitous route."

"And sometimes people are looking so hard for magic—and love—they'll see it anywhere." He shoved the last case into the trunk, glowering when it didn't fit into place and he had to adjust the others. "Doesn't it bother you? The way she calls it her love story and not theirs?"

Lucy shrugged. "That's just Lena."

"Is it?" He shook his head. "I know people like that. They're the same ones who care more about the wedding than the marriage. People who think the perfect love story is more important than the person you have it with."

A throat cleared behind them, and they both whirled.

Tyler stood on the sidewalk a few feet away, holding one of Dean's lavalier microphones in his hand. "You forgot this inside." He handed Dean the microphone, his expression a neutral blank that gave them no clue how much he'd overheard. But he must have overheard *something*.

Lucy's heart leapt into her throat, but it was Dean who spoke.

"Tyler, look, I didn't mean..."

Tyler smiled slightly and shook his head. "We're good. Don't worry about it."

But Dean was obviously still worrying about it as he watched Tyler retreat back to the flower shop and Lena. He groaned, leaning against his rear bumper. "You think he heard?"

"Honestly? Yeah. At least part of it. But he didn't seem offended."

"That I implied his bride cares more about living out the Cupid story than she does about him?"

"Depending on how much he heard, he might not have realized you were talking about Lena," Lucy pointed out—though she knew that was wishful thinking.

"I wasn't entirely." Dean turned back to rearranging the gear in the trunk of his car. "She just reminded me of someone."

Lucy thought he must mean one of his parents, or one of their former spouses, but then he added two little words that shifted everything.

"My ex."

He'd talked about generic exes last night. How they'd teased him he didn't have a heart. But this time, the word sounded different. There was a weight to it. This was *the ex*. And suddenly what he'd said about caring more about the wedding than the marriage hit hard. Had he been married?

"You were...?" She didn't know how to finish the question, but he finished it for her.

"Engaged? No. Not really. I was just seeing someone—someone I trusted, someone I thought knew me and understood how I felt about marriage— and it turned out the entire time, she'd been planning our wedding behind my back. Or rather *her* wedding. *Her* dream. She even put down a deposit on a venue. She was that sure she could change my mind. Change *me*." He slammed the trunk shut, all the gear safely stowed inside. "And that"—he jerked his chin toward the florist—"sounded just like her. She would have loved the Cupids. The big fairy-tale love story. Do you know, after we broke up she kept the wedding venue, the date, everything? All she did was change the groom."

Lucy's heart ached for him. "Dean, I'm so sorry that happened, but Lena is crazy about Tyler. Just because she likes the story doesn't mean that's all that matters to her."

"Don't worry," Dean assured her. "I'm not going to sabotage the piece. It's gonna be cute and light and nothing is going to hurt How Sweet It Is."

"That wasn't why I said—"

"Lucy, it's fine. Leave it alone."

But it didn't feel fine. It felt like he was pushing her away. Like distance was opening up in between them.

And maybe it should.

Had she been just like his ex? Expecting him to change his mind?

She'd been fooling herself to think what was be-tween them was anything more than business. Because no matter how many times she'd protested to Nana and Lena and anyone else who asked, she *had* started to think that. She felt a lot more than professionalism for Dean.

She'd been falling for him, and there hadn't been any magic involved. Just her own heart, leading her in the wrong direction. Because Dean had been very, *very* clear, that he didn't want this. He didn't believe in it.

And convincing him otherwise? Changing his mind? If taking him to meet happy couple after happy couple hadn't done it, would anything?

No. It was too big a risk to throw her heart at him, knowing he didn't want it.

So maybe it was for the best that this was almost over. She just had to get through the live feed on Valentine's Day. Then the focus would shift off the Cupids for another year. She'd stop thinking about love all the time. And she'd stop feeling *this*.

Whatever this was.

Chapter Thirty Eight

"*D*ID SOMETHING HAPPEN WITH YOU and Lucy?"

Dean jerked, staring at his cell phone like it might bite him. "What? Why would you ask me that?"

On the other end of the line, Georgie sighed. "It's nothing. She's just been really quiet the last couple days. I wondered if you guys had a fight."

Guilt rose up the back of his throat. It hadn't been a fight, exactly, but the way they'd left things still felt wrong. And the silence since was getting to him. His life felt out of balance without Lucy shooting him text messages that always devolved into debates that left him grinning.

He was still scheduled to see her for the live feed on Valentine's tomorrow evening. Lena and Tyler's Happy Couple segment would air tonight, and he had no reason to talk to her. So why did he want to so badly? Why did he want to apologize for something that required no apology? He hadn't done anything wrong. He'd just been his usual jaded self.

Keeping his distance was the smart thing to do.

Obviously, they'd already gotten too involved. He kept having these *feelings* for Lucy—and then remembering that those feelings couldn't be trusted. They didn't last. And people let you down.

No. Much better that he stayed away. No apologies. Even if everything felt off.

"No fight," he told Georgie. "We're just done with the Cupid success stories. No reason for us to see one another before the live feed tomorrow."

Georgie hmmed. "I heard about that big live broadcast. From my boss. Because my brother never tells me anything, but apparently he tells *her* everything."

He winced. "Okay, okay, I should have said something."

"But you didn't want to jinx it? Because of the anchor thing?"

"I'm not superstitious," he insisted. Though he absolutely was.

The truth was, he'd been too busy thinking about eating one of the Cupids on-air to worry about jinxing his chances at making anchor, but he still should have told Georgie. He was just so used to being steady and strong for her that it felt foreign to admit he was nervous or uncertain.

"Speaking of superstitions," he continued before she could argue, "are you still planning to eat one of the Cupids?"

"It's just a chocolate, Dean," Georgie said softly. "Whether it leads to anything more or not—whether I fall in love or get my heart broken or don't—you can't blame the chocolate. The Cupid is just a way of being brave. Of putting myself out there. Of admitting to myself and the world that I want to love someone. And I want them to love me back. That isn't some horrible thing."

He couldn't wrap his head around it. "How can you still think that after everything that's gone wrong for us because of love?"

"Because a lot of things have gone right, too. I still see the good—all the things you don't want to let yourself see because you're trying to avoid the hurt. You were always braced for impact so you never let yourself enjoy the fun parts. But if you spend your life avoiding the possibility that something will go wrong, you're going to miss the chance for things to go right. Is that really what you want?"

In the past, he would have just said yes. Now... "I don't know."

It was easier to just see his life as work and Georgie. Easier to focus his energy on those priorities and not take the risk of wanting more. What could possibly make that risk worth it?

"Are you going to be mad at me if I eat one of the Cupids on Valentine's?" she asked.

"What?" Shock jarred him out of his spiraling thoughts. "Of course not. Georgie. I'll always support you. Even when it scares me to watch you do the romantic equivalent of skydiving. I'm always behind you."

"I know you are." She paused, hesitating. "Are you sure you don't want to try a little romantic skydiving yourself? It could be fun."

He groaned through his laughter. "I'm pretty sure my parachute is faulty."

"I could say something about making sure the person you're going with has a parachute strong enough for both of you, but I think we've stretched this metaphor far enough."

He chuckled. "Good call."

Through the phone, he heard the sound of papers shuffling, then a muttered, "Shoot."

"What's wrong?"

"Oh, I just can't find my notebook. I think I must have left it at How Sweet It Is this morning. I set it beneath the register so I could make notes as things come to me while I'm working, but now I can't find it and I don't have time to get it right now."

"Do you want me to pick it up for you?" he offered.

"Are you sure you wouldn't mind? It's out of your way..."

"No, it's no problem. I'm almost done here. And I can go over the plans for the live feed with Lucy while I'm there."

"Oh, that would be so great," Georgie gushed gratefully. "Lucy said she'd be working late tonight, trying to stockpile Cupids, so she should be able to let you in."

He would get to see Lucy. Though there was no way he was admitting to his sister that was the primary reason he'd jumped at the chance to do her this favor. He needed to make sure things were good between them, so there wouldn't be any awkwardness for the live feed.

That was it. Just business.

And he kept telling himself that as he quickly shut down his computer and packed up his things, impatient to get to Watson Corners.

Chapter Thirty Nine

*L*UCY HAD SO MANY CUPIDS boxed up and ready for delivery tomorrow that she was starting to run out of places to store them. The little white boxes with their gold embossed labels were stacked in towers on every available surface. The sight should have lifted her spirits. She should have been giddy thinking about all those couples falling madly in love—and about the sudden surge in the shop's bank balance.

Things had never been better for How Sweet It Is—not even in her great-grandparents' day. But still an uneasiness whispered in the back of her thoughts, and she wasn't nearly as happy as she should be.

She'd thought she was over her nerves about publicizing the Cupids, but she must not have been as comfortable with that as she'd thought. She refused to think this unsettled feeling might have anything to do with Dean. He might be coming to the store on Valentine's to eat one of the Cupids on camera, but he was still the same cynic he'd been when he first walked into the shop and called her a fraud. She needed to remember that.

But when a knock came at the back door, her stupid heart still leaped.

She forced herself not to race toward the sound, moving slowly and deliberately. She looked through the peephole, and when she saw Dean standing on the back step her heart gave a traitorous little throb.

He'd always been handsome. That wasn't anything new. So why was she noticing it more than ever now?

She opened the door, her expression schooled to blandness. "Dean. Hi."

"Hey." He shifted uncomfortably, awkwardness humming in the air between them. "Did Georgie mention I was coming by? She left a notebook, apparently?"

"She didn't say anything, but I think I know which notebook you mean. She leaves it under the register sometimes. Come on in."

He trailed her down the short hall to the kitchen, drawing up short when he saw the leaning towers of Cupids. "Wow. Looks like you're ready for Valentine's Day."

"I hope so." She waved a hand at the stacks. "These are all earmarked for delivery. I haven't even started on the batches that will be sold in the shop. And now that I see them all stacked up, I'm realizing we probably need half a dozen more delivery drivers for the day. Normally, Nana or I will just do a quick delivery run, or Lena's dad will help out when he isn't doing runs for the flower shop—but we don't normally have this many." Not that Dean wanted to hear her yammer about any of that. "Come on. The notebook should be out front."

She pushed through the swinging door, crouching down to better see the shelf beneath the register. There were stacks of boxes ready to be filled with chocolates—and a brown leather-bound notebook.

"You could hire some extra help for the day," Dean suggested.

"In all the free time I have to be posting ads and vetting candidates." Lucy smiled tiredly and held up the notebook. "Is this the one?"

"I think so. Thanks." Dean took it from her hands, flipping it open to reveal Georgie's writing filling the pages with formulas and equations. "Maybe one of your happy couples knows someone who can help out. I'd offer myself, but I have a certain live feed to do on Valentine's."

"You've already done more than enough. And I shouldn't be complaining to you." She led the way back to the kitchens. "I'm so grateful for the business. None of this would be happening if it weren't for your stories. Even if you were only covering them under duress."

He grimaced. "I'm sorry about the other night. I was..."

"You were fine." Her face heated at the realization that they were going to talk about this. "Perfectly professional. And I'm sorry about your ex. I didn't realize..."

"Of course you didn't, because I never told you. And I shouldn't have snapped at you."

"You didn't," she assured him. "And there was no reason you should have told me."

"Except we're friends."

She swallowed, her face warming even more for some inexplicable reason. "So you're not mad?"

"At you? No. Never. It was just listening to Lena talk about *her* proposal and *her* engagement stirred up a bunch of things I'd convinced myself didn't bother me anymore."

Lucy bit her lip. "You must have really loved her a lot."

"I thought I did. But we would have been all wrong for one another. I've never once wanted to win her back, and as far as I know, she's happily married to someone else right now. She was definitely caught up in the idea of getting married and being in love, not so much in loving *me*—which is what made me so resistant to the Cupids. People can convince themselves of anything. Convince themselves they're madly in love when really they just want to feel it so badly, want someone to love them so badly, that they trick themselves into seeing something that's not there. They don't need a magic chocolate making things worse."

"I can still make you a fake Cupid," she offered. "So you don't have to eat a real one on the air."

"No." Dean shook his head. "No, that isn't what I want." He looked at the stacks of Cupids, a little self-deprecating smile quirking his lips. "I might have taken you up on that when I first came here to do this story. Real or not, I didn't want any part of Valentine's magic." He met her eyes. "But now..."

He trailed off, right when she was desperate to know the end of his sentence. Her heart hung on the words.

Had he changed his mind? Had she changed it? Was he still anti-Cupid, or when he came into the shop tomorrow to do the live feed, was it possible he would try one for real? Really open his heart?

Over these last couple weeks, arguing with Dean, defending the chocolates, and talking up the benefits of love, Lucy had started to think that Lena and her grandmother and everyone else who told her she was playing it too safe with her heart might be right. Her decision to avoid the Cupids had stopped feeling responsible and practical and started feeling cowardly. For the first time, she'd been tempted to leap.

She'd been trying so hard, for so long, not to lose control. Not to take a chance. But had she been protecting herself from something wonderful?

Just like refusing to promote the legend of the Cupids had been an attempt to protect the shop from a curse—one she was starting to think might not even exist. By fearing it, had she kept the shop from the success it could have had all along—and the opportunity to spread that much more love?

She'd taken the leap with the shop. She'd let Dean do the stories, and the results had been amazing. Was it finally time to take the leap with her heart? If she and Dean ate the Cupids together...

"Don't Wait Too Long" began to play on her phone, as if her Pandora station knew they needed a push.

Dean hadn't looked away from her eyes—and she couldn't have torn her gaze away if she'd tried. There was something in that look. Something that made her feel like they were dancing again, just as they had the other night when it felt like she had never belonged anywhere like she did in his arms. When it had felt like she didn't even need the Cupids to tell her that *this* was where she was supposed to be.

He'd pulled away then. He always pulled away.

But he wasn't pulling away now.

"Dean?" she whispered, not even sure what she was asking.

He blinked slowly, lifting one hand as if to brush something off her cheek—but she was certain there was no chocolate there. "Lucy..."

The buzzer screamed through the kitchen, jerking them both out of the moment.

Dean stumbled back a step, and Lucy's gaze jerked toward the back door—where the buzzer was sounding again. That syncopated pattern, quick and agitated.

"Lena," she said aloud, frowning.

Lena wouldn't stop buzzing until the door opened. She never did.

Lucy snatched up her phone, turning off the music. Her heartrate—already fast, thanks to Dean—accelerated even more as soon as she saw the sheer number of texts she'd missed since muting the notifications.

"Something's wrong," she told Dean, opening the Happy Couple group text even as she moved toward the door.

What she saw was enough to stop her in her tracks, even with Lena leaning impatiently on the buzzer. The shrill noise perfectly matched the alarms suddenly going off in her brain.

"Oh, God," she whispered, frozen as she stared at the screen.

"Lucy?" Dean came up beside her, but she was barely aware of him.

It was a story. But not just any story. It was the takedown story that Dean had never done.

Kate Kelly, the thwarted web series reporter with

the Selfie Stick of Doom, had evidently not gone away quietly. She'd done some digging and found sources to speak out against the Cupids. The title, in massive black letters, read THE CUPID CON.

The buzzer came again, penetrating Lucy's fog of dread. She moved robotically toward the door. As soon as the latch released, Lena burst inside. Her face was flushed, eyes wild behind her cat's-eye glasses, as she flung herself against Lucy.

"The wedding is off," she moaned. "It's over. I never should have eaten one of the Cupids!"

Lucy sucked in a shocked breath, her heart lurching into her throat as a single thought drowned out all others. "Oh, God. It's the curse."

Chapter Forty

$\mathcal{D}$EAN DIDN'T BELIEVE IN CURSES any more than he believed in magic, but from the shocked expression on Lucy's face as her arms closed around her friend, she absolutely believed the Curse of the Cupids had fallen down on her head.

She quickly rallied though, her expression settling into calm determination as she focused her attention on Lena.

"It's going to be okay," she comforted the florist. "I'm sure it'll all work out. We'll have cocoa bombs and talk it through." She gently guided Lena down the hall, and Dean flattened himself against the wall so they could pass.

"Should I stay?" he asked, the words so soft they were barely audible over Lena's hiccupping tears.

Lucy quickly shook her head. "No, there's nothing you can do."

"Oh God, you're working, and I'm interrupting you!" Lena moaned as soon as she saw the piles of chocolates in the kitchen. "I'm the worst friend ever."

"You're a great friend who's always there for me,"

Lucy countered. "And I'm here for you. Go pick out your favorite cocoa bomb. I'll be right behind you with the milk."

Lena shuffled toward the front of the shop like she was sleepwalking, and Lucy moved quickly toward the refrigerator, not even looking at Dean. The leather of Georgie's notebook creaked beneath his hands, he was holding it so tightly.

"This is exactly what I was afraid of," she muttered as she yanked out milk and began filling two mugs. "The magic is backfiring. Gigi warned me, and I didn't listen."

"Lucy, you know this isn't magic." Dean waved a hand toward the front of the shop where Lena waited. "Anyone who looked at the two of them could see this coming—"

"No, Dean. Most people who looked at them saw two people who were madly in love—one of whom was a little dramatic about it. Only you saw some big facade." She put away the milk with a little more force than necessary. "And now it's all falling apart, and it's my fault. I knew this could happen. I should never have let you do the story. I shouldn't even be selling them."

"Don't be ridiculous. Of course you should sell them. You have to—"

"So you can get your live feed? Your promotion?"

His brow bunched in a frown. "That isn't why I'm here."

"Then why are you here, Dean?" she asked suddenly, setting down the mugs of milk with a thud. Her eyes caught his, pleading for something he wasn't sure he knew how to give. "Why do you keep coming back here? What do you want from me? Because I can't defend the chocolates to you right now. My friend needs me. And you need to leave."

His throat closed as he clutched the notebook, the leather creaking again. He didn't know what he would have said, even if he could have gotten the words out. Had he done this? Infected her with his doubts?

He'd never seen her like this. He'd seen her worried but never truly disheartened. Never defeated. He hated this helplessness, unable to do anything for her. She was like his personal lighthouse, a beacon guiding him toward optimism, but now the light was out, and he was lost. She didn't need his doubt right now. And he didn't know how to offer anything else.

So he left.

Lena was sitting on the floor when Lucy emerged from the kitchen with two mugs of steamed milk. Lucy had pushed Dean and his unwelcome cynicism from her thoughts as soon as he'd walked out of the kitchen, focused on heating the milk and taking care of her friend. She wouldn't allow herself to worry about anything else right now. Not even the curse. Even if that worry tried to whisper in the back of her thoughts, a quiet voice of dread.

Lena had stopped sobbing and was now staring listlessly at the cocoa bombs in the display case in front of her. With Lena, the quiet might actually be worse. It was certainly more out of character.

"Hey," Lucy said gently, kneeling down beside her.

"I couldn't pick," Lena said.

Lena. Who always knew exactly what she wanted exactly when she wanted it. Lucy's worry dialed up to eleven.

Lucy picked for her, selecting two of the cocoa bombs and dropping each one into a mug of hot milk. Lucy sat on the floor beside her, and they watched as the little chocolate orbs bounced and floated on top of the milk until the chocolate shell melted and the ball released a burst of marshmallows and cocoa powder. The rest of the chocolate shell vanished, leaving a perfect mug of cocoa.

"It's sort of hypnotizing," Lena murmured, as Lucy grabbed a spoon from a drawer and gave each mug a quick stir.

"Do you want to tell me what happened?" she asked gently, passing over one mug of decadent cocoa.

"It all started with that stupid interview," Lena whispered. "I never should have done it. I never should have encouraged you to talk to Dean or written that stupid post. Or even eaten a Cupid at all."

Lucy's throat tightened on the reminder of the curse, but she pushed her own worries into the background, focusing on Lena. "What happened, Lene?"

"We watched the segment tonight. Tyler and I," she said, staring down into her cocoa like it held the answers to all the mysteries of the universe. "I kept telling myself it would be romantic, that it would feel like a celebration of our love—but then it wasn't what I thought it would be." She looked up then, grimacing. "I had this idea of what our love story was—that we were both so completely, instantly in love with one another that the rest of the world just ceased to exist. I was so sure. But he went out with her again."

"What?" Tyler had eyes only for Lena, Lucy was sure of that. There had to be an explanation.

"He admitted it tonight." Lena sniffled and took a long sip of cocoa. "It wasn't just that she texted him and he texted back. They met for coffee. He kept saying it was just coffee and they were just friends, but he never told me about any of it before. He let me think both of our original Cupid dates had been busts and that we were this perfect, fated couple, when all along he hadn't been sure about me. Not the way I was about him."

"Not many people are as sure about things as you are," Lucy offered gently. Lena was a force of nature, but that was what Lucy loved about her. It was what Tyler loved about her, too.

"I know. I know I can be a lot. I've been told by countless exes how exhausting I am. But Tyler always seemed to like that about me."

"He does, honey. He loves you."

"And I love him! So why did he do this?"

"What did he do?" Lucy asked gently. "Besides go out for coffee a year ago?" Because there had to be more to the story. Lena might be dramatic, but even she didn't get this worked up about coffee. Something else was happening here.

"He just went along!" Lena exclaimed, and Lucy rescued the cocoa she was gesturing with before it could spill all over Lena's dress. "He went along with her—because she wanted to go to coffee. And he went along with me because I wanted to fall madly in love and get married and have babies." She took the cocoa back but still didn't drink, staring into it hopelessly. "Did I want this too much? Did I force him into it? What if all he's been doing this entire time is going along? What if he doesn't really love me and he's just too nice to tell me he doesn't?"

"Sweetie..." Lucy's chest ached sympathetically as she realized what was really going on. Lena was so bold, sometimes it seemed like she didn't have any insecurities—until an innocuous coffee date made her question everything.

"No," Lena insisted, spiraling now. "You know how he is. He's *nice*. He's way too nice for me. I'm pushy and dramatic, and it's hard to say no to me. He always says he can't say no to me."

"Because he loves you," Lucy reassured her, taking the cocoa from her again and gently setting it aside so she could hold Lena's hands.

"Is that it? Or do I make him feel like he can't talk to me about things? Like this coffee date? Why would he lie about that for a year?"

"Maybe it just never came up. It didn't seem like it meant anything to him."

"But it changes everything! He wasn't sure! I had this whole idea of who we are, and I was fooling myself the entire time."

Lucy gave Lena a *don't you think you're exaggerating* look. "Coffee doesn't mean he had doubts. And even if he did, does it really matter how he felt a year ago? Isn't what really matters how he feels now?"

Lena pulled a face. "You sound like him. Do you know he actually asked me if the story of us was more important than our relationship? Like this is all about me losing our perfect Cupid love story!"

Lucy cringed internally. She had a pretty good idea who had planted that particular seed of doubt in Tyler's mind. Dean hadn't even been surprised when Lena had shown up declaring the wedding off. He'd probably barely restrained himself from saying *I told you so.*

She shoved away the thought of him. Lena was her focus now. "Did he really call off the wedding?" Lucy asked gently. She'd noticed the conspicuous absence of the ring on Lena's hand.

Lean's face flushed, and she studied their linked hands. "No. I might have thrown the ring at him at one point. I just..." She looked up, meeting Lucy's eyes, her own pleading for understanding. "He let me think he was sure about me from the first second. He let me think that for a year, and this is how I find out? I never doubted our instant connection or that he liked me just the way I was, because I thought—this is the Cupids, he's my person, of course he doesn't think I'm too much. But what if the Cupids really did mean for him to end up with *her?*"

Lucy shrugged. "What if the Cupids weren't magic at all?"

"*Lucy.*" Lena gasped, gaping at her. At least she got out of her doom spiral.

Lucy held up one palm. "I'm not saying the legend is wrong, but what if you had never eaten a Cupid? You love Tyler, right?"

"Of course I do."

"So why does it matter who some chocolate wants him to be with? Wouldn't making a life with him *still* make you the happiest you've ever been?" She took Lena's hand again, wrapping her fingers around

Lena's. Both of their hot cocoas sat abandoned and lukewarm on the floor. "Can I give back some advice you gave me?" she asked gently. "Don't let fear stop you. You're scared he doesn't love you the way you love him. You're looking for a reason to pull the rip cord because it's easier than sticking it out and falling even further—but he's going to be there to catch you, Lena. He's crazy about you. You have to talk to him."

Her best friend looked at her with enormous, lost eyes. "But what if he doesn't want me back?" she whispered, broken.

Chapter Forty One

DEAN KICKED HIMSELF THE ENTIRE drive to Georgie's apartment building.

He hadn't handled that well. He didn't know what he should have said, but telling Lucy she was being ridiculous had been a guaranteed loser of an idea. Even if she was overreacting.

He'd taken the time, sitting in the parking area behind the shop, to watch the video of the "exposé" of her shop he'd tracked down with a quick search of the internet.

It was vague. Full of innuendo but no actual accusations. From the way Lucy had paled when she read the headline, he'd been worried, but it sounded like a whole lot of nothing from a reporter who was trying to get some clicks. It would blow over.

But he couldn't get the look on Lucy's face out of his head.

She'd looked extinguished. Determined to help her friend, but beneath that determination, he'd glimpsed something he'd never thought he would see in Lucy Sweet.

Defeat.

And it was killing him.

It was just so *wrong* on her face.

He tried calling her when he arrived at Georgie's place. Then tried texting her when she didn't answer. No response.

Georgie buzzed him in. He shuffled her notebook between his hands as he rode up in the elevator, but as soon as she opened the door, he realized the notebook was the furthest thing from her mind.

"Did you see this?" she demanded, waving her phone past his face so fast he barely had time to register the headline on the screen. "Who is this woman? Seriously, who posts a takedown piece calling love a fraud on the day before Valentine's?"

"Before about three weeks ago, I would have," Dean admitted. He held up the notebook. "Here you go."

Georgie's eyes locked eagerly on the leather. "Did you see Lucy? How is she? Has she seen it? She isn't responding to anyone's texts on the Cupid loop."

"You have a Cupid loop?"

"Answer the question, Dean!"

"Which one?" When she snatched the notebook out of his hand and tossed it on the couch, glaring, he relented. "She's seen it. She got some kind of notification on her phone about it right before I left."

"And you *left*? Why would you leave?"

"Lena showed up. She was upset." *And Lucy practically kicked me out because I said something stupid.* Though he didn't admit that part. "She thinks there's a curse."

Georgie gasped. "Gigi's curse! I didn't even think

of that." She spun away from him, pacing to the other side of her cozy studio apartment, then back toward him, demanding, "How is she? Is she okay?"

"She's upset," he admitted. Though the word felt inadequate.

Defeated. She was defeated. And he hated seeing her like that. It felt so wrong for her not to believe in the magic, even for a second.

"No wonder she isn't answering our texts." Georgie looked toward the window, as if she could see through the night and across the miles to How Sweet It Is. "Do you think I should go down there?"

"Your midterms—"

"Dean, not everything is about school!" she snapped at him. "Haven't you figured that out yet? Lucy is my friend. How Sweet It Is is important to me. And that has nothing to do with magic."

Except it did.

Only the magic wasn't the Cupids. It was Lucy.

She was the one who lit up the shop. She was the one who made people want to keep coming back. She was the one who lit *him* up.

"Dean?"

He jerked, meeting his sister's questioning gaze. "You're right."

"I am?"

"How Sweet It Is is important." *Lucy* was important. "But so is the magic. She has to believe." He had to find some way to make her believe. Because she'd made *him* believe. And he needed to give that back to her.

Georgie's worry suddenly melted into a huge smile.

"You just figured it out, didn't you? That you're crazy about her?"

"Of course I am," he grumbled. "How was I supposed to resist?"

Georgie squealed, leaping up to tackle-hug him. He pretended to be indifferent to her enthusiasm as he set her back on her feet, but he couldn't quite smother his smile as she beamed at him.

"Your powers of denial were strong, but I knew you'd figure it out eventually."

He snorted. "Thank you for your faith in me. Now how do we restore Lucy's?"

Chapter Forty Two

*L*UCY CLOSED THE DOOR BEHIND Lena and headed back toward the kitchen. She was emotionally exhausted after the ups and downs of the night, and for a moment, she just stared at the towers of Cupids, a heavy sense of dread beginning to throb in her gut.

She needed to make another batch. She should have been making Cupids for the past two hours. But instead of reaching for her ingredients, she picked up her phone. She'd set it on the counter when she was steaming milk for Lena's cocoa bomb and hadn't heard any of the notification pings since.

There were a dozen texts, but the *CUPID CON* story was still queued up on her screen, and it was all she saw.

She clicked play and listened, barely processing what she heard. Her brain was too fatigued to sort out all the details, but the gist of it was all too clear. False promises of love. Fraudulent guarantees. It was all her fears. Everything she'd been afraid people would say about How Sweet It Is if they advertised the Cupids.

How could it be anything but the curse?

Lena's relationship had fallen apart. Who knew how many other relationships were on the rocks? Maybe that's what all the messages were about on the Happy Couple Loop. And even if everyone else was fine, even if the curse was all in her head, this story wasn't. How could she responsibly sell the Cupids tomorrow? She'd been so careful with her words, but what if she'd slipped? What if she'd accidentally guaranteed love—or if her grandmother had when she wasn't around? What if there were disappointed customers and lawsuits—

Okay, probably not lawsuits. That was her fears running away with her. But the shop's *reputation* could be killed, even if no one actually sued. Could she risk it?

And if it was the curse, if the magic was backfiring, how could she responsibly allow anyone else to try a Cupid? Wouldn't she just be setting them up for heartache? She loved the Wall of Love. She loved being part of those love stories. But it all felt so fragile now, and she couldn't escape the voice in the back of her head whispering that it was all her fault. She'd gotten greedy. She'd wanted success too badly. And now...

The only safe choice seemed to be to stop making the Cupids at all. Stop selling them. Tell everyone that she hadn't been able to get the secret ingredient. And refund any of the money necessary to disappointed preorder customers.

It would be a financial hit. A nasty one. But she was relatively sure the shop could survive it, at least for a little while.

That had to be the safer choice.

She stared at the Cupid boxes piled high and sank on to her stool in defeat. At least Dean wasn't here to gloat. He'd been right all along. She was doing more harm than good by promoting the legend of the chocolates, encouraging people to rush headlong into love. Look at what had happened to Lena and Tyler. Lena had *counted* on the Cupids, she'd *relied* on them, and now the reality had set in. The reality that there was no magic.

At least not anymore.

"Lucy?"

Lucy flinched at her grandmother's call. Nana Edda was a true believer. She credited the Cupids with meeting the love of her life, her husband of nearly five decades. She'd always wanted Lucy to spread the gospel of the Cupids.

She was going to be so disappointed.

Her grandmother entered the kitchen, her face already a mask of concern—so at least she'd heard about the story already. At least Lucy didn't have to tell her.

"You saw the story?" Nana Edda asked gently, coming to take the phone from Lucy's hands and set it aside. "It's not so bad," she soothed. "Lots of conjecture and innuendo."

"She calls it a con." And wasn't it? Wasn't it all an illusion?

"I know what you need. A nice Mexican cocoa to perk you up."

"I just had a cocoa bomb with Lena—whose engagement might be breaking up, in case you were wondering if the curse had already taken any casualties. And I'm still not sure I trust you with the cayenne after what you did to Dean," she said, trying for a joke that fell woefully flat.

Nana Edda ignored her attempt at humor. "You don't really believe this is the curse."

"Gigi warned us."

"Gigi didn't know the rules of the magic any more than anyone else does. No capricious fairy gave her the recipe and vowed to curse her if she ever tried to profit from it. She was superstitious. Just like you. And too cautious. Just like you. And she found that recipe like magic—just like you. Nothing on that recipe card ever said it was forbidden to share the love with as many people as possible, unless that part was written in invisible ink."

"But she knew—"

"She was scared of not being accepted here," Nana Edda interrupted. "Scared of being thought of as the crazy foreign lady who believed in magic chocolates. Scared of how people would look at her and what they'd think of her. What are you scared of, Lucy?"

Lucy averted her eyes, unable to meet her grandmother's steady gaze. "It's not about fear."

"Isn't it?"

"It's so easy for you!" Lucy threw up her hands. "You've always believed in them! And it's never been on your shoulders if the shop fails!"

"So what if the shop fails?" Nana Edda asked.

Lucy gasped. "How can you say that? It's our history. Our heritage. This is our *family*."

"These walls? This building?" She shook her head. "It's just a place. And yes, this place has memories. Yes, it's special. But it isn't our family.

It isn't our traditions. Those aren't going anywhere even if we can't afford prime Watson Corners real estate anymore. Our legends, our history, our *recipes...* those are all in you." She put one hand over Lucy's, squeezing gently, her other hand gently cupping Lucy's cheek. "*You* are the family legacy. Whether How Sweet It Is stays open or not. Do you know how proud Gigi was that you became a chocolatier? That you surpassed even her abilities?"

Lucy shook her head, the words beyond credibility. "I didn't..."

"It made her and your grandfather so happy that you loved this place the same way they did. That you loved making chocolates and making people happy. But none of us ever wanted the shop to be a millstone around your neck. None of us ever wanted you to put your own happiness on hold so you could try to keep this place open. That isn't what will keep our family legacy alive. *You* do that. By letting yourself be happy."

Lucy's eyes welled, but she still shook her head. "I just don't want to lose it."

"And you won't. Look at everything that's happened in the last few weeks. Doesn't that feel like fate? Like Gigi and your grandpa watching over us?"

"But the curse..."

"It's just an idea, sweetheart. It only has the power we give it. Just like the magic."

Lucy frowned at her grandmother. "I thought you believed the magic was real."

"I do," she insisted. "But it doesn't matter whether the magic is real or not. What matters is if we believe in it. If we open our hearts."

Lucy studied her grandmother's familiar face, but instead of comfort, she just felt *exhausted*. Her heart didn't feel open. It felt like she was worn out, tired of fighting this fight on her own.

"I can't," Lucy murmured.

Her grandmother had always believed. She would always believe.

But Lucy couldn't. Not anymore.

Chapter Forty Three

*D*EAN RANG THE DOORBELL FOR Tyler's condo, glancing guiltily at the time on his phone. It wasn't technically too late to drop by unannounced, but there probably wasn't a good time to drop in on a guy whose engagement you might be partially responsible for breaking up.

The more Dean had talked to Georgie, the more convinced he'd become that he'd played a role in messing things up—not just undermining Lucy's confidence with his constant doubts but also undermining her best friend's relationship with his comments to Tyler the other night. He needed to know if he'd somehow caused this, and he needed to apologize.

Dean glanced at his phone again, hoping this was the right place. Edda had texted him, worried about Lucy, and Dean had coaxed Tyler's address out of her. He wanted to get the full story about what had happened with Tyler and Lena before he went to Lucy to lure her back to the Land of the Believers—a task he couldn't have been worse suited for, but one at which he was determined to succeed.

The door opened suddenly, and Dean quickly shoved his phone in his pocket, snapping to attention. "Tyler. Hey. Sorry to just show up. I know this probably isn't a good time, but I was hoping I could get just five minutes. I think I owe you an apology."

Tyler blinked, one hand still gripping the edge of the door, his expression mostly neutral with a dash of surprise. "Sure. Yeah. Come on in," he said mildly, pushing the door open farther.

Calm and smiling slightly, he didn't look at all like a man who had just lost the love of his life.

"Can I get you something to drink?" Tyler asked as he guided Dean toward the small den off the entryway.

Dean almost glared at him. Didn't he realize that Lena was absolutely nuts about him? Yes, she was also a little over the top, but Dean had seen firsthand how wrecked she was by the idea of losing him. That wasn't a woman who only cared about how her relationship looked.

"Nothing, thanks," Dean said curtly. He didn't sit, moving instead to stand behind one of the high-backed chairs, gripping the backrest. "I don't know what's going on with you and Lena, and I know it isn't any of my business, but I need to apologize. When I said she loved her love story more than she loved you—it wasn't even you two I was thinking about. I shouldn't have projected my past onto you. And I'm sorry if that messed things up for you guys."

Tyler's widening smile made the words break off in his throat.

"Why are you smiling?" Dean demanded.

Tyler just grinned, shaking his head. "Dean. You

have nothing to apologize for. It's not like I never noticed Lena's obsession with our perfect love story before. I know her. I know exactly what I'm getting into. Lena loves our story. But she loves me more."

"But...aren't you...? Didn't you break up? She showed up at Lucy's saying the wedding was off."

Tyler arched one eyebrow. "Have you met my fiancée? Honestly, I never expected to make it all the way to the altar without at least one 'we're calling off the wedding' fight. It came a little sooner than I expected, but maybe she's gotten it out of her system now."

"Out of her system? She broke off your engagement."

"And then she came home, and we talked about it, and now she's upstairs reading a book."

"A *book*?"

Tyler just smiled. "You don't have to apologize, Dean. You aren't to blame for anything except giving Lena a chance to talk about our story on camera—and giving me a chance to clear the air about something that would have undoubtedly come up at some point down the line. We're better than ever."

"But Lena..."

"...needed to realize we were more than the Cupids. You can't rely on meant-to-be. The chocolates were our starting point, but any successful love story is built on a lot more than that. Though the faith helps—believing in us, that we can get through this, whether a chocolate helps us do that or not."

Dean shook his head. "But Lucy thinks there's a curse. She thinks the magic is tainted and that it broke you two up."

For the first time since Dean's arrival, Tyler frowned. "I thought Lena texted her." He moved to the door of the den, calling up the stairs. "Babe? Did you clear things up with Lucy?"

Lena came clattering down the steps a moment later. "Of course. I told her she needed to work on her maid-of-honor speech because the wedding is definitely back on. Why?"

"Did she respond?" Dean pulled out his phone, frowning at the recent message from Lucy's grandmother. "Edda said Lucy was fixated on the curse and was spiraling. I came over here to get you guys back together so I could convince her love still conquers all."

"So there were ulterior motives behind your apology," Tyler said with a wry grin, utterly unoffended.

Dean flushed. "I did mean it." He looked up at Lena. "And I should tell you, too, that I'm sorry I implied you loved your love story more than you love Tyler."

Her eyes widened, and she laughed. "Well, that's silly. A love story is only as good as the love of the people in it." Then her gaze landed on him, far too knowing. "Wouldn't you agree?"

He wasn't about to answer anything incriminating. Not yet. "I need to talk to Lucy."

Lena beamed. "Excellent idea. Just let us know if you need backup."

Chapter Forty Four

*T*HE CHOCOLATE MOLDS ALL SAT empty.

She needed to be making Cupids. Lucy sat in her kitchen and stared at the empty molds, feeling numb. She'd planned to make them all night. It was the only way she was going to have enough for the rush they expected tomorrow as well as the delivery orders.

Her hands needed to be busy. But they sat limp in her lap, and she could only stare at the empty molds.

She didn't know what to do.

Even if she could bring herself to make them now, would they even be magic with her own faith in them crushed?

Her phone continued to buzz occasionally with texts from the Happy Couple Loop, but Lucy hadn't been able to bring herself to look at any of them. Not since she'd seen the story. She couldn't handle any more evidence of things falling apart.

Her grandmother had finally retreated upstairs, undoubtedly trying to get some sleep before the busy Valentine's frenzy, but Lucy had stayed behind, sitting in the kitchen that had once been her favorite place in the world and trying to remember what it had felt like when she believed.

This place had been magic to her once. And not just because of the Cupids. It was home—in a way the string of apartments she'd shared with her mom after her dad's death never had been.

And she didn't know how to protect it.

Was she risking too much if she sold the chocolates? Was she dooming How Sweet It Is if she didn't? She needed to make up her mind. She needed to start working toward tomorrow, whether that meant making Cupids or cancelling orders, but she just sat and stared at her kitchen, paralyzed by indecision.

A creak on the floorboards in the front of the shop caught her attention, and she frowned, turning her head toward the sound.

She knew the sights and sounds and smells of How Sweet It Is better than she knew her own apartment. Nana Edda had a key to the shop, and she'd given Georgie one last week, but Nana was upstairs, Georgie was at home, and neither of them was in the habit of dropping by in the middle of the night. Lucy strained her ears, listening for a long moment but hearing only the familiar hum of the refrigerator.

She'd almost convinced herself she was imagining things when the creak came again.

Lucy snatched up a palette knife, her breath going short. The knife was for tempering chocolate and didn't have any pointy parts, but it was better than nothing. She crept toward the swinging door.

Had she locked the front door? She must have. But it was so automatic, she never actually remembered doing it. And it was hours ago—before everything had happened with Lena and the curse. Could she have forgotten?

That would be the perfect culmination of the curse if some thief snuck in. The money from the registers was all securely locked in the time-lock safe, but a robber might not know that.

She should call the cops. She shouldn't have left her cell phone face down on the counter on the opposite end of the kitchen. Lucy glanced back at the phone. She should go back for it. If this were a robber—

Her gaze was still on the phone when the swinging door opened.

It thumped against her and ricocheted back. She screamed, bringing the palette knife up defensively.

On the other side of the door, a deep voice called out. "Lucy?"

A *familiar* deep voice. "Dean!"

He caught the swinging door when it swung in his direction, peeking through the opening. "Sorry. I didn't mean to startle you."

"So you broke into my shop in the middle of the night? I thought you were a chocolate bandit, here to steal all the truffles."

Dean's eyebrows arched high with amusement as he stepped into the kitchen. "Black market Cupids?"

"Don't laugh. You scared me."

"I'm sorry. I didn't hear music, so I thought you must have gone upstairs already. Georgie lent me her key, and there was a van blocking the alley, so it seemed easier to come in the front. I tried texting."

She grimaced. "I haven't been looking at my phone."

"A lot of people are worried about you." Something

almost like sympathy moved across his face, and she couldn't look at it.

Her gaze landed instead on the piles of Cupids—which now seemed to be taunting her. "You were right," she heard herself saying, the words seeming to come from a foggy distance. "All that skepticism turned out to be smart. Score one for Team Down with Love."

"I don't want to be right—not about that," he said, before adding softly, "and I don't want to be on that team anymore."

She looked over at him then, frowning. "Isn't this what you were warning me about? That love back-fires, that it hurts?"

"That was self-preservation talking. I thought you saw right through me on day one."

"I did. But now..."

Dean met her eyes, his gaze serious. "I was wrong."

"What?" She shook her head, looking away from those persuasive eyes. Nothing was computing to-night. The one thing she could always rely on was that Dean was the skeptic. But now that she was try-ing to agree with him, he was changing his tune?

"I was wrong. About love. About the Cupids. All of it." He seemed to be searching for words. Dean, who always had a quick retort. "Lucy, you have to believe."

"Why?" she asked wearily. "Because you won't get your live feed if I don't?"

He didn't take the bait. "Because it's who you are. I don't care if we go live or not. We can cancel it right now. I'll find some other way to impress Nora."

"Dean." The hopelessness of the situation tried to

swallow her. "I haven't made a single Cupid chocolate tonight. I can't…"

"Lena and Tyler are back together."

"It isn't just about them."

"I saw that story. It's just smoke and mirrors."

"Isn't that what you said the magic chocolates were when we first met?"

"I'm not the person I was then," he insisted. "You dragged me all over town teaching me what love is and showing me that putting more of it into the world is a good thing—even if there might be heartaches and struggles along the way. That sometimes love does need us to believe in it."

"The Happy Couples were very persuasive."

He shook his head. "None of those stories made me believe. *You* made me believe."

She finally let herself look at him. Really look at him. His dark-chocolate eyes were warm, as intent and persuasive as always, but there was something else there now. A softness behind the intensity. A gentle pleading—like he was willing her to see something. To know something.

To believe.

And not just in the chocolates.

In him. In this thing that had been stretching between them since the second she'd first set eyes on him in her shop. Even when she'd been mentally throwing daggers at him, this had been there, under the surface. The pull. The draw. Maybe it was just stubbornness, neither one of them willing to let the other win—but maybe it was something else. This thing that had been building beneath the surface, that she hadn't been brave enough to look at head on. This connection.

Lucy wasn't brave. The shop had been the only risk she'd ever taken. The only thing that had ever mattered enough.

Until now.

She'd always been scared of taking a chance. Too scared to try the Cupids herself. But the magic hadn't waited for her to be brave enough.

It had sent her Dean.

Dean, who argued with her and supported her and challenged her and made her laugh—and made her better. She loved who she was when she was with him. She loved...

He took a half-step closer, unspoken messages shifting in his eyes, his gaze growing even warmer as one of his hands gently caught hers. She felt that brush of skin shivering down to her core, a bolt of heat. "Lucy..." he whispered. "*You* are the magic. And I—"

A loud thud behind the swinging door made Lucy jump—and whatever Dean had been about to say so quietly, so seriously, vanished into a wry grimace.

"I think the reinforcements are getting impatient," he explained sheepishly.

"Reinforcements?"

Dean's gaze flicked to the swinging door.

As soon as Lucy's world expanded beyond Dean and the feel of his hand on hers, she could make out the shuffle of footsteps and low hiss of whispers trying to shush one another on the other side of the door. Her face began to heat as she realized just how much she'd blocked out the rest of the world.

"You may as well come in," Dean called out, a grin curving his lips. "We can hear you."

Her grandmother poked her head through the door

first. "We weren't eavesdropping," she announced preemptively, as if anyone would believe her.

Then Nana Edda pushed the door open all the way, and Lucy's jaw dropped as she saw the crowd huddled in the doorway behind her.

She'd expected Georgie—Dean had said he'd borrowed her key—and maybe Lena and Tyler, since Dean somehow knew they were back together. And they were there, with nervous, hopeful smiles. But the "reinforcements" didn't stop there.

Pablo and Mark crowded into the shop behind them, along with Claire and Malcolm, several of their kids, and half a dozen of the other Cupid success stories. There were so many people in the little front room, they were probably bordering on fire code violations. And they were all here for How Sweet It Is—for *her*—in the middle of the night.

Lucy's eyes were already welling up when the eager crowd shifted, and another face popped up in the back.

"*Mom?*"

Her mother grinned, her arm linked through her husband's, as she called out, "Edda told me the Cupids had gone viral. I figured you could use an extra couple of delivery drivers on the Big Day, so Gary and I came back early. Then we got a text from a nice young man..."

Lucy's throat squeezed as emotion pushed against her desire not to become a big blubbering mess in front of all the people who cared about her. She looked over at Dean, belatedly realizing she was still gripping his hand. Her grasp on her emotions became even more tenuous when she saw him watching her with a soft smile.

"Did you do this?" she whispered.

"Your grandmother mentioned you were way behind on making Cupids for tomorrow. I figured it was time to rally the troops. They all still believe in the chocolates. And in you. You're our general. We'll follow you anywhere. Just tell us what to do."

Since she'd taken over the shop, she'd always felt like she had to do everything herself. Like she was the only one who could make the Cupids, the only one who could keep How Sweet It Is afloat. Her friends and family weren't chocolatiers. They hadn't spent decades at her great-grandmother's knee or graduated from culinary courses in Belgium and France—but they *believed*. She could show them the rest.

She didn't have to do it alone.

Lucy bit her lip, looking out over all the smiling faces, and her own smile burst through as she dashed the moisture away from her eyes.

"All right, team," she called out, beaming. "Time to make some magic."

Chapter Forty Five

*T*HEY SLEPT IN SHIFTS, CRASHING on the beds and sofas upstairs when they grew tired.

Lucy supervised every detail, vigilantly guarding against seized ganache and air bubbles—but even she managed to get some rest. With all hands on deck to prepare the biggest batch ever, Cupids quickly began piling up, and the laughter never stopped.

Instead of French jazz, Lena had put on a station filled with upbeat love songs, and they all sang along as they worked—some more in tune than others. Lucy's mother, who explained to Dean that she was a disaster with chocolates, volunteered to fetch and carry.

Pablo claimed custodianship of Lucy's computer and set about designing the most efficient delivery routes for the following day, printing out carefully detailed spreadsheets and directing his designated minions on exactly which orders were to be loaded into which cars in which order.

The van which had been blocking the alley when Dean arrived turned out to be the one Lucy's stepfather had rented to help with deliveries, and several other volunteers had brought their own cars. As one set of helpers replenished the stock of Cupids for the busiest day of the year, another carefully loaded the preordered chocolates.

Malcolm and Tyler turned out to be chocolate-tempering savants, while Mark and Georgie demonstrated deft piping skills. Lena put her artistic talents to good use, decorating the tops with drizzles of raspberry chocolate, and Dean found himself in charge of checking the finished chocolates and putting them on trays for display. Lucy came over periodically to peer over his shoulder and make sure the finished product was up to her glossy, perfect standards.

The rich, sweet scent of chocolate filled the shop, even more than usual. Or maybe Dean was just more aware of it. Everything felt brighter. Sweeter.

He hadn't had a chance to tell her how he felt.

Ever since their army of helpers had interrupted them, he hadn't had a single private moment with Lucy. It had been right on the tip of his tongue—the truth he'd realized tonight when he'd thought about why it was so vitally important to him that Lucy believe in love and happily-ever-afters—but he didn't want to tell her in a crowded kitchen with over a dozen people watching.

He kept catching her eye, brushing a hand along her back whenever he got the chance. He was hyperaware of her, and he knew she was just as conscious of him, but everything unspoken between them looked like it was going to stay unspoken for at least a little while longer.

Her arm bumped against his as she came up beside him again, reaching past him to pluck one of the less-than-perfect Cupids off the tray and relocate it to the not-for-sale pile.

He caught her studying the others on his cookie sheet with an eagle eye. "Checking up on me?"

"Checking up on everyone," she corrected with a smile. "These are the Valentine's Cupids. They have to be perfect."

He glanced over at the clock and picked up one of the chocolates. "It's after midnight. You could test one out. See if it works."

A rosy flush suffused her cheeks as she plucked the Cupid off his palm and set it back on the tray. "Save them for the paying customers. Even with all this, I'm worried we won't have enough."

"Then we'll make more," he assured her. "Don't worry."

"We should set aside one for your live feed tomorrow," she suggested. "Just to make sure we don't run out before you get your moment." She grabbed one of the flat boxes, folding it with deft motions and writing his name on the top. "Here. So none of the clerks tomorrow sell it by accident."

Since several of the clerks for tomorrow were Cupid-success volunteers and it was likely to be chaos, it was a good idea. Dean dropped the chocolate into the box, and Lucy sealed it, setting it on a high shelf where it would be out of the way.

"There," she declared, smiling softly up at him. "One Channel Five Cupid Reserve."

He met her gaze, his lips quirking upward. "You know you're finally going to have to tell me," he commented casually, "since I'm seeing how they're made now. What is the secret ingredient? Did you spike the ganache with the juice of a special flower found only in the wilds of the Amazon? Do you order special vanilla pods from orchids that only grow in Tibet?"

"I don't know if I can trust you," Lucy said. Dean averted his eyes so she wouldn't see the flash of hurt in them. But then Lucy leaned even closer, her shoulder brushing against his as her breath whispered against his cheek.

He met her gaze then, and her face was so close that for a moment, he forgot what they were talking about. That ring of darker blue around the soft gray blue of her eyes held all of his attention. How had she come to mean so much to him in just a few short weeks?

"Are you sure you want to know?" she asked low, the words only reaching his ears.

"I do," he murmured back. He wanted to know everything about this woman. He'd always loved mysteries, uncovering secrets, but the idea that she might actually trust him with her most precious one made his heart beat harder in his chest.

She leaned infinitesimally closer, her lashes veiling her eyes, as her voice became just a breath of air— more a feeling than sound. "There isn't one."

He was so caught in her spell the words didn't register at first. "What?" he asked, dazedly.

"They're just regular raspberry chocolate truffles." Her lashes lifted, unveiling those blue-on-blue eyes, and she held his soul in the palm of her hand as she whispered, "The magic is that we believe. That's the secret ingredient."

Three weeks ago, he would have mocked that kind

of faith. Two weeks ago, he would have snorted his skepticism. But now, it just made sense.

It was like something he'd already known clicking into place. Awareness of a truth that had always existed. Of course it was about belief. That was what magic was, what love was. It was more than a feeling. It was a faith in the connection. Trust. Belief. It was letting yourself be fully vulnerable to another human and believing that they would still be there for you.

And he was a believer now.

He'd leapt out of the airplane—parachute or no. And he'd never felt so free.

His gaze dropped to her lips, the rest of the world had long-since receded from view. There was only Lucy—and this feeling. This faith.

"Whoops!"

Lucy's gaze snapped away from his, her head turning instinctively toward the sound of something going wrong in her kitchen.

She looked back to Dean with an apologetic little smile before moving away to investigate the ganache makers. His body swayed after her, as if physically pulled by the invisible tether of that *almost* moment— but he turned his attention back to the next tray of Cupids ready to be examined.

There would be time tomorrow. He would make sure of it.

He glanced over, but Lucy's attention was completely occupied explaining something to Malcolm, her back to Dean.

He snatched the box with his chocolate for tomorrow—or rather, later today—off the high shelf and popped it open, quickly palming one of the Cupids from the tray in front of him and dropping it inside the box alongside his. Just in case Lucy decided she wanted to try a Cupid with him after what he had to tell her.

His heart thudded hard, but when Lucy glanced back over her shoulder at him, he'd already sealed the box and set it back on the high shelf, and he was back to pretending to be concentrating fully on quality inspection.

Chapter Forty Six

*V*ALENTINE'S DAY WAS HANDS DOWN Lucy's *favorite* day of the year, but this was a Valentine's unlike any other.

It was so much better.

She'd been nervous, so incredibly nervous about negative rumors because of Kate Kelly's story. She'd worried it would drive customers away. But before they even opened, there was a line around the block and the buzz of excitement, of possibility, was thick in the air.

Across the street, Lucy spotted a giant handwritten sign on the specials board at La Vie Douce advertising *Consolation Cakes – Come Get Cheered Up If Your Cupid Is A Bust*—but even that couldn't dampen her mood.

The clock showed three minutes to opening. The frosted-glass door was still locked. Lucy stood in the center of the shop, facing her army of helpers. Lena had left for a few hours to get the flower shop ready for their own busy day, but she'd rushed in the back door a couple of minutes ago, not wanting to miss the excitement of opening. Several of the others had departed to see to their own obligations, with hugs and well wishes, but there were still nearly a dozen smiling faces looking back at her.

Lucy looked over at the Wall of Love, her gaze moving over each of the pictures in turn before ending on her great-grandparents. She'd been trying so hard to make them proud, seeing only the bank balance when she thought of keeping How Sweet It Is alive—but this was the real success. All these people, brought together by love, and hope, and chocolate.

Lucy met the eyes of each member of her battalion. "Thank you," she said, the words heavy with the sheer magnitude of her appreciation. "I never could have done this without you. Thank you all for being the best chocolate makers, and delivery organizers, and quality checkers a girl could ask for. And thank you for believing, and for reminding me what the real magic of this place is—the way it brings us together."

She glanced behind her at the door—and the eager customers visible through the frosted glass. "It's about to get crazy in here. But this is the best part." Her gaze snagged on Dean's in the crowd. "Thank you for sharing it with me."

He smiled, those dark-chocolate eyes crinkling at the corners, and Lucy grinned back.

The clock ticked over to the top of the hour. "Here we go." Lucy couldn't stop smiling as she unlocked the door, flipped the sign—and the madness began.

Malcolm stationed himself at the door in his self-appointed role as crowd control. As the first customers rushed inside, Lucy quickly retreated behind the counter. Her grandmother, mother, and Georgie were already taking the first orders. Gary gave a salute and a grin and headed out the back to start the deliveries, leading Pablo and the other Happy Couple volunteer drivers. It was Valentine's Day. And everyone wanted to be part of the love.

Dean had his camera on his shoulder, documenting the first rush.

Lucy grinned at him and turned to help her first customer, but Lena was suddenly there, catching her hand and tugging her into the little corner in front of the kitchen door. "I have to get back to the florist—it looks like we're going to be slammed today—but I wanted to wish you a Happy Valentine's Day..." She shot a meaningful look toward Dean, who was fully focused on his camera, angling to get a better shot. "And *good luck.*"

She hugged Lucy quickly and darted through the swinging door and out the back before Lucy could protest that she wasn't hoping for any magic with Dean. Though it was just as well she didn't get the chance to say it. No one would believe her. She didn't even believe herself anymore.

But it was still hours before he would eat his Cupid, and as soon as she greeted her first customer, she was far too busy to think about her own romantic future. At least not much.

The hours flew by like seconds.

The shop was filled with laughter and energy. She saw a few customers blushing and making eye contact, striking up conversations and wandering out together. Others had met in line and grinned as they made their purchases together, toasting one another with their chocolates. Still others picked up two or more and rushed out, obviously on their way to spread the love elsewhere.

One woman in her nineties bought nearly a dozen, planning to give one to each of her grandchildren. Several people with wedding rings on their fingers bought two and had them boxed up to bring home to their spouses later.

But the one thing every customer had in common was the hopeful smiles.

Dozens of customers were excited to see Dean in the shop, gushing to him about how they'd been avidly following his series on the Cupids and couldn't wait to see him eat one of the chocolates live on television later in the day. The network had been teasing the live feature on all of their newscasts for the last twenty-four hours.

Dean had so many eager interview subjects, he set up his camera in front of the Wall of Love and had a queue of people who wanted to be included in the next Cupid feature.

More reporters came by. Not Kate Kelly, but several Lucy had responded to that morning, letting them know that if it wasn't too late and they were still interested, they were welcome to come by the shop that day. A few replied that it was too late for them but asked if they could put her on their list for lead-up-to-Valentine's feature next year, while others showed up to document the Valentine's enthusiasm.

Lucy gave so many interviews, her throat grew raw and her cheeks ached from smiling so much—though that probably would have happened anyway, just from all the laughing with customers she was doing.

She *loved* the vibe in the shop today. It felt like anything was possible.

Even a truce with La Vie Douce across the street.

Lucy didn't know how it happened. All she knew was that as soon as her grandmother saw the Consolation Cakes sign, she'd marched over to the bakery with a box of Cupids and somehow managed to broker a peace. Five minutes after she left the bakery, the specials board was erased, and a new message appeared: *The Perfect Place to Take Your Cupid Match for a Romantic Get to Know You Date.*

Nothing could stand in the way of Nana Edda on a mission.

Even with all the Cupids they'd made, around lunchtime, Lucy realized they were starting to run low and retreated to the kitchen with a couple helpers to make yet another batch—or four.

She was in the kitchen, eyeing the steadily diminishing supply of raspberries, when Dean entered, lugging his camera equipment.

"Is it okay if I leave this stuff in the office?" he asked.

"Of course. Are you leaving?"

"I talked to Nora, and we're going to incorporate a bunch of the footage from this morning into the segment tonight. I need to get the video over to her and edit it."

A whisper of disappointment flickered through her. "So you won't be...?" Her gaze moved to the box with the chocolate they'd set aside for his broadcast.

"Oh no, we're still going live," he assured her. "That is, if you're still okay with it."

"Yes, of course."

He met her eyes. They weren't alone in the kitchen, but suddenly she was sharply aware of him.

Some unspoken message was alive in his dark-chocolate gaze. "Are you sure?"

There were so many things he could have been asking with those words. If she was sure the curse wouldn't bite them for doing the live feed. If she was sure she trusted him to go live and say whatever he wanted with no filters about the magic and love.

If she was sure she wanted him to eat a Cupid while standing right in front of her...tempting fate...

"I'm sure."

Chapter Forty Seven

"*THIS IS GREAT MATERIAL.*" Dean looked up from the editing bay where he'd been reviewing the new footage from this morning to see Nora standing in the doorway, watching over his shoulder.

"It's still too long," he explained. "There are too many good quotes to choose from."

"How long?"

"Ninety seconds over what we discussed."

Nora nodded. "Leave it. We'll poach from one of the other segments."

Dean arched his eyebrows. Nora was a notorious stickler for timing, always wanting to keep the broadcast moving along. "Really?"

"It's Valentine's Day." She held up a finger. "But I still want that live feed tight. Two minutes. Including chocolate eating."

"You got it."

Nora leaned against the doorjamb. "You aren't going to beg me not to make you eat the scary love chocolates on camera?"

"I'm trying this new thing. Being open to possibilities. Figured it was worth a shot."

"I like this new Dean." Nora cocked her head. "So do the execs. It was unanimous. You're our new morning guy."

Dean's jaw dropped, and his breath whooshed out. "Don't joke about that."

Nora grinned. "We'll make the announcement tomorrow."

Dean stood, wanting to hug his boss but knowing that would be completely inappropriate. "Nora, thank you. Thank you for your faith in me. You won't regret it."

"Yeah," Nora agreed. "I don't think I will." She nodded toward the editing bay behind him. "Better hurry up and get that cut. You have a live feed to get to, anchorman."

The parking around How Sweet It Is was a disaster.

He should have known. He should have planned for this. Luckily, his equipment was already at How Sweet It Is, and the camera operator who would be helping him with the live feed had already arrived and started setting things up, but Dean still had to park all the way on the other side of town and jog through the streets of Watson Corners in his dress shoes that most definitely were not designed for running.

He glanced at his watch as he ran. He was going to make the live feed—it was getting close, but he should have time to spare—but he couldn't wait to get back to How Sweet It Is. He couldn't wait to see Lucy and tell her his news.

It felt like everything was falling together.

Everything except parking.

Dean was winded by the time he reached Main Street. There was still a line out the door at the chocolate shop, but it was shorter than it had been this morning.

Dean nodded a greeting to Malcolm as he slipped through the front door, moving directly to where Marnee, the camerawoman Nora had assigned to the live feed, was setting up. He touched base with her, made sure she had everything she needed, and then allowed himself to look for Lucy.

And his heart thudded hard in his chest.

She was wearing the Valentine's dress. She'd done her hair and makeup, but it was her smile that hit him right in the heart, just like it always did.

She finished helping the customer she'd been serving and met him at the edge of the counter. "I wasn't sure you were going to make it."

"I couldn't find parking. But I would have left my car in the middle of the street if I had to. I wasn't missing this."

Her eyes met his as she gripped his arm. "Don't worry. You're going to get the anchor job. I know it."

"I already did."

Her eyes flared wide. "What?"

"Nora just told me. It's mine. They're announcing it tomorrow."

"Dean!" She leapt up, her arms closing around his neck as his locked around her waist. He hugged her close, laughing as she squealed with delight. "I knew it!" she insisted when he set her back on her feet.

"How have things been here?"

"*Busy.* We've been making more batches, and we're still barely keeping up. Our latest batch is setting now, but they won't be done in time for your live feed. I'm glad we set that one aside for you."

Dean thought of the two chocolates tucked away in that box and grinned. "Me, too."

Lucy looked past him, her eyes widening, and suddenly gripped Dean's biceps. "Dean!" she whispered. "Look. Georgie."

He turned to see his sister standing a few feet away in front of a tall Asian woman with short dark hair. The woman was smiling tentatively, but it was Georgie's expression of nervous excitement that made his heart stop in his chest. She looked so scared, like this mattered so much, and he wanted to protect her from anything that would ever hurt her.

"You came," Georgie whispered.

The woman's smile quirked mischievously. "You've been talking about this place and these chocolates nonstop. How could I miss it?"

"Would you..." Georgie swallowed. "Would you like one of the Cupids? I set a couple aside for us."

"I'd love that. I mean...scientifically speaking, I think this phenomenon really requires serious, in depth, personal analysis. If you'd be interested in that kind of thing."

"I absolutely would," Georgie whispered.

She pulled out the Cupids she'd stashed and made her way around the counter so she and her crush were standing together. They each took a Cupid, meeting one another's eyes and sharing a nervous, hopeful grin.

"On three?" Georgie asked.

The other woman nodded. "One..."

"Two..." Georgie whispered.

On three, they both bit into the chocolates.

On four, Georgie's crush smiled and swayed forward for a kiss.

When they broke apart, Georgie was blushing furiously—and Dean felt a pressure inside his chest like he was either about to have a heart attack or burst into tears.

"Definitely magic," Georgie's match murmured, lacing their fingers together.

"You okay?" Lucy asked softly at Dean's side, her hand still gently holding his arm.

He cleared his throat roughly. "Of course. Though you won't convince me the Cupids made them fall in love. There was obviously something there beforehand. Georgie's had a crush on her for weeks."

Lucy grinned. "Uh-huh."

"She seems like a nice girl," he said gruffly.

"You know, I'm impressed, Dean Chase. People falling in love left and right, and you haven't even broken out into hives yet."

"I've changed."

She met his eyes, her own warming. "I know," she murmured. "Me, too."

He'd been here for most of the day, watching the magic unfold, but it had never felt more like magic than it did in this moment. His gaze dropped to her lips.

And Edda appeared suddenly at her side. "We just got a phone order for three dozen. Do we even have three dozen left?"

Lucy's hand dropped from his arm as she moved to handle the new crisis. "We should," she told Edda. "Just barely. What time do they need them?"

Dean headed over to check on the live-feed setup. It was getting close. He'd meant to tell Lucy how he felt and ask her if she wanted to have a Cupid with him *before* they were on live television, but she was being pulled in so many different directions today that he might have to save the mushy feelings stuff for after hours.

She and her helpers frantically packaged up Cupids and more customers kept a steady line out the door as the clock ticked closer to his live feed.

The Cupids ran out. A groan rose from the lined-up patrons, who were informed that another batch should be ready in thirty minutes.

Which was twenty minutes after his live feed was scheduled to end. Dean was incredibly grateful they'd thought to set aside that special box last night. He made his way back to the kitchen to grab it.

The shelf where he'd left the little white box was empty.

Dean frowned, until he realized Lucy must have already moved the reserved Cupids.

He headed back out front, not wanting to bother her when she was busy, but with no Cupids to actively sell, there was a lull. Georgie was taking orders from the people in line on a tablet, so they'd be ready to box and go as soon as the chocolates set.

Dean found Lucy studying the rest of the display cases—which were also picked over after the busy day.

"Hey." He gently brushed her arm. "Did you bring the Cupid we set aside out here?"

Lucy frowned, uncomprehending. "What do you mean? It isn't still there? It was just there."

She rushed past him to the swinging door, but when they pushed through, nothing had changed. The shelf was still empty.

Lucy stared at it in horror. "Oh no," she whispered as Dean realized the awful truth.

The last Cupids were missing.

Chapter Forty Eight

"WHAT DO YOU MEAN YOU sold it?"

Cassie, one of the volunteer helpers, looked absolutely miserable as she protested, "I didn't know it was a special box!"

"It had Dean's name written right on top."

"I didn't even look at the lid. I was in a hurry. We were trying to fill that big order for the Valentine's party, and we were two short. I was looking for an extra two, and they were right there."

Hope flared in Lucy's eyes. "No, that must not be the right box. There was only one inside—"

"There were two."

With the words, Dean broke Lucy's complete focus on Cassie, and she turned to him with a question in her eyes. "There were?" she asked.

"Two," he confirmed, with a wry little smile, his eyes silently admitting he'd snuck another one in the box. That he'd wanted to have his first Cupid with her.

Her eyes widened, her cheeks flushed, and she

didn't tear her eyes off his until Cassie moaned, saying, "I'm so sorry."

"It's not your fault," Dean assured her. "It's been crazy in here today, and everyone is just doing their best to keep up."

"Okay," Lucy said, gathering herself. "The ones we set aside are gone. The chocolate hasn't set enough for the next batch to be handled without melting all over our hands. And you go live in..." She glanced at the time. "Six minutes."

"What about the flawed ones?" Dean asked. "We could use the rejects. We won't do a close-up. No one at home is going to be able to see air bubbles or cracks."

Lucy was already shaking her head. "We sold them. The first time we ran out this afternoon, we gave customers the choice between an imperfect Cupid at a discount or waiting for the next batch to be ready. Nana said the magic was no different, so enough people took the imperfect ones that we ran out."

They were really all gone. How could they all be gone?

The kitchen door swung open, and Edda rushed in, frowning when she saw Lucy and Dean and half the volunteers congregating in the kitchen. "What are you doing back here? Isn't the live feed about to start?"

"We're out of Cupids," Lucy explained.

"Could you use a different chocolate?" Pablo asked. "Just for the broadcast? If you don't show it off on camera, no one watching will know the difference."

"But I would know." Disappointment welled up.

Dean had long since stopped wanting to expose the myth as fake. Now he just wanted a piece of that magic for himself, but it suddenly felt like the universe was conspiring against him.

"You could always have a real one later," Mark suggested, "as soon as the next batch sets."

Dean frowned, practicality taking over. "We might have to do that. Which ones look the most like the Cupids?"

Lucy sighed, the disappointment in her eyes matching his. "I'll get them."

"Wait," Nana Edda held up a hand. "I have an idea."

She bolted out the back door, but when Dean turned a questioning look on Lucy, she just shrugged. "I have no idea what she's doing." She gestured toward the front of the shop, where his audience awaited. "It's almost time."

Dean headed out front and took his mark, putting in his ear monitor and checking in with the station, while Lucy picked out two non-Cupids from the display case.

He'd wanted this moment, a live feed at a big local event, the kind of thing reserved for the anchors. This, he knew, even more than the announcement tomorrow, was his coronation as the heir-apparent to the morning anchor job. He'd been pointed toward this moment since he first sat down at his high school anchor desk. This should be the realization of all his dreams.

But his dreams had shifted. Or maybe they'd just gotten bigger.

He still wanted to be anchor, but he wanted so much more now. To be part of the community. To be the voice people relied on because he delivered the news not only with competence and control, but also with compassion. To be there for Georgie, so she could chase her dreams and take all the risks she wanted knowing he would always have her back even if she fell flat on her face.

And Lucy.

She made him want to be a better man. He couldn't imagine his future, his dreams, without Lucy there at his side, arguing with him about the nature of love and teaching him to believe in magic.

She appeared at his side, holding a decorative plate with two chocolates that *almost* looked like Cupids. If he hadn't been quality testing them all night, he might not have noticed the difference. But he did notice. And Lucy did too, as evidenced by the regret in her eyes.

The clock clicked toward the live feed.

"Will you still eat one with me?" he asked, his eyes on the fake chocolates. Ironically, she'd offered to make him a fake Cupid and now that it was all they had, all he wanted was the real thing.

"If you want." Lucy smoothed her hands nervously over her skirt.

"You're going to be amazing," he assured her. "Lee Ann will throw it to me, and I'll do a little intro—say I'm here with the owner of How Sweet It Is, ask you how business has been, and then we'll do the chocolate tasting. Nora wants us to keep it tight, so it won't be a long segment. It'll be over before you know it."

Lucy nodded, still looking a little green, and Dean caught her hand, giving it a squeeze. "You've got this."

The front door burst open, admitting a massive bouquet of red roses. And Lena.

"Delivery!" she singsonged. Then she lowered the flowers enough to see over them, and her eyes widened. "Am I too late? Are you live already?"

Dean grinned. At least one thing was going according to his plan. "You're just in time." He tucked his microphone under his arm to take the bouquet from Lena. "Thank you."

Lucy's eyes were wide when he turned to her. "What's this?"

Dean smiled and extended the roses. "Lucy Sweet. Will you be my Valentine?"

The entire shop released a collective, "Aww."

And Lucy's nervous expression softened into something Dean was scared to put a name on. Scared because he wanted it so much—and he didn't want to get ahead of himself.

Chapter Forty Nine

*L*UCY HAD NEVER BEEN ANYONE'S Valentine before, even before they started selling the Cupids. Her previous relationships had never lined up with the holiday—which had always been convenient in the past, since Valentine's was such a busy time at the shop, and she didn't really have time for falling in love anyway. But as her heart turned to gooey melted chocolate at the sight of Dean holding those flowers, she realized just what she'd been missing. *Him.*

"Lucy?" Dean prompted, when she didn't immediately respond, and she smiled through the swirls of emotion making everything warm and golden.

"I'd love to."

His smile was blinding—until his eyes flared with sudden panic, and he shoved the flowers at her, bobbling the microphone. "We're on in five seconds!"

Lucy quickly took the flowers, tucking them against one shoulder, the chocolate plate sitting on the little pedestal Dean had set up for the Cupids. Lucy just hoped the camera wasn't focused too closely on them, even though she wasn't sure anyone but her would spot the difference. Well, her and Dean. He knew the Cupids as well as she did now.

He began to speak, using what she'd come to think of as his reporter voice, introducing her, introducing the shop, talking about the magic of Valentine's Day. She managed to respond coherently to his first question, though she was relieved when he took back the baton—chatting back and forth with someone only he could hear through his earpiece.

Lucy shifted the gorgeous red roses in her arms, her eye catching on a simple white square tucked in amongst them. The card wasn't Lena's handwriting. It was Dean's. He'd taken the time to write out the card himself when he and Lena had apparently conspired for this moment, but that wasn't what made her breath catch.

It was the words.

Written in Dean's now-familiar writing—after their trivia night, she would never forget those long slashing strokes—were four simple words.

You are the magic.

And her heart just stopped. How could it hold up against an assault like that? How could it be expected to beat properly when this man—this cynical, funny, smart, protective, sweet man—thought *she* was magic?

"And now, the moment we've all been waiting for," Dean said, bringing Lucy back to the present—and the man she'd hopelessly fallen for. "The Cupids!"

Dean looked at Lucy, looked at the chocolates on the pedestal, and then back at the camera, something shifting in his expression, softening.

"Three weeks ago, I have to admit, I didn't really believe in the magic," he said to his home audience.

"I'd been burned by love before and chose to focus on the ways it could hurt us. I felt it was my duty to protect the people I cared about from that hurt by shielding them from love. It wasn't until I was assigned to come to this shop—until I met Lucy and all the people here at How Sweet It Is—that I realized love is a lot more than being rash and reckless and impulsive. It's about second chances, believing in one another, supporting one another. I've learned a lot in the last few weeks—and I think that might be magic," he joked self-deprecatingly. "So now I'm ready to try a little more magic. Lucy? Will you try it with me?"

She grinned, reaching for one of the chocolates—she'd almost forgotten they weren't the real thing. "I'd love to."

Dean picked up his chocolate, his eyes never leaving hers.

"Wait!"

Nana Edda burst through the swinging door from the kitchens at a run, holding a Cupid box.

Like magic.

"When I took the Cupids over to La Vie Douce this morning, the owner said I'd brought more Cupids than they had staff. They had exactly two left!" Edda rushed over to them, blocking the camera with her back while she snatched the not-Cupids out of their hands and popped them into her own mouth, replacing them with real, actual Cupids, before darting back out of the way.

Lucy looked up at Dean, feeling the weight of the Cupid in her hand. The rest of the world—the shop, the live feed, all of it—seemed to have faded into the distance. "You ready for this?" she asked him.

"With you?" His dark-chocolate eyes met hers, the edges crinkling with his grin. "Absolutely."

Lucy had never had a Cupid on February 14th before. She'd never wanted to risk her heart. She'd always been so cautious, putting the shop first and shoving everything else to someday. But now someday was here.

And nothing had ever felt so right.

She lifted the Cupid to her mouth as Dean did the same, his eyes never leaving hers. She couldn't stop smiling, and his grin seemed to have a thousand secret messages just for her. With one arm wrapped around the roses, she bit into the Cupid chocolate—at the exact moment Dean bit into his, his dark-chocolate gaze locked on hers.

The chocolate was perfection. The two flavors of ganache, chocolate and raspberry, mingled together, decadent and sweet and smooth. They melted on her tongue as she popped the second half into her mouth and chewed. Dean ate his second half, his eyes crinkling at the edges. The moment seemed to stretch out, somehow incorporating every moment they'd ever spent together. The first second she'd seen him, right there in front of the Wall of Love. Their arguments, their interviews, making chocolate together that first time, and making chocolate together last night. Love and magic and possibility. So much possibility, as if the future stretched out in front of them, if only they were brave enough to take it. And now, finally, Lucy was feeling *very* brave.

Dean's throat worked as he swallowed. Lucy did the same. And then simultaneous grins burst out on both their faces.

They moved together at the exact same moment.

She tipped her face up, he lowered his head, his hand coming to brush her cheek, and his lips settled gently, perfectly, *finally* on hers.

The kiss tasted of chocolate. And hope.

A cheer went up, and Lucy jumped, startled by the reminder that they were not, in fact, the only two people in the world.

That they were, in fact, in public. And on *live television.*

Her face was flaming as they broke apart. Lucy ducked her chin, too happy for the embarrassment to take hold completely, though it was definitely part of this intoxicating mix of emotions.

Dean tucked her against his side as he turned to face the camera again and wrapped up the live feed, beaming the entire time. It felt like an eternity, but it could only have been a few seconds later when Dean announced, "We're clear!" And the entire shop gave another loud cheer.

Lucy looked around, laughing with a mix of relief and sheer joy. They were no longer on television, thank goodness, but they were still surrounded by the smiles and happiness of everyone she loved. Her mother was there, with her arm around Gary. Lena and Tyler, Pablo and Mark. So many success stories. So much love. Her grandmother stood closest, her hands clasped in front of her chest, her eyes damp, and the biggest smile on her face. She always did cry at happy endings.

But this didn't feel like the end. It felt like the beginning. Like anything was possible.

Dean set down the microphone, and Lucy looked up at him. "Well. You ate a Cupid. How does it feel?"

With both hands free now, he put his arms around her, pulling her close. He grinned, lowering his face toward her. "Like magic."

And he kissed her. And if this one was anything to go by, his kisses were going to just keep getting better.

Epilogue

*O*NE YEAR LATER...

"Are you sure you made enough?"

Dean looked around at the stacks of spare Cupids Lucy had been preparing for the last week—and was only half-teasing. The legend of the Cupids had continued to grow over the last year, with national news outlets picking up the story after Dean and Lucy's kiss during the live feed had gone viral.

Nora had hassled him a little about going over on time, but she'd quickly conceded that it was Valentine's Day, after all, and the viewers had loved it. So much so that Dean was scheduled to do an entire episode of the morning newscast "Live from How Sweet It Is" this morning. He had a feeling it was going to become an annual event.

Not that he was complaining.

He loved How Sweet It Is. Loved the magic of Valentine's in the shop. And loved the owner.

Who was currently eyeing the multitude of Cupids as if she might be tempted to squeeze in another batch before they opened in fifteen minutes. "Do you think we need a few more?"

Dean put his arms around Lucy, pulling her close and distracting her with a kiss so she would stop worrying for five seconds. "You have enough Cupids to feed the entire state," he assured her when he lifted his head. "It's going to be fine. Better than fine. Perfect."

Relief filled her smile. "What would I do without you?"

"Luckily, you don't have to find out any time soon." He brushed another kiss on her lips—because he couldn't resist.

The ring box was burning a hole in his pocket. He almost pulled it out and dropped down on one knee right then and there—but the shop would be opening any minute, and he knew Lucy needed to be focused entirely on How Sweet It Is. He'd planned a whole romantic dinner for after the shop closed tonight.

It was the anniversary of their first kiss, the anniversary of the first time he'd told her he loved her—that night, after the live feed when it was just the two of them.

He'd been waiting for months to propose, wanting it to be on this day that was so special to them. He could wait another few hours. But impatience was making him jittery.

"Quit canoodling, you two!" Nana Edda exclaimed as she swung through the door into the kitchen. "It's almost time!"

Dean took Lucy's hand, and together, they made their way to the front of the shop, where his camera operator and producer waited, along with Georgie and the two full-time employees Lucy'd had to hire this year to keep up with demand.

The online business had exploded after their Valentine's Day broadcast went viral, and How Sweet It Is now shipped their products all over the world. Lucy and Lena had even recently signed a partnership deal with an online floral delivery service to pair How Sweet It Is chocolates with floral arrangements for special occasions. Lucy had a meeting in a few weeks to discuss stocking her chocolates in high-end grocery stores in the area—though the Cupids continued to only be sold directly from How Sweet It Is.

And there was nothing like the energy in the shop on Valentine's Day. Several of the Cupid couples had arrived to help again this year, in a new Valentine's tradition. Tyler and Lena, who'd tied the knot back in September, had dropped by earlier, but they were busy at the flower shop today.

"The Wall of Love is getting pretty crowded," Dean commented as he took his mark, putting in his earpiece. "After this year, we may need another wall."

Lucy lifted a stern finger at him. "Don't jinx it."

He laughed. "I wouldn't dare."

"And no guarantees," she reminded him. "We only promise people the *possibility* of finding true love with a Cupid. Don't go waxing poetic about the magic and getting carried away just because you're madly in love with me."

"I'll try to restrain myself," he promised, "but you know how hard it is to contain a true believer." He winked at Nana Edda and Lucy rolled her eyes. "You ready to eat another Cupid on air with me?" he asked. "The show's social media has been going nuts asking for another Lucy Sweet sighting."

"One Cupid." She held up a single finger. "Then I have to help customers. The morning rush is no joke, and I can't spend your entire broadcast making eyes at you just because social media wants me to."

He laughed. "Deal."

"Thirty seconds," his producer warned. Lucy gave him a quick kiss on the cheek before darting off to open the shop.

The first eager customers rushed through the door as Dean smiled for the home viewers and wished them a good morning and a Happy Valentine's Day. The actual eating-of-the-Cupid had been scheduled toward the end of the broadcast—timed so that Lucy wouldn't be quite so busy and so they could tempt their viewers to stick around until the very end.

When the show went to its first commercial break, Dean glanced around and caught sight of Lucy, her smile brilliant as she laughed with a customer. Then Nora spoke in his earpiece with some changes to the next section, and Dean was too busy working for a few minutes to gawk at his girlfriend.

The show passed quickly, as it always did, as if time on camera ran at a different pace than the rest of the day. Before he knew it, it was time for the Cupids. On the last commercial break, his producer grabbed Lucy, and the love of his life brought over the Cupids—one for each of them.

"Such a sentimental romantic," Lucy teased, her eyes glinting.

"You know I'm a sucker for a love story," he agreed. A voice spoke in his ear, and he repeated the message. "Ten seconds. You ready?"

She smoothed her hands down the skirt of her new Valentine's dress, simple and red and stunning.

But, as always, it was her smile that blew him away. And the fact that it was directed at him. He always felt lucky when she smiled at him.

Dean introduced the Cupids, explaining once again about the legend and filling new viewers in on what had happened last year, how he'd met Lucy. Then they each took their Cupids, smiling at one another as they popped the delicious sweetness into their mouths. He pulled Lucy into his arms for a quick kiss. When they broke apart, he bumped against one of the display cases, barely registering a soft thud as something hit the ground. He'd pick whatever it was up later. Right now, he needed to sign off.

But Lucy bent down. "Oh, Dean, you dropped—"

She broke off, and he looked over. The sound of his producer's voice in his ear went fuzzy and distant when he saw Lucy standing there.

Holding the ring box on the palm of her hand.

Wide blue-on-blue eyes lifted to his. "Dean?"

"That was for later."

Her eyes flared impossibly wider. "Later?"

He grinned. "I guess the magic had other ideas."

He plucked the box off her palm and sank down to one knee. He was vaguely aware of the camera operator scrambling to realign the shot—but he had eyes only for Lucy. He opened the box, revealing the chocolate solitaire diamond nestled inside.

"Lucy Genivee Sweet...my Chocolate Siren..."

"Oh, my goodness..." One hand flew to cover her mouth, her eyes welling.

"You taught me what love is, what magic is, and who I want to be. I want to be the man who loves you like crazy for the rest of his life." He smiled. "Will you marry me?"

She didn't make him wait. "Of course I will."

A delighted laugh burst out of him, riding a wave of pure happiness—but it was completely drowned out by the cheer from everyone around them as he rose to his feet and kissed her, all in one motion. When he pulled back to slide the ring onto her finger, he was dimly aware of Anna's voice in his earpiece, telling the audience from the studio that Dean looked like he was a little busy right now, so she would sign off for the both of them.

"We're clear," his producer called, and there was another rowdy cheer.

Lucy just laughed in his arms, her face flushed with happiness. "Are you trying to go viral again?" she teased.

He laughed. "I'd planned to wait until after dinner, but the Cupids weren't having it."

"Oh, sure, blame the magic. You know you loved being courted by the national networks."

"I did," he admitted. Last year, after the video of them had taken off, he'd been offered jobs at a number of national shows. Who knew being part of a human-interest story could be even better for his career than covering them? "But I turned them all down to stay close to Watson Corners. My heart is here, after all."

Lucy sighed happily. "My fiancé. Such a romantic."

Dean grinned, his gaze going to their picture on the Wall of Love. It looked good there. Right next to her great-grandparents.

He'd been looking for a story to propel him to the national stage, but what he found instead was a reason to open his heart—and someone who helped him see the magic in every single day.

Maybe it wasn't the Cupid chocolates that made them fall madly in love with one another last Valentine's.

But maybe it was...

The End

Thanks so much for reading
Sweeter Than Chocolate. We hope you enjoyed it!

You might like these other books
from Hallmark Publishing:

A Royal Christmas Wish
The Secret Ingredient
South Beach Love
Love By Chance
A Simple Wedding
Dater's Handbook
Moonlight in Vermont

For information about our new releases and
exclusive offers, sign up for our free newsletter at
hallmarkchannel.com/hallmark-
publishing-newsletter

You can also connect with us here:

Facebook.com/HallmarkPublishing

Twitter.com/HallmarkPublish

Turn the page for a free sample of

the Secret Ingredient

NANCY NAIGLE
USA TODAY BESTSELLING AUTHOR

Chapter One

ELLY McINTYRE DIDN'T CARE IF the town of Bailey's Fork, North Carolina was too small in some folks' eyes. It was big enough to have kept the Main Street Cafe open through four generations of McIntyres. It also had bragging rights for the winningest high school football team in the region for ten years running and held the honor of the largest loblolly pine in both Carolinas, and that suited her fine.

The fact that she and Andrew York had professed their love by carving their initials in the bark of that tree had made Kelly McIntyre almost famous...for a little while.

Kelly straightened her short black-and-white apron and retied its red sash over her blue jeans. She lifted the tall glass dome from the cake people came from miles around to get and sliced a wedge, letting it fall over right into the center of the shiny red plate. Today's flavor—Southern Seven-layer Caramel. Her specialty. For that, she could still feel a little famous.

"Here you go." Kelly placed the plate in front of Fuzzy Johnston. "Mrs. Johnston out of town again?"

His eyes twinkled. "She'd never let me have this."

He sank his fork into the frosting, then lifted it to his mouth. "Only live once, don't you know?"

"Your secret is safe with me," she teased. "You *are* going to eat some real food too though, aren't you?"

He nodded while swallowing the rich cake, then chased it with a sip of coffee. "I'll have the chicken-fried steak, please."

She jotted the order on her pad. "Do I need to even ask if you want mashed potatoes and gravy?"

"Nope." He grinned, looking quite pleased with himself. Fuzzy owned the biggest chicken farm around, and rumor had it his wife cooked chicken six ways to Sunday, which was why when she was out of town, Fuzzy always ended up here in the cafe for something a little different. "And fried okra."

"I'll put this right in." She tucked her pad into her apron pocket and headed to the kitchen. "Fuzzy's usual." Kelly pushed the ticket onto the clip and spun it.

Andrew snapped the order up and then stage whispered from the pass-through, "For someone who complains that his wife won't fix him anything but chicken, you'd think he might switch it up when he got the chance."

She loved that twinkle in Andrew's green eyes. His light brown hair was damp, which made that one piece of hair fall forward, giving him a tough-guy look. But she knew the ooey-gooey sweet side of him. "He did switch it up. He had cake as an appetizer." She spun away with only a quick glance back, knowing Andrew would pick up on the playful jab.

Andrew leaned forward at the pass-through. "He *loves* my chicken-fried steak and gravy."

"He ate a big slice of *my* cake, first," she challenged.

"Saving the best for last," he said with a playful smirk.

She turned and propped a hand on her hip. "I seem to remember helping you get that chicken-fried steak recipe just right." Kelly had helped him with as many recipes as he'd helped her. It seemed like there was nothing they couldn't perfect together.

Andrew straightened, his white apron splattered with grease and barbecue sauce. "Did I tell you that you look real pretty today?"

She swept a loose tendril of hair behind her ear. "Now you have." She never tired of hearing him say that. With a smile on her face, she turned, and then looked over her shoulder. "Thank you." He still made her heart race. She swept her thumb against the band of the diamond engagement ring on her left hand.

"Hey," he called after her. "Mom texted me. She and Dad are coming in for dinner tonight."

Kelly walked back over to him. "Great." They'd hardly ever come in since Andrew had started work at the cafe. "What's up?"

"They want to celebrate. Mom said it's a surprise. Something about my great aunt."

"That's the one who lives in France, right?"

"We haven't seen her in a couple of years. Not since the last time Dawn and I went for the summer. Maybe she's coming for a visit," he said. "Mom would love that. Will you save some cake for them? They love your chocolate cake."

"Of course. I'll put two slices aside right now. I can't let my future in-laws down. How would that look?"

"Very bad."

"My thoughts exactly." She placed two slices in the cooler to hold for the Yorks.

"Thanks, beautiful." He blew her a kiss, then got to work on the order.

I'm the luckiest girl in the world. She and Andrew had known each other since grade school, but it wasn't until high school when he'd landed a job bussing tables here at the cafe that the two of them had started dating. He loved to cook, and she loved to bake, so they spent nearly all of their extra time in the kitchen of the Main Street Cafe making up recipes and testing out ideas. They never tired of it, or each other.

The dinner crowd started to roll in, and the noise level grew exponentially. She pulled another order from the call window. With three plates balanced up each arm, she made it across the diner and dropped them off at table fourteen. "Can I get you anything else?" Everyone was already digging in, so she whisked back into the kitchen to pick up the next order.

Andrew tapped the bell at the window and shoved two more plates of the daily special under the heat lamp, giving her a wink before turning back to the cooktop. Kelly's dad barked an order, and Andrew hopped to it without a single grumble. Andrew loved being in the kitchen as much as he loved her, and she loved watching him cook.

Kelly spotted the Yorks as they walked in. There was no mistaking Andrew's father. Except for slight graying at the temples, father and son looked just alike. Tall, athletic, with wide lean-on-me shoulders, light brown hair and green eyes. His mom wore her signature cowboy boots, jeans and pearls with that ever-present smile and an air of kindness you could sense a mile away.

"Good evening. How are y'all doing tonight?" They weren't big talkers most of the time.

Mr. York gave her a nod.

Mrs. York said, "It's so good to see you. We're doing great."

"Follow me. I'll get you seated." She grabbed two menus as she passed the register.

"Thank you, Kelly," Mrs. York said with a smile.

"I might recommend the savory fried pork tenderloin," she said as she seated them in a booth. The pork tenderloin wasn't only the special on tonight's menu, but it was one of her favorites of Andrew's recipes. When Andrew's dad tasted that, he'd have to finally admit his boy really did have a future as a chef, something he hadn't been supportive of.

"Works for me," Mr. York said.

Andrew's mom scoured the menu, which was funny because she always ordered whatever her husband was having. "Let's keep it simple. I'll have the same."

"Great. I'll be right back with your sweet teas." She walked over to the kitchen window and waved toward Andrew. "This is your parents' order."

Andrew gave her a half smile.

"Wait right there." He handed a dish through the window. "Appetizer. Not on the menu. For my folks."

"This looks delicious." She took the platter. "You're so thoughtful. I love you for that, you know."

"I do what I can." He swept at his brow.

Were the beads of sweat on his forehead from the heat of the kitchen or his parents' arrival? She couldn't blame him for being nervous; she was too.

The trio platter had Andrew's homemade pimento cheese, a heaping serving of made-from-scratch hushpuppies, and a spicy bean salsa that he'd been tweaking for over two weeks. "We might have to add this to our future menus." Whenever they perfected a recipe, she'd laminate it and put it in their binder full of recipes they'd use in the restaurant they'd someday own together. This looked worthy of the appetizer section.

He nodded toward the dining room. "If Dad likes it, it'll please anyone."

"They'll love it. Don't you worry." She zipped by her other tables to deliver the appetizer.

His dad raised his head. "We didn't order that."

"On the house," she said as cheerfully as possible. "I think you'll like it."

He scowled and muttered something about not ruining his dinner with filler that she pretended to ignore. Mrs. York dove right into the platter.

Thankfully, when she brought out his dinner, he seemed much more ready to indulge. "How did you enjoy the appetizers?" she asked.

"Fabulous!" Mrs. York said.

Mr. York glanced at the near-empty dish. "Never was one much for hushpuppies, but everything on that plate was good. Probably won't be able to finish my dinner now."

"No worries. We can box your leftovers if needed."

The cafe was busy, but she kept an extra-close eye on their table to be sure to get their dessert to them before they asked for it. When she did, Mr. York didn't even complain.

"Can I get anything else for you two tonight?" she asked.

"No," Mr. York said quickly, then rubbed his stomach.

Mrs. York placed her hand atop her husband's across the table and softly said, "Not a thing, darling. Thank you so much. That was the best cake. So moist. And all those layers? It had to take hours to prepare. You're an amazing baker."

"She is, isn't she?" Kelly heard Andrew say behind her.

She turned and reached for his hand. "Hey."

His blue button-down shirt was wrinkled from where the apron had been tied against it for hours in the steamy kitchen. "My special girl." He pulled her in close.

She resisted the urge to kiss him right there in front of his parents. "Thank you." As she held his gaze, she knew he was thinking the same thing at that moment.

Kelly turned back to his parents. "I'm so glad you enjoyed it." A customer across the way was waving her down. "I need to get their check to them. Excuse me." She left, but she had one ear cast toward their table. Call it female intuition, but every nerve in her body was on alert. Something was up.

She heard his mother's giggle, followed by, "Tell him, honey."

"I thought you wanted to tell him. Aunt Claire is *your* aunt." His voice was impatient.

"What's going on?" Andrew asked.

"Aunt Claire called tonight," his mother said. "You know how excited she's been about your cooking and all. Well, she's lined up the opportunity for you to go to Paris to study under one of the best pastry chefs in the world."

"What?" Andrew's voice carried across the cafe. Kelly glanced over. He looked flat-out dumbfounded. "But I'm not a baker. Kelly is the baker. I'm a chef. There's a difference, Mom."

"You're no chef, just a short-order cook. But maybe you'll be as good as Kelly when you get back," his dad said. "With any luck."

Kelly gulped. What was wrong with that man? Insulting his own son like that? Andrew had a natural talent in the kitchen. It was something to be proud of. Andrew had expressed his disappointment in his father not appreciating his career choice, but it wasn't until today that she realized how much he disapproved. Her heart ached for Andrew.

"You'll be able to stay at Aunt Claire's while you're there," his mother said. "The owner of the school is renting the carriage house for the executive pastry chef teaching this special curriculum. I have no idea what this is costing her, but she's covering every dime. It's a once-in-a-lifetime opportunity."

Andrew pulled up a chair to the end of the booth. "Wow."

"Unless you've got second thoughts about the whole cooking thing," his dad said. "You can always come back and work at the shop with me."

"I have a job, Dad." He fiddled with the bottom of his shirt. "And Kelly is here."

Kelly tucked herself out of their view. Ever since Andrew had refused to work with his father in the family business, his dad had hated all of Andrew's ideas. Truth be told, Andrew was an awesome mechanic, but he didn't enjoy doing that kind of work. After a long day turning wrenches, he'd been filthy and in a foul mood. When he was in the kitchen, his whole demeanor changed.

Andrew's mom pressed her hand on his arm. "I need to let Aunt Claire know if you're coming. The Pastry and Baking Program begins the first week of July."

"So soon? Kelly and I had plans this summer." He tugged at his shirt collar.

"I'm sure those plans can wait. You two have your whole lives ahead of you. The program runs from July to December. Only twenty students get in. Aunt Claire pulled some serious strings."

"It does sound like a great opportunity..." He leaned back in the chair, looking down at his hands. "But I don't want to be a baker. It would be a big waste of time and money."

"We'd never be able to send you to something like this." His mom sounded almost apologetic. "Aunt Claire says that if you do well, there could be other scholarship opportunities too."

Kelly could see how torn he was. He pressed his fingers into the palm of his hand, the way he did when he was deep in thought. Paris was so far, but if she were faced with this decision, she'd jump at it.

Read the rest! *The Secret Ingredient* is available now.